NO DARKER CRIME

John Creasey

Master crime fiction writer John Creasey's 562 titles (or so) have sold more than 80 million copies in over 25 languages. After enduring 743 rejection slips, the young Creasey's career was kickstarted by winning a newspaper writing competition. He went on to collect multiple honours from The Mystery Writers of America including the Edgar Award for best novel in 1962 and the coveted title of Grand Master in 1969. Creasey's prolific output included 11 different series including Roger West, the Toff, the Baron, Patrick Dawlish, Gideon, Dr Palfrey, and Department Z, published both under his own name and 10 other pseudonyms.

Creasey was born in Surrey in 1908 and, when not travelling extensively, lived between Bournemouth and Salisbury for most of his life. He died in England in 1973.

THE DEPARTMENT Z SERIES

No Darker Crime

Department Z

John Creasey

house of stratus

This edition published in 2017 by Ipso Books

First published by John Long Limited 1943, revised by Arrow in 1969

Ipso Books is a division of Peters Fraser + Dunlop Ltd

Drury House, 34-43 Russell Street, London WC2B 5HA

CHAPTER 1

'SOMETHING OF INTEREST'

Dear Mr. Garth,

*If you will call at The Elms, Brookside Road, Wimble-
don, about 7 p.m. today, you will hear something which I
am sure will interest you greatly.*

There was no signature to the note. Nor was there any
address. But the postmark was 'Wimbledon' and David
Garth assumed it had been sent from The Elms. He drew
his almost flaxen eyebrows together as he tried to recollect
any acquaintance in Wimbledon—and to imagine what the
matter of interest might be. His face, too long in the chin
and nose to be quite handsome, cleared as he decided that
it was of no importance. Dropping it on to the table, he lit a
cigarette and glanced at his watch.

'Five to five,' he mused. 'I wonder if it's any use looking
up Anne?'

He eyed the telephone in the corner of the long, narrow room, which was furnished with a variety of oddments
inherited or acquired on his travels. A court cupboard in
lovely, mellowed walnut, a Chippendale tripod table, two
slung-chairs, their sound leather seats barely marked after
two hundred years of usage, a beautiful gate-leg table, and,

1

flanking the fire-place, two vast and very comfortable hide armchairs. A shaft of Autumn sunlight threw into bold relief the delicate inlay-work of a walnut Regency bookcase.

It would be pleasant to see Anne again, he reflected although now that she was engaged she might feel it would be indiscreet to meet him. His long, sensitive lips curved; without more ado he stepped to the telephone and dialled a Chelsea number.

The voice that answered made his heart leap, although he had believed himself quite cured of his infatuation for Anne Duval. 'I'll give you three guesses,' he told her.

She did not recognise him; or perhaps affected not to.

'Who did you say …?'

'It's David,' he said, shortly. 'I wondered if …'

'David!' she exclaimed. 'David, I …'

There was a hint of excitement in her voice. Then she paused and her tone became flat and indifferent. But she carried it too far when she concluded: 'Oh, you mean David Garth? Hallo, David.'

'No, that's too bad!' he protested, not entirely joking. 'Once we were as one, but now you have the nerve to pretend you can mistake me for same other David. Anne, are you doing anything tonight?'

'I'm afraid so,' she said, a little too promptly. 'I've a dinner appointment. I'm terribly busy, these days, David—war work, you know.' She spoke quickly, as if to prevent him from interrupting. 'And the fact is, I *have* met several other Davids, recently—George knew them. Have you seen George, lately?'

'Does he respect the laws of ministerial discretion enough to forget to tell you I've been to America?' demanded Garth. 'Anyway, since it's been in most of the papers and on the radio …'

'I don't get much chance to read the papers, these days,' she told him. 'Did you have a good journey?'

'Not a U-boat either way. Thanks for asking.'

'Oh, that's all right,' said Anne.

That startled him more than anything else. The Anne he had known so well would have seized on that note of raillery and snapped back some witty rejoinder and they would have laughed together. That was one of his pleasantest memories of Anne Duval—the ease of laughing with her. After their estrangement and her engagement to the more solid—and stolid—George, he had often reproached himself because he had taken Anne, and life, too lightly.

'I do wish I were free,' she added, after the slightest of pauses. 'Perhaps if you ring again—in about a week, say—I'll have an hour or two to spare. Sorry—I can't stop now. Goodbye, David!'

He replaced the receiver with mixed feelings.

That evasive, contradictory reaction was so unexpected from Anne. It contrasted not only with his memories of her, but also with that first eager 'David!' It was as if she had allowed her feelings free rein, then suddenly regretted it.

'The truth is,' he reflected wryly, 'she thinks I might be too disruptive an influence, so she's playing safe. I've received my *congé* and that's that. The question is what to do with the evening?'

He glanced at the note again, with a mild stirring of curiosity. It was written in a bold, flowing hand, with green ink on mauve paper. The over-all effect was flamboyant.

Undecided still, he dropped the letter on to the table again, and wandered across to a small bureau near the window. The writing flap was down and there was a pile of newspaper cuttings on it.

In the sunlight, his blond hair was creamy gold. His eyes— blue, dark-fringed, wide-set and deceptively sleepy-looking—

scanned the top cutting. It was from the *New York Daily Mirror* and it had a headline an inch deep:

GARTH SAYS NOW OR NEVER
English Spokesman Rates U.S.A.

'David Garth, dreamy-eyed, handsome, lazy-looking, belied his appearance and put pep into his speech at Ligham Hall last night. Question—does Garth, from Ministry of Propaganda, Whitehall, speak for himself or for the British Government? If for himself, one day he will be caught with his pants down. But Garth is nobody's fool. Internal quarrels and isolationist U.S.A. outlook, he said, will only lead to another world war. Others have said the same but not with such vigor and feeling. Don't be taken in by his pretty blue eyes. Garth's dynamite. Maybe we need some.'

Garth smiled briefly and looked at the next cutting from the *New York Times:*

David Garth Speaks for Himself
Not Views of Whitehall, He Says

'Asked by a *Times* reporter whether his speech at Ligham Hall should be regarded as official, David Garth said NO in Capital letters. We question the wisdom of permitting official spokesmen to make unofficial pronouncements in public.'

He picked up another, from the London *Daily Telegraph:*

Mr. David Garth To Return
Lecture Tour Cut Short

'It is understood that Mr. David Garth, distinguished critic and, more lately, lecturer for the Ministry of Propaganda, is to return from the United States, where some of his recent speeches have caused some misunderstanding. Mr. Garth's return is for private reasons and it is hoped that he will be able to return to the United States before the year is out.'

Garth shrugged, dropped the cutting, and turned to gaze out of the window into Jermyn Street.

He was sardonically amused by this evidence of the delicacy of the panjandrums in Whitehall—while appreciating the fact that an official reproof, sharply delivered to him personally had not been made public.

Actually, he had been recalled for speaking too bluntly; but secretly, he had a shrewd idea that some of his superiors applauded his plain speaking. Yet that did not excuse him for using his position to make statements which might arouse ill-feeling.

'Still, as a private citizen, I wouldn't have gone over at all,' he mused. 'I wonder if they'll let me resign?'

He knew it was much more likely that he would be sent on a lecture tour in England, with careful instructions on what not to say. They might have released him for the Army, but a motoring accident had left him with a stiff left arm and he had been rated Grade 3 since his 'medical', two years earlier.

The telephone startled him.

He went across and lifted the receiver.

'David Garth speaking.'

A man spoke. A stranger to him, his voice quiet, but with a note of authority; a voice which commanded immediate respect.

'Good-evening, Mr. Garth. You won't know me, but I must ask your indulgence in a matter which you may find somewhat startling.'

'I say, who …?'

'Before you ask any questions, Mr. Garth, would you mind telling me: have you received an invitation, unsigned, to visit a house of which you have never heard?'

'Good Lord!' exclaimed Garth, amazed.

'Then you have?' The voice held evident satisfaction. 'Mr. Garth, there is no time now for explanations, but I will be greatly obliged if you will go to the Regent Palace Hotel lounge at once. There, you will be met and given some explanation of this unusual request.'

'But …'

'You might find in this an opportunity for re-establishing your reputation at the M.O.P.', went on the other, drily. 'On the other hand, you might find an outlet for even more direct self-expression! Don't ignore this request, will you?'

The line went dead while Garth was still seeking an effective reply. Frowning, he replaced the receiver, lit a cigarette and took the note from the table again. As he read it, the unknown caller's message ran through his mind.

He had to admit it had been cleverly phrased. He was feeling pretty sore about his recall and the probability that for some time to come he would be closely watched, and all his speeches scrutinised for any departure from the orthodox. Now, he had been offered two alternatives—vague ones, it was true, yet with possibilities. Moreover, the speaker had implied that he had some official connection, perhaps with the M.O.P. itself....

He read the note again, slowly:

Dear Mr. Garth,

If you will call at The Elms, Brookside Road, Wimble-don, about 7 p.m. today, you will hear something which I am sure will interest you greatly.

It was half past five, and he had nothing else arranged. A visit to the Regent Palace, only a few hundred yards away, would at least do no harm, he decided.

He walked through to Piccadilly and along to the hotel, entered the crowded foyer through the revolving doors, and approached the lounge.

There were few more popular meeting-places in the centre of London, and a hum of conversation filled the large, ornately-ceilinged room. Several women sitting alone eyed his tall figure, immaculate in dark-blue hopsack, with unconcealed interest. But no one made any deliberate move to attract his attention.

Frowning, Garth looked about him, wondering how he could be identified amongst so many. And even if he were, he thought, it would surely be impossible to talk without being overheard. He strolled the length of the wide passage between the massed chairs and sofas, alert for anyone who might seem to be regarding him with especial interest.

No one approached him.

He retraced his steps as far as the lounge doorway, beginning to wonder whether he could possibly be the victim of some hoaxer. A waitress passed him and handed a note to a hall-porter, and a moment later, the man came over to him.

'Excuse me, sir—would you be Mr. Garth?'

'I am,' Garth said,

'Your friend's sent a message, sir, to say he's sorry he can't get down to see you, but will you be good enough to go to Room 316? That's on the third floor, sir ...'

He broke off, as he was button-holed by a vociferous middle-aged woman plaintively demanding that he find her a seat, and Garth nodded and strode off towards the lifts. Up on the third floor, he followed the deserted corridors until he reached the door of 316; then, for the first time, doubtful of the wisdom of going further, he paused and reached for his cigarettes as he considered.

He was just about to light one, when a man turned the corner. Tall and well-built, he wore a Savile Row suit with a casual elegance that matched Garth's own. He looked somewhere about thirty-five and was clearly in the pink of condition. His face creased into an engaging smile as he drew up.

'I've beaten you to it, then?' he said, cheerfully. 'Don't look dumbstruck, old chap—we're quite harmless!' And gripping Garth's right arm, he turned the handle of the door and pushed it open.

Propelled into the room, Garth stared confusedly at a man on the bed.

It was as if the man from the passage had contrived to pass him, take off his coat, and lain down on one of the beds. But the grip on his arm remained firm until the door was closed.

'It's all right,' he assured Garth, as the man on the bed laconically raised himself and swung his feet to the floor. 'We're two separate people. And we're not even brothers ...'

'Which is no cause for regret,' remarked the second man. 'We are ...'

'Cousins,' supplied the first. 'It's always quicker to get it over this way, I think. Look carefully and you will see the subtle difference. My hair is a shade lighter ...'

'Only it has more oil upon it,' quoth the man on the bed. 'My eyes are darker, too.'

'Oh, yes?' murmured Garth, glancing from one to the other as they eyed him expectantly. Then he realised how futile the comment must have sounded. But he *felt* futile. With other men who acted so outrageously he might have felt annoyed, yet there was an engaging good humour about this couple which invited reciprocity. He made the effort:

'I suppose I haven't strayed into an asylum?' he asked, drily.

The man on the bed beamed approval.

'No asylum.' He spoke more quickly and crisply than his cousin: 'Some would say that such should be our lot, but Fate is kind … Everything all right, Mark?'

'Yes,' added the other. 'He wasn't followed—neither was I. The trouble with us,' he added, to Garth, 'is that we have suspicious minds. In the simplest things, we see great possibilities for evil.' He grinned. 'No, don't say it! We're going to explain, partly, at least. Sit down and light that cigarette and make yourself at home.'

He indicated the only easy-chair in the small room, and Garth crossed to it and seated himself with a good-humoured shrug.

He was a pretty good judge of men. And the one thing obvious to him, about this pair, was that their facetious back-chat was only a façade. And men of the calibre he sensed them to be would not have gone to such trouble to get him here and meet him unseen, without some very good reason.

Their precautions against being seen with him, indeed—while undeniably quickening his interest—gave him a feeling of faint disquiet. He waited with mounting curiosity as the second man seated himself on the upright chair near the bedside telephone. Then the man on the bed announced, solemnly:

'I will now unfold the mystery.'

'Never mind the mystery,' interrupted 'Mark'. 'Get to the point!'

'What, put the cart before the horse?' protested the other. Then grinned again, as he added: 'Although I agree—Garth will probably start throwing his weight about, if we don't start somewhere. The point first, then. We want you to go to Wimbledon tonight, Garth, but not as a free agent. We want you to go as a representative of—er—a small department in Whitehall, to which we have the honour to belong.' More seriously, he concluded: 'If you're convinced that it's worth while, can you go?'

Garth hesitated before saying:

'Yes, but …'

'Ours the "buts"!' said the other, promptly. 'If you can go, and are convinced you should, will you still go when I tell you that the venture might hold more than a modicum of danger?'

Chapter 2
Garth is Warned

G arth looked into the speaker's eyes.

The glimmer of a smile in the drily expectant expression, as well as the steady regard of the silent 'Mark', tempted him to say 'yes' without wasting time.

Innate caution made him refrain.

'What kind of danger?' he countered, mildly enough.

'Oh, the physical kind,' said the other, casually. 'But the thing is ...' He paused just enough to give emphasis to his words: 'The last man who went along was a friend of ours. He left the house, but didn't rejoin us. He was found dead—a bullet in the head. No evidence that he was shot by anyone from The Elms. Many questions were asked, and Frankenstein was put through it pretty well; but he managed to head us off.'

Garth clutched at the name: *'Frankenstein?'*

'It is not a real name,' said the man who talked so coolly of sudden death. 'You might call it a nickname for the monster. He calls himself Franklin and we haven't been able to prove that he owns any other names. But we think ...'

'Just a minute,' Garth cut in. 'It's time I had a chance to speak.' Neither of the others demurred, so he went on: 'Are you seriously asking me to believe that a friend of yours accepted an invitation like the one I had this afternoon, only to be killed after he'd been to the house? Now, come ...!'

'Your turn to be interrupted, old son,' said the other, quietly. 'You are right, except on one point. He went there and was killed. We think Franklin killed him, or at least arranged his murder. But he did not receive an invitation: someone else did, and our man went in his place. A mild deception—and there was every hope we'd get away with it. We didn't. You have a better chance because you are the man whom Franklin actually approached, and we've done our darnedest to be sure he doesn't learn that we've been in touch with you. On the other hand, it's only fair that you should know the possibilities.'

'I want to know a lot more than those,' retorted Garth. 'Who the dickens *are* you?'

'He's Mark and I'm Mike,' said the other, promptly. 'We can tell you more when we know you're with us, which won't be until after you've been to Wimbledon. We can tell you that it's all quite above board. And we're allowed to tell you that certain parties are very anxious indeed to learn more about Franklin and his "items of interest"—and we've been detailed to find out. It's as simple as that. We have to make it mysterious for the time being, old son, because'—he smiled engagingly—'suppose Franklin were to suspect that you'd talked to us? Suppose he were to exert some kind of pressure to find out who sent you? I mean—if you didn't know, you couldn't tell. The simple ways are best.'

Garth felt his restraint breaking.

'Look here!' he snapped. 'If you think you're going to scare me by talking this bilge, you're dead wrong. If there's a good enough reason for my going to Wimbledon I'll go, but I'll take a lot of convincing that there is!'

'M'mm...' murmured the man who called himself Mike. He gave a lopsided grin. 'The sad thing, old son, is that we have to convince you by our earnest manner and honest, confidence-inspiring, ugly faces. We haven't authority to go any further, yet. Although we can tell you this,' he added, as if visited by sudden inspiration: 'We know of four people, at least, who've received a similar kind of letter. All of them very soon after a trip to America on private or Government business—a peculiar coincidence, at a time when Anglo-American understanding was never more important.'

He grimaced, bleakly. 'There are saboteurs on both sides. I don't mean the honest-to-God American politicians with an isolationist complex—we think they'll see straight and come round, sooner or later. But there are others whose motives are considerably more dubious. And we think Franklin might be connected with them.'

'Is this secret service work?' Garth demanded, his irritation suddenly fading in what he thought was understanding.

'Your guess is as good as mine,' said Mike, politely. 'Other people than Government agents are anxious to make sure that Anglo-American post-war relations are very healthy. We might be working for private interests, might we not? Anyway, we simply can't answer questions at the moment. Get away from Wimbledon with some information about Franklin's proposition to you, pass it on to us—and then we'll play ball.'

Garth said, 'How did you know I had such a letter?'

'Ah,' grinned Mike. 'That would be telling!'

'I'm beginning to think I'm a damned fool for even listening to you!' Garth glared at the man called Mark. 'You're both a lot too casual about it all to expect to be taken seriously.'

Mark smiled, more restrainedly than his cousin.

'We're not really as casual as we might seem. Look'—He took out his wallet, extracted a photograph, and leaned across to hand it over. 'Evidence!' he said, abruptly.

Garth picked it up and stared at it, tight-lipped. It was of a man: big, good-looking—and obviously dead. There was a small hole in his forehead, and a trickle of blood ran down from it.

'As he was when we found him,' added Mike, harshly. 'Listen to me, Garth. You're a free agent. We're not trying to compel you to do anything. We've shown you how care-ful we have to be—we've warned you. Now, it's up to you. We shall have to try someone else if you won't come in. That will mean delay, which in itself might prove disastrous. Don't ask us how—we can't know, at the moment. And if we did, we wouldn't tell you until later. Is that all clear?'

Garth eyed him steadily.

There was no point in saying that the whole situation seemed bizarre, fantastic: the obvious was not a thing to dwell upon, with these men. They wanted a decision and expected it quickly. And somehow they had convinced him not only that it really mattered, but that they were working for a good cause. He was at a loss to understand why he should feel so sure, and it was that very perplexity which influenced him as he hedged:

'How long can you give me to decide?'

'It will take you three-quarters of an hour to get to Wimbledon,' Mike pointed out. 'It's turned six, already, and you were to be at Wimbledon about seven.'

Slowly, Garth said:

'The man who asked me to come here obviously knew I was feeling sore about the M.O.P. recall—he suggested this might be a means of rehabilitating myself. Is it?'

Mike smiled, gently, almost mockingly.

'It might be. But on the other hand, he might have thought it a smart way of ensuring your interest.'

He was going to give nothing away obviously. Yet despite his normal caution—almost, indeed, despite his better judgement—Garth found himself believing all he had been told, and certain that he was mixed up in something of very great consequence. But still he hesitated. Then as he caught another glimpse of that photograph, and lighting the cigarette, he said abruptly:

'When and where do I meet you, afterwards?'

The words were hardly out of his mouth before he felt the clammy hand of sudden, cold awareness flush his neck. But Mike's smile had widened and he slipped from the bed and strode across to clap him on the shoulder, as Mark rose quickly from his chair.

The eyes of both men were glowing, and for the moment they looked even more alike.

'Nice work!' exclaimed Mike.

'Good man!' added Mark, with feeling.

'I felt sure we could count on you, when I saw you,' Mike admitted. 'But thanks, just the same. Glad to have you aboard.'

'We can't make arrangements now,' Mark told him. 'But we'll see you within an hour of your return—we'll send you word. And you're going to return: there's no reason at all to think that Franklin has spotted us. That's if you keep mum, of course. But you won't give anything away.'

'Do you know how to get to Wimbledon?' demanded Mike.

'Train from Waterloo is best,' said Mark. 'And you'll get there quicker by Tube than cab, I think. But please yourself. And one other thing ...'

'You won't be altogether alone,' supplied Mike.

'We shall be watching,' explained Mark.

'Watch-dogs of the bull-dog breed!' grinned Mike. Then added contritely: 'Garth, I know we're an exasperating pair—but you've given us reason to feel cock-a-hoop. Oh, and it isn't likely that you were seen, coming up here—but have some explanation ready, in case you're asked. An appointment you had to put off—any old story, provided it will cover you. All right?'

'I … I suppose so,' said Garth, dazedly.

'Of course it's all right,' declared Mark. 'The probability is that your interview will go like clockwork. You've just two things to remember, old son. First—you want information, all kinds of information. If you can give us a *verbatim* account of what takes place, so much the better. Second, you've gone to see him because of the letter. You don't know his name—forget Franklin. You don't know that we exist, as far as he's concerned. Right?'

'Yes,' Garth nodded, wryly; still somewhat dazed.

'Then off you go,' urged Mike. 'Our blessings, and all that kind of thing!'

And Garth found himself walking along the bare passage before he had properly realised that he was out of the room.

He decided to take their advice and travel by Tube, and headed for the nearest entrance.

The train for Waterloo was crowded. And when he finally reached the station, he found the next one to Wimbledon due to leave in five minutes, and spent a frantic couple of minutes on the platform before he found a vacant seat—wedged in between two corpulent, elderly men.

Perspiring freely, not altogether with the rush and warmth of the evening, he lit another cigarette and attempted to marshal his thoughts. From the moment he had left the Regent Palace, his mind, had been filled with a series of kaleidoscopic impressions; now, for the first time he could settle down to consider the situation dispassionately.

The first thing that occurred to him was that even now it was not too late to withdraw. The second, arrived at after some moments of cogitation, was that he could not be dispassionate. There had been an air of fantasy about the interview—for that matter, about everything that had happened since the letter had come. As he ran through each item, he realised, wryly, that Anne's coolness was a contributary factor to his presence here.

In spite of the sense of urgency which the cousins had impressed upon him—and a natural apprehension occasioned by a vivid mind-picture of the dead man—he found himself thinking of Anne as much as the project ahead. Why had she uttered his name as if with real pleasure, only to change so abruptly? It was a problem that increasingly worried him the more he pondered it …

He reached Wimbledon at ten minutes to seven.

It was only when he was outside the station and looking about for a taxi that the vague apprehensions born of the cousins' persistent warnings came to a head. Yet when he finally managed to hail a taxi, he climbed into it unhesitatingly.

'Do you know Brookside Road?' he asked the driver.

'Know every inch of Wimbledon, sir,' the man assured him. 'But it's a long road—what part did you want?'

'I don't know the number,' said Garth. 'The name of the house is The Elms.'

'Oh, The *Elms*, that's an easy one! Right near the common, sir—be there in ten minutes.'

Ten minutes, thought Garth, grimly.

There was still time to withdraw—to have the man take him somewhere else. But he knew as he settled back that he would not do so, that he would see this thing through. Now, however, he began to feel irritated in retrospect, by the manner of the cousins. They had deliberately scared him. Surely it would have been better had they persuaded him to go without dropping so many hints of danger and without producing that photograph in evidence?

He smiled wryly.

The photograph had been a last-minute resort, when he had proved difficult to convince. Not that he blamed himself for that—everything considered, he had had plenty of justification for wanting to know more about the mission. It was surprising, indeed, how little they had in fact told him; how cleverly they had played on his susceptibilities. First, that intriguingly-phrased telephone message; then, the cousins' emphasis on the likely involvement of Anglo-American relations—a particular obsession of his, as they would know well enough, of course, from reports in the Press.

The taxi passed along tree-lined avenues of pleasant houses. Here and there, he saw gaps and bomb-damaged buildings; but Wimbledon on the whole looked friendly and inviting.

The sun was still some way from the horizon and on Wimbledon Common itself, groups of adults and children strolled over the sun-swept grass.

Here, most of the houses were large; standing in their own ground, well back from the road.

The taxi turned left, then slowed down to enter the driveway of a house hidden by massive beech trees. Garth's jaw tightened. From now on, he had to watch every word he said, every action he made. He felt cooler and less afraid; it was as well that the first flush of fear had come earlier.

Then he saw the house: a square, squat building, bare of creepers, stark-looking against the soft background of trees. Its plaster coat had broken away in places, leaving wide, bare patches of brick. The garden seemed to consist entirely of shubberies and tall trees; but these were neat enough. The drive itself was well-kept, too. And as the cab drew up at the pillared entrance the polished brass letter-box and knocker gleamed in the sun.

'Here you are, sir!' said the driver, unnecessarily.

Garth paid him, adding a good tip. And only half-conscious of noting the elderly, weather-beaten face and shrewd, blue eyes, asked, in a moment of inspiration:

'Are you busy, tonight?'

'Not all that,' said the man. 'Like me ter wait, sir?'

Garth nodded.

'I'll send word if I'm likely to be too long,' he promised.

'Okey-doke, sir!'

As he shut off his engine, Garth stepped into the porch and stretched out a hand to press the bell. He was startled when the door opened before he could do so, but the neatly-dressed maid had a reassuring smile.

'Good evening, sir,' she greeted him. 'Are you Mr. Garth?'

'I am,' he said.

'You're expected, sir. Will you please come this way?'

He entered, and she led him across a large, gloomy hall and up a wide staircase. The landing window admitted more light than the front door, and he noted that the landing itself was spacious. Two wide passages led from it, and he followed the girl along the further one.

She stopped at the second door they came to. It was large and yellow, somehow out of keeping with the place; for it looked new. She did not tap, but pressed a bell-push. Then pausing only for a moment, she turned the handle, stepped just over the threshold and stood back for him to enter the room.

'Mr. David Garth, sir,' she announced, and a man rose from a large desk by the window. A vast man, whose shaggy outline seemed to put the room into shadow.

'Ah, Mr. Garth!' he said warmly. 'I am delighted to see you, sir—so glad you were able to come! All right, Ethel.'

The door closed as the huge man extended a hand.

CHAPTER 3

THE MAN WHO CALLED
HIMSELF RYALL

No greeting could have been warmer or more reassuring. The huge man's grip was firm but not too powerful, although his hand enveloped Garth's. Then motioning him to a comfortable easy-chair, he took two silver boxes from the desk.

'A cigar?' he invited. 'Or a cigarette. I can recommend both.'

'A cigarette, thank you,' said Garth.

'Good, good!' beamed the man. 'Are you comfortable? Good. Now I've no doubt that you are puzzled by my somewhat unusual method of inviting you here—and much to my dismay, I remembered after posting the letter that I had not signed it. Like most of us, these days, I am a very busy man, Mr. Garth—I'm afraid I don't pay the attention to detail I should.' He smiled widely; and his large, white teeth were thrown into sharp relief by a massive black beard and moustache. 'I hope you will forgive the discourtesy, my dear sir!'

'Of course,' murmured Garth.

'Very good of you,' beamed the other. 'Now, sir, my name is Ryall—spelt R-Y-A-L-L.' His voice was deep but soft;

he uttered the name naturally enough and Garth hoped he did not show his surprise, for he had expected 'Franklin'. The deception—either on the part of the cousins, or the remarkable man in front of him—made him suddenly more aware of the delicacy of his position.

'Well, Mr. Ryall?' Garth lit up, casually. But he was glad of the excuse to avoid the other's piercing gaze.

Nothing about the man who called himself Ryall was less than striking. His unusually large, pale grey eyes had a singular luminosity which was only emphasised by the startling blackness of his jutting brows. Above them, the forehead was high, broad and remarkably unlined. Wiry, dark hair grew in tufts high on his cheeks and covered the backs of his powerful hands. There was physical strength far beyond average in the man, Garth thought. And not only physical strength; there was real 'power' there.

The huge man's clothes were hopelessly out-of-date, he noted. His shoulders were too squarely-tailored; his too-long coat was waisted and had lapels of watered silk. He wore a Gladstonian butterfly collar, and his black tie was drawn through a plain gold ring. As he seated himself now behind the big desk, his beard covered his collar and cravat.

'You must be very curious, Mr. Garth?' he suggested, and beamed again.

'I am,' admitted Garth. 'Otherwise I should not have come.' He felt it wise to be a little aloof. 'May I ask if you are likely to keep me long, Mr. Ryall?'

The big man's eyebrows rose.

'I do hope it is not an inconvenient evening for you, Mr. Garth? I had hoped you would be able to dine with me. But if you have another engagement....' He paused, still smiling; although without much humour, Garth was certain.

'Good of you,' murmured Garth. 'It is simply that I have a taxi waiting ...'

'My dear sir, that is easily attended to!' Ryall leaned forward and pressed a bell-push. 'We can call a cab for you as soon as we have finished our talk. Ethel,' he added, as the maid appeared at the door. 'Pay off Mr. Garth's taxi, please.'

'Yes, sir,' she said in her pleasant voice, and went out again.

As the door closed, Garth felt that a link with the outer, ordinary world had gone. He wished now that he had pretended to have a later engagement; or at least declared himself unable to stay to dinner. But he relaxed a little as Ryall leaned back, his huge hands spread wide on the desk before him.

'Now that is settled, Mr. Garth, I shall explain my motives in inviting you here. I want it clearly understood that the proposition I am going to put to you may not be attractive. If it is not, then you have only to tell me and we shall forget the whole thing.'

'I see,' said Garth, pointedly non-committal.

'Good!' Ryall was a shade too hearty. 'Now, there are contributary reasons for my wishing to see you, of course, and thinking that you might be of service to me. And also,' he added sententiously, 'to your country. We can serve England in many ways, sometimes in the limelight of publicity, with the accompaniment of guns and martial music—the war has produced many heroes. Or we can serve the country quietly; sometimes—in fact very often—without being appreciated. But you will realise that, won't you, Mr. Garth?'

Garth said defensively: 'I don't quite understand you.'

'I think you do,' Ryall told him, gently 'I have followed your career with much interest, Mr. Garth. I know that you are one of the most brilliant and polished orators of the

day. I have even heard you speak—and I may say I have
been as greatly impressed by your command of words, as
by your studied use of rhetoric. You have the power to sway
multitudes—but perhaps you do not realise that?'

'I should hardly have thought—'

'My dear sir, I understand you!' Ryall slapped the desk
with a heavy hand. 'You know your powers, but you have
received a sharp reprimand—I can read between the lines
of newspaper reports, believe me! You feel you have been
badly treated—of course you do. And I agree with you. I
agree fully with everything you said in America. I only wish
that your superiors—as they like to call themselves!' he
amended, with fine scorn—'realised the importance of
speaking frankly to our friends across the Atlantic.'

Garth thought: *So the cousins were right.*

Although still wary, he could not believe Ryall had
any suspicion of the other interview: the man was too
self-assured. It would be wise, he decided, to appear to sub-
mit to the influence of his undoubtedly powerful personal-
ity. The more he agreed with him, the more he was likely to
learn. And since Ryall had plainly selected him because of
his alleged sense of grievance against his superiors:

'I'm glad you do,' he said warmly. 'It's time someone—oh,
forget it! I shouldn't have talked so freely,' he mumbled,
with apparent embarrassment.

'I don't agree with you,' Ryall told him. 'It is your spon-
sors, not you who were wrong. You said what needed saying.
If it cannot be said through Government spokesmen, then
it must be said through other channels. Let me assure you,
Mr. Garth: I have studied Anglo-American relations for a
long time. I have interests in both countries. In my opinion,
only frankness will serve. Like you ...'

Ryall's voice dropped, became confidential: 'I have fallen foul of the pundits in Whitehall. I have grown tired of trying to convince them of the correct way to approach the people—let me emphasise that: the *people*—of the United States. That being so, I have decided to endeavour to approach them myself. I have influential friends whose only interest is the promotion of a *bloc*, such as the already-proposed United Nations, to ensure world peace for many years to come. And the corner-stone of such an organisation can only be Anglo-American amity. Don't you agree, Mr. Garth?'

'In principle, yes,' he began. 'Of course! But I don't see …'

Ryall waved a hand grandiloquently.

'In principle, Mr. Garth—that is what matters! We have a common interest and a mutual understanding of the problem, and we have suffered in like fashion from the conservative—perhaps I should say the traditional Establishment—approach to the problem. What we have to discover, then, is an effective method of combating the influences which block progress. Can we agree on that?'

Garth hesitated.

'Yes … But I ought to be frank, Mr. Ryall. I am in the service of the Ministry, which means that I am not at liberty to make commitments outside it.'

As before, Ryall waved his objection aside.

'A difficulty, my dear sir—and as such, made to be overcome. Have I studied your career, especially your later speeches, rightly? Do I understand that, deep within yourself, you feel a sense of frustration, an aching awareness of the wrongness of our present methods? Am I not right when I say that in your opinion we are heading for misunderstanding—for a repetition of the folly which brought calamity upon the world?'

Ryall spoke as if he were addressing a meeting, and Garth was aware of the power of the man's own rhetoric.

He was deliberately presenting an unanswerable case—while subtly implying that he and Garth were far superior intellectually to those with whom they differed. It was easy to imagine the effect Ryall's words would have on a self-centred individual suffering from wounded vanity over an allegedly unearned reprimand.

All the time, the huge man was eyeing him narrowly, and Garth could imagine the questions running through his mind. Was the spell working? Was Garth as gullible as he hoped? Was the poison of revolt beginning to take effect?

'Well, Mr. Garth?' Ryall prompted.

Garth gulped, hesitated, then seemed to let a pent-up store of grievance come flooding out.

'As a matter of fact we do think along similar lines, Mr. Ryall. I can't understand how they can't *see* that we're in for serious trouble if they don't adopt a more realistic attitude. They're so unbelievably*blind*! If you'd heard some of the idiotic ...'

He broke off then, as if determined not to let pangs of conscience deter him, he drew a deep breath and plunged on: this time, falling into a 'platform manner' quite as effective as Ryall's own.

He expected to be interrupted, but Ryall sat back as if this were exactly what he wanted. Realising this, Garth grew more vehement in his condemnation of the Government's methods: spreading his criticism to Washington and working himself up until finally he had risen from his seat and was striding about the room, one hand raised and clenched, his face pale, his eyes glowing. Long practice had taught him when such histrionics were necessary on the platform; his knowledge had never been more useful.

Abruptly, he stopped.

Self-consciously, he drew a hand across his forehead: and sinking into the chair again, shot an apologetic glance at Ryall.

'I'm afraid I've let my tongue run away with me,' he grimaced. 'I do feel strongly about it—and needless to say it isn't often I can say exactly what I think.'

'I quite understand,' purred Ryall. 'And I am very glad to know how deeply you do feel. Now, I think perhaps an *aperitif?* We shall have ample opportunity for talking further, over dinner. A friend and very dear colleague of mine will be present—an American whose views coincide with our own.'

'Look here,' said Garth, hastily. 'All this is strictly between ourselves, Mr. Ryall! It's definitely confidential—I can't afford to make more trouble for myself.'

'Not a word will be breathed to anyone who might carry tales to the Ministry,' Ryall assured him. 'My dear fellow, secrecy—to some degree—is necessary for us all. We do not want to find ourselves hampered on every side! You can rely absolutely on my discretion—and that of Paul Russi. You will like Russi: he is a man after your own heart. Perhaps not surprisingly, he is on the staff of the Ministry of Propaganda in Washington, so you see you have much in common.'

'Russi?' echoed Garth. 'I don't seem to know the name. I did meet a number of their chaps, but ...'

'Russi has been in England for some time,' said Ryall, smoothly. 'Come, my friend!'

He rounded the desk as Garth got to his feet, and strode to the door.

Until that moment, Garth had not realised just how massive the man was; nor how tall. He was six-feet-three at least:

his breadth of shoulder and thickness of waist was deceptive. He quite dwarfed Garth's five-feet-eleven.

Following him downstairs, Garth noted another thing. Ryall moved swiftly and with a peculiar lightness; it was almost as if he had reason for stealth.

The dining room seemed, for that house, surprisingly modern, with light walls and a pale beige carpet. The furniture was of fumed oak and the table, set for three, sparkled attractively with crystal and silver and damask napery. The whole impression was of freshness and of wholesome conviviality. And Garth, always sensitive to atmosphere, began to wonder if his suspicions of the man were not entirely baseless. There seemed no tangible reason to attribute dark motives to Ryall—or to Russi.

The American was standing by a cocktail cabinet, a shaker in one hand and a bottle of gin in the other. He finished adding the gin before he looked up and smiled.

A man of medium height in pale grey, American-tailored wild-silk, the most striking thing about him was his completely bald head. The contrast between his baldness and Ryall's singularly hirsute appearance was quite dramatic. Russi's face, too, was in equally compelling contrast: clean shaven, with full, red lips and fresh, pink cheeks he looked like an overgrown child.

'Ah, Russi!' said Ryall. 'I want you to meet our good friend, Mr. David Garth. Garth, this is Mr. Paul Russi, of whom I was speaking.'

Russi's hand looked soft and white, but his grip was firm and his voice unexpectedly deep and resonant.

'This is a real pleasure, Garth,' he drawled. 'I guess I haven't missed a speech of yours. You sure know how to hand it out. What'll you have?'

Garth smiled: 'What are you mixing?'

'Manhattan.'

'I'll have a Manhattan.'

'And you, Mr. Ryall?' asked Russi. Garth was surprised by the 'Mr.'.

'As usual, lime-juice and soda,' smiled Ryall. 'But don't trouble, my dear fellow: I shall mix it myself.'

There was no doubt, decided Garth, that Ryall himself struck the only false note in the next hour. He did not join in the conversation to any great extent, and his interpolated comments almost invariably steered the subject back from trivialities to the major point: Anglo-American understanding and its mishandling by the Government.

Russi did most of the talking.

It was impossible for Garth to judge what it was all leading up to. But helped by those timely comments from Ryall, Russi was obviously trying to secure his interest so as to make him fall in with their proposition, when it came. And they titillated his interest very astutely: there were times when he found himself warming to the American for his apparently genuine concern.

Yes, he thought, it was cleverly done …

Over a Benedictine, he himself waxed expansive, deliberately adding fuel to the flames in his eagerness to encourage them to get to the point. If there were any sort of chance of breaking the stranglehold officialdom had obtained, he was careful to intimate, he would take it eagerly: there were limits to what the Government should be permitted to do.

When he paused, at last, Russi regarded him with a gentle smile. His eyes seemed innocent of guile, although by then Garth was quite certain the man was, in his way, as clever as Ryall.

'You really think that way, Garth?'

'Of course I do!' said Garth, warmly.

Russi glanced at their host.

'What do you think, Mr. Ryall?' he asked mildly. 'Shall I tell our friend what we have in mind?'

'I think, my dear fellow,' murmured Ryall, 'I shall broach the subject myself. I, perhaps, can present it in a way which may do it less justice than you would contrive, but which might in some respects make it clearer to Mr. Garth.'

'That suits me,' said Russi, amiably.

'Thank you,' Ryall finished his liqueur, selected a cigar and took a silver cutter from his pocket. 'Now ...'

There was a tap at the door.

Garth was exasperated by the interruption: he was on a knif-eedge of expectancy. But Ryall looked up sharply and called: 'Come in!'

The neat maid opened the door.

'Mr. Brown is on the telephone, sir,' she said. 'He would like to speak to you.'

'Oh,' said Ryall.

Garth was watching him closely, although trying not to make it obvious. He saw the grey eyes narrow as Ryall rose to his feet, murmured an apology, and went out. As the door closed behind him, Russi shook his head admiringly.

'A very great man, Mr. Ryall.'

'A most impressive one, certainly,' said Garth. 'Have you known him long?'

'Long enough, I guess,' Russi shrugged. 'When you know more about him, you'll realise what I mean.' Smoothly, he led the talk into more general matters, while Garth waited with increasing tension for Ryall's return.

He thought he heard his light footsteps near the door. Then they faded and he fancied he heard another door open and close. A moment later, there came the sound of a car engine. He frowned, and the American rose abruptly.

'I hope he hasn't been called away,' Russi began. 'He's busy on a hundred different jobs and never knows where he'll be called next. He ... ah!'

The door opened—but to Garth's sharp disappointment, only the maid appeared.

'Mr. Ryall sends his apologies,' she said, 'and says to explain that he has been called away on an urgent matter. He asked me to tell Mr. Garth that he will call on him tomorrow.'

'Oh,' said Garth, flatly.

'Hell! That's too bad!' Russi grimaced as the door closed again. 'You were on tip-toes, Garth, weren't you?'

'I suppose I was.' Garth tried to dissemble. 'I suppose he has that effect on one. Can you give me an idea of what he was going to talk about?'

Russi laughed.

'I could, but I don't propose to. I'd say Ryall would be mighty annoyed if anyone were to steal his thunder—he's made that way. I guess it doesn't matter all that much either: there's no urgency in it. And he's right—he can tell the story much better than I can.'

It was obviously useless to press him—and bad tactics too, Garth decided.

Hiding his disappointment well, he chatted on for some ten minutes more with the American. He found it no hardship. Ryall had impressed him deeply, but there was something vaguely repulsive about the man. Russi, on the other hand, had a genial friendliness which his chubby face and easy smile served to emphasise. He found himself quite liking the American: there was no chance that he could ever like Ryall.

When the maid came again, it was to announce that a car was waiting for Mr. Garth.

It was a different taxi from the one which had brought him from the station—a limousine with a hackney-carriage licence. And Russi, who saw him to the door, told him the driver had instructions to take him right to Jermyn Street.

Not until he was sitting back in the comfortable interior, did Garth realise how summarily he had been dismissed. Had any other host disappeared without offering a word of personal apology, he would have thought it a pretty poor show; somehow with Ryall it seemed in no way surprising. But Russi had played his part in the dismissal smoothly—perhaps too smoothly?

As he was driven along the edge of Wimbledon Common, Garth began to wonder whether the exit had been deliberately staged to keep his curiosity at a high pitch.

He dismissed the possibility as hardly likely.

Far more probably that Ryall had received news from 'Mr. Brown' which had caused him some disquiet; surely only an emergency would have taken him away at such a time and in such a manner. He recalled the way Ryall had looked up at the maid's knock—almost as if he had been prepared for some kind of interruption, but was not pleased by it. The atmosphere in the room had changed at once.

He was still deep in thought when the car deposited him at Jermyn Street little more than half an hour later. But as he mounted the two flights of stairs to his flat, a feeling of anticlimax swept over him.

The mysterious cousins would no doubt get in touch, but he would have little to tell them; he no longer looked forward to their next meeting. Thoroughly disgruntled, he let himself into the flat.

The door of his lounge-cum-study was open.

The sight of it really startled him. He knew he had not only closed but also locked it—the room held many of his most prized possessions, and he had gone to the trouble of having a special lock fitted.

Alarm and apprehension merged in him as he moved toward it. Then began to subside, as he suddenly envisaged finding 'Mike' or 'Mark', or both, beaming blandly up at him: it was the kind of thing one might expect of them, he felt.

He pushed the door wider. The two hide armchairs were empty and he could see nothing, but the door struck against something and he cannoned into it in mid-stride.

'Damn!' he said, feelingly, and stepped through to look behind it.

Then he stood quite still.

A cold chill of fear started at the base of his spine and ran upwards. And suddenly cold from head to foot, he stared at the huddled figure of a girl which lay between the door and wall—and felt quite certain that she was dead.

She lay on her face, with her knees tucked beneath her. Her clothes were dishevelled and one shoulder of her blouse was torn to reveal a patch of creamy skin. A mass of dark hair spread tumbled forward on the carpet, leaving her neck bare.

He saw no sign of injury.

As the momentary paralysis eased, he went down on one knee to check whether by any chance she was still breathing. And only then did the truth strike him.

He let her head fall again, as her name sprang involuntarily to his lips.

'Anne!' he gasped. *'Anne!'*

And her voice, over the telephone, seemed to echo in his ears.

Chapter 4
No Need for Panic?

S he had been killed by a knife-thrust to the heart.

When he had recovered from that first shock of recognition, Garth knelt again—and saw the knife-handle sticking out. With a queer sense of unreality, he recognised the knife itself—a memento of Madrid that he had picked up in the early days of the Spanish Civil War, with a stiletto-type blade and a solid handle ornamented with delicate Moorish inlay-work.

There were red stains on the torn white blouse, and she had obviously struggled. Her face was in set lines of fear; almost of frenzy, and there were scratches on her face.

Garth straightened up again.

The shock of the discovery still affected him: he could not think clearly. He crossed unsteadily to the cabinet and poured a stiff whisky, which he drank at a gulp. Then stood there, the glass still in his hand, staring helplessly towards the murdered girl.

Why had she come here?

And who had been waiting to kill her?

Above all, *why had she been killed?*

The whisky began to work, and the mental paralysis passed. He ought to send for the police, he thought. Then stared at the knife. He had not touched it, but the way it jutted up from her breast made him feel sick.

If he summoned the police, would they take his word that he had discovered her there? Or would they suspect him of killing her?

He moved towards her again.

He had not thought to check whether her flesh was cold. Now he touched it. There was still warmth in her body: she had not been dead for long. That made it even worse. If he sent for the police even Ryall and Russi would provide no real alibi: no assurance, that he had not killed her since he returned.

This is madness!' he said, aloud, getting a grip on himself. 'They've got to know! I can't ...'

The telephone shrilled out.

He stared at it, uncomprehending at first. It rang again and he moved towards it automatically, glancing at his watch as he went. A little after five past nine. Darkness was falling: he should pull the curtains. Five past nine, he thought stupidly, as the bell rang again. Four hours since he had talked to her in the hope—he admitted it, now—of reviving their old association; of displacing George in her affections.

George Kent—what would *he* say?

Several windows along the street showed lights, so it was not yet black-out time. He lifted the receiver and managed to keep his voice steady.

'Hallo?'

'On the dot, as promised,' said a familiar voice. Mike's voice. 'Don't talk freely, now. Did you see him?'

Garth said: 'Yes, I ...'

'Good man!' The eagerness remained, contrasting bitterly with the dead girl behind him. 'You know Mrs. Parmitter, don't you?' Without waiting for an answer Mike went on: 'Call there in an hour—I'll be waiting. She's at ...'

'Stop!' Garth cried desperately. 'Don't go!' He drew a deep breath. 'Are you still there?'

'Yes …' Mike suddenly sobered. 'You don't sound too happy, old man?'

'I can't come, do you understand? I can't come! Something's happened here. I can't talk about it over the telephone, but something's happened. I can't come.' He remembered suddenly that he must not let even Mike know what had happened. And now he could see lights going out as black-outs were drawn. It would soon be dark: he could get the body out of the flat. He was panicking, now—telling himself it was useless to hope the police would believe he had found her there: useless to do the right thing.

'Oh,' said Mike. 'Like that, is it?'

'I can't come!' Garth repeated, desperately. 'I'm out of this show now, do you understand?'

As he replaced the receiver, he saw two people walking along the street below. They were glancing up at him and he realised they could see his face: perhaps even his expression. Hastily, he drew the curtains and then dabbed his perspiring forehead with his handkerchief. He turned, and saw Anne again. Saw her hair, so dark and lovely: hair that he had loved. As he had loved her. There had been bitterness in his soul because she had preferred the steadier George to him. But what was that bitterness, to this? And now what?

'Oh, God—what shall I do?' he asked aloud.

Reason insisted still that he should call the police. But the knife was his—almost certainly his finger-prints were on it. The special lock which he had believed could only be opened by his key—he had only one, and that was in his pocket. Like a drowning man snatching at a straw, he took out his key-case. Yes, the key was there. He thought wildly of what an unanswerable case could be built up against him.

Motive—jealousy; had he not once been engaged to Anne? Opportunity.... The weapon....

'*This won't do,*' he ground out, between clenched teeth. 'It just won't do!'

Then he heard footsteps, outside the flat door.

He stood rigid, his hands clenched, staring towards it. There was only his flat on this floor, and the one above was used as an office; it was never occupied during the evening. The people outside might be firewatchers; but it was hardly likely they would be on duty so quickly after black-out. He began to tremble uncontrollably.

There was a ring at the doorbell.

Should he pretend he was out?

But the caller might well be a friend in whom he could confide. And he felt in urgent need of the opinion of another person, who would be more dispassionate. He crossed to the door, deciding that he would close it when he reached the hall and if necessary take the caller into the little morning-room. Then if ...

He stopped short as the bell rang again.

If he put his hat on and picked up his gloves, he thought wildly, it would appear that he had only just come in—had not yet been into the larger room. He could bring the caller in and they could make the 'discovery' together! He forgot that the taxi-driver would know what time he had arrived; that his call from Mike might be discovered. He picked up his hat and gloves, put on his hat, and then opened the door on a third, louder ring.

The bald-headed American friend of Ryall's stood smiling at him.

'Russi!' he exclaimed, really shaken.

'Hallo, Garth. I guess I should have called you up, but ...'

'It ... it doesn't matter,' said Garth. 'Come in.'

Now that the emergency was on him, he did not know what to pretend. Russi must realise there was something amiss: he could not go through the farce of opening his study door and 'discovering' Anne convincingly, now. As they stood in the little hall, the American regarded him curiously.

'Are you feeling all right?'

'I … yes,' said Garth, hoarsely. 'Thanks. Of course I …'

'Well, you sure look like you'd seen a thousand ghosts.' Russi's mellow drawl was soothing. 'I had a call from Ryall, who asked me to bring a message along as I was passing.'

The words made little impression on Garth.

If he told the police what had happened, he would have to name Ryall and Russi. And when questioned, Russi would certainly remember the queerness of his manner now. It was useless to attempt deception and he desperately needed to confide in someone—anyone. And here was a man whose detachment was unquestionable, and who—because they thought along the same lines, ostensibly at least—would probably be sympathetic.

Abruptly, he admitted: 'You're right—I'm not feeling myself. I've had a shock.'

'Not bad news, I hope?'

'Bad enough,' said Garth harshly. 'I think I can … can rely on you. When I got back here, the flat had been burgled …'

'Say, that's bad!' Russi looked startled. 'Nothing taken that matters I hope?'

'I haven't looked,' Garth admitted. It was no use, he was behaving like a fool, yet he somehow felt better for the sympathetic American's presence. All that 'Mike' and 'Mark' had said should have made him suspicious of the man's intentions; even of the coincidence of his arrival.

No such thought even passed through his mind.

'Come with me,' he said.

He opened the door of the lounge and went in, then held it for the American to step through and pointed to Anne. Russi's brows contracted as he looked down.

Garth watched him closely, tensely.

The round eyes narrowed, the tentative smile faded from Russi's lips. He stared for a long moment, then turned back to Garth. His face had lost all friendliness now; was cold and suspicious.

'Say, what is this? What are you trying to pull?'

'Listen to me,' Garth urged him. 'That is ... was ... a friend of mine. I came back here to find the flat burgled and this door open—and Anne lying there, killed with *my* knife! She couldn't have been dead more than half-an-hour. I may be crazy, but—if I go to the police...'

He broke off, unable to utter the obvious.

Russi's expression grew softer. He took out a cigarette-case and proffered it, then flicked a lighter into flame and lit up for Garth and then for himself.

'It's bad,' he said softly. 'I guess I can see the way your mind's working. It looks like someone is trying to frame you, doesn't it?

'*Frame* me?' Garth echoed, blankly.

'Sure. Unless ...' Russi went down swiftly on one knee, beside the body. 'Maybe she did it herself. But the way she's been righting doesn't figure. Yes, I said "frame you", Garth. If anything like that was dumped in my flat, I guess I'd wonder who wanted me in bad with the police and would like to see me fried. Any ideas?'

His words made the whole thing worse, not better.

Garth drew a weary hand across his eyes, and then crushed out his cigarette in the nearest ash-tray, staring at the American. It must be true of course. This had been done deliberately. To get him arrested on a charge of murder, presumably. Some enemy ...

No, it was fantastic!

'I can't believe it,' he muttered shortly. 'No one dislikes me enough for that!'

'Someone doesn't love you much,' Russi pointed out, laconically. 'Did she have another boy-friend?' He seemed altogether too casual, and Garth wished him anywhere but there. 'Because my guess is she had, and you maybe took her away from him ...' Russi paused, expectantly.

Garth spoke with an effort.

'Let's keep our feet on the ground. The fact is, it was the other way round—and a long time ago. And I can't believe ...' He broke off. 'Oh, what's the use? I'll have to call the police right away.'

Russi said an incredulous:

'*What?*'

'You heard me.' Garth snapped roughly.

'I guess I didn't believe I'd heard right.' Russi shook his head. 'I'll admit your police are different from ours, Garth, but if I wanted a one-way ticket to the electric chair, that's what I'd do—ring them up and tell them about this! You *didn't* kill her, did you?'

'Don't be a fool! Of course I didn't!'

'Then why fry for it?' demanded the American. 'It's not your pigeon—and you surely won't be much use to Ryall if you're up on a charge of murder. Although I guess he'd want to help you all he could.'

'Why don't you tell me what you would do, not what you wouldn't?' Garth demanded fiercely.

'That's easy.' Russi was very calm. I'd get her out of here as fast as I could. The black-out's on. There's no moon. You could get her away—dump her some place where no one would find her till morning. Get that knife out, if its yours. No one would know where she'd been ...'

'Someone might have seen her come here.'

'Sure. And they might not have seen her go away. You couldn't have answered the door if you hadn't been here, could you?' He looked at his watch, then at the small gold one on Anne's wrist. The glass was broken, but it was still going. Calmly, he bent down, unstrapped it, turned it back to a little past eight, deliberately bent the minute-hand and banged the watch against the wall.

Then he held it to his ear and nodded with satisfaction.

'It's stopped,' he said. 'Now listen to me, Garth. I want to see you through this—I guess I'll be wanting your help later, and I can't have it if we don't get the girl away from here. We can put her somewhere the cops will find her in the morning. They'll see her watch and think that was the time it happened. You were at Wimbledon at five minutes after eight: no one can argue about that. I'll say so; so will Ryall, the maid, the cab-driver. The only thing you have to worry about is getting her out of here.' Cryptically, he asked: 'Any ideas on that?'

Almost against his will, Garth said:

'There are several bombed buildings nearby ...'

'You've said it!' Russi's eyes glinted. 'I remember I passed one in a cab. We'll wait till it's properly dark and take her down. Is there any way of getting her there without going through the main streets?'

'Yes ... But ... if we're caught ...'

'Aw, forget it!'

'If we're caught, I mean, you'll be involved!' Garth snapped.

'And if we're not, neither of us will be,' said Russi. 'If we are, then what difference does it make? You tell the truth and that watch gives evidence for you. And she must have *been* killed some time after eight. *Rigor mortis* won't tell them much—they can't argue to an hour or two about the time of death.'

Carefully, he wiped the back of the watch on a handkerchief, removing the finger-prints. Then with equal care, he polished the leather strap and, holding it with the handkerchief fastened it back on the dead girl's wrist.

Garth watched him—fascinated, at first, and then with dawning realisation.

Russi, he suddenly recognised, was far too accomplished in his self-appointed task. The care he took, the way his mind sprang to and dealt with all the dangers, suggested that he was not unused to such emergencies—or too great a knowledge of this particular one.

It was as well that he was paying careful attention to the watch, for Garth's eyes in that moment betrayed his sudden comprehension of the whole truth.

Then Russi straightened up.

'I guess we're all set, now.'

'Yes …' Garth grimaced, wanly. 'I … I don't like it.… '

'Give yourself a drink,' said Russi, shortly. 'Where's your nerve? Do you want to get yourself into trouble?' There was a faint, badly-concealed truculence in his manner, very different from the easy friendliness of the Wimbledon interlude and his first show of concern here at the flat. Garth noticed the change, and it confirmed his suspicions.

He was fully alert, now.

The shock of that sudden recognition of the truth had brought him to a far greater awareness of the dangerous business in which he was involved than even the death of Anne. The fact that she was dead, that all this discussion was about her dead body, did not seem real. That part of his consciousness which dealt with Anne would not accept the facts; was still completely numbed. For the rest, his awareness of crisis deepened; he was putting himself in Russi's power.

He was certain, now, that Russi had known what he would find when he reached the flat: that Russi and Ryall were framing him.

He did not quite know, then, why he allowed himself to be an accessory to his own victimisation. But at all events, he found himself going along with Russi's plans: concentrating on selecting a suitable hiding-place—somewhere that could be reached without much difficulty, and without using the main streets.

It should be easy enough.

A hundred yards along Jermyn Street was a turning which led to a small, quiet square where there were several bombed houses—cleaned up now, but with piles of debris still on the sites. An ideal place—and it would take him no more than five minutes to carry Anne there....

Russi looked up to ask:

'What time shall we start?'

'Well—we'd better not go any earlier than ten o'clock,' Garth cautioned, and was glad to find that his new-found self-control seemed to be gaining in strength. Russi would think that his own coolness had given him confidence. And he would let him think so.

It was half past nine by the time they had finished. Anne's body was wrapped now in an old mackintosh, and Russi had drawn out the knife and cleaned it. During that operation the nearness of Anne and all she had meant to him nearly wrecked Garth's poise. But Russi's almost inhumanly casual attitude to the whole affair angered him so deeply that the momentary weakness passed.

The waiting period was intolerable.

At a few minutes to ten, Russi finished a whisky-and-soda, glanced at his watch, and got to his feet.

'This is when we start. Will you carry her, or shall I?'

Garth said steadily:

'I shall.'

'Suits me. You going the back way?'

That startled Garth. The back stairs were little used and certainly would not be known to a casual visitor: further evidence, he felt bleakly, that Russi knew more about the flat than he professed. In his own mind, he had already decided that the best route would be via the front door. The darkness should be complete enough to hide his burden from the casual glance of possible passers-by.

He raised Anne in his arms.

For a moment, his heart contracted. But he gritted his teeth, and when Russi opened the door for him, he walked through steadily enough. The staircase was empty and Russi led the way, a few steps ahead of him. As they reached the open front door the American whispered a warning and a moment later, Garth heard the deliberate tread of a policeman passing nearby.

'Come on!' Russi murmured, when the coast was clear, and Garth followed him into the pitch-dark street.

The dim light thrown by Russi's torch was just enough to show the way without touching on Garth or his burden. A couple passed them on the other side of the road, giggling together; but they reached the corner of the little square without meeting anyone else. They hurried across it, Russi still leading the way, and reached the far corner. Garth was planning to turn right, and make for the bombed-out shell of a building which he knew was surrounded by a low, easily-surmounted wall.

It was then that someone suddenly shone a torch into Russi's face.

CHAPTER 5
ALL SAFE?

Garth, a few steps behind, stopped immediately as he saw Russi clearly silhouetted in the beam. He could see the outline of the man who held the torch too—and as he heard him speak, thought: *Police!*

'What do you reckon you're doing?' Russi demanded, in a high-pitched voice. 'Put that light out!'

'Sorry, sir!' The voice was deep, respectful. 'I'm looking for ...'

'You're not looking for me!' snapped Russi. 'And I don't like being dazzled—who are you?'

'I am a police constable, sir and ...'

'A cop, huh?' said Russi disparagingly. Then he proceeded to protest volubly, making far more out of the incident than it warranted, obviously to give Garth breathing-space.

As the two voices alternated, Garth turned and crossed the road. But he found the going difficult without the torch to guide him. He reached Jermyn Street again and turned left: there was another alleyway leading to the building he had in mind.

But there were too many footsteps; too many people about. Walking too fast, he cannoned into a man and apologised hastily and with real alarm.

His heart was hammering against his ribs now.

Every footstep seemed a policeman's; every moment he expected a light to shine on him, a voice demand to see what he was carrying. Once, he missed his footing and nearly fell. He reached the other alley at last, and hurried along it. He was just able to discern the white paint on the kerb, but did not know whether he had reached the right building—when he heard a heavy footstep ahead of him.

He stopped at once and stepping cautiously to one side found himself in the wide porch of an empty shop. There was no likelihood of his being seen from along the street, but if a patrolling policeman should happen along, it would be disastrous. Knowing that he had come to the end of his tether, he laid Anne's body on the ground and pulled the mackintosh away.

Her face and blouse were pale blurs in the darkness as the footsteps, heavy and deliberate, drew nearer.

Garth went down on one knee. His fingers sought her face, ran over her smooth cold forehead. Very softly, he promised:

'All right, my sweet. I'll make them pay for it!'

As he rose again, the footsteps stopped and he saw a beam of light flick into a doorway up ahead: a policeman, checking the shop doors.

He was perspiring freely as he reached Jermyn Street again. He could hear no voices: presumably Russi would have returned to the flat.

He reached it himself to find the American waiting tensely in the little hall.

'All safe?' he asked sharply, and Garth nodded.

'I ... I think so.'

'What in hell do you mean, *think* so?' snapped Russi. 'I didn't go through all that for fun! And shut that goddam door!'

Startled by the outburst, Garth obeyed automatically, then walked silently to his drinks cabinet and poured two stiff whiskies. Russi followed: he looked very pale, now, and his hands were unsteady.

'I think you need this,' Garth told him, coldly.

'Reckon so,' muttered Russi. He swallowed the neat whisky at a gulp. And as he set the glass down, his large, round eyes were suddenly icy hard. Garth was sure that he saw the man now for what he was: evil, dangerous, and clever.

'Now listen, fella,' he went on, harshly. 'You'll be in bad if they ever trace this business to you. Ryall and I will speak for you, but you might be in bad. Don't forget it!'

Garth said coolly:

'It applies to both of us, doesn't it?'

The American stared at him. There was a venomous glint in his eyes and Garth realised just how much he was meant to feel himself in this man's hands. Ryall and the maid and the driver of the second taxi would doubtless deny everything, if required—even all knowledge of his visit to Wimbledon. Yet he felt cool and detached and quite unfrightened. He had glimpsed the importance of what was happening, and was suddenly convinced that he had taken the right line.

He knew it for certain, when Russi's eyes dropped, and his manner changed.

'Sure—it goes for both of us, right enough. I guess I owe you an apology, Garth. But that cop had me scared.' He crossed to the cabinet, gesturing for permission, and poured himself another stiff whisky. He swallowed it down, and was suddenly more affable: more the man Ryall had introduced. 'I hand it to you, man—you're cool! I thought our number was up when that cop stopped me. You picked a bad spot—there's been a burglary around here.'

'Oh?' said Garth calmly, and the American shook his head admiringly.

'You've sure got a cool head on you! Anyway—you know the story if the cops question you? You were at Wimbledon—and I've never been here. Forget the message from Ryall,' he emphasised: 'I've never been here.'

Garth shrugged.

'I'm unlikely to mention your visit,' he said. 'Unless ...'

He paused deliberately.

'Unless what?' snapped Russi.

'You let me down,' Garth told him.

Russi gaped; then pulled himself together, affable again.

'Now listen, Garth: I'm not a fool. I don't know a thing about it. You were at Wimbledon: you didn't leave till about twenty of nine—and I haven't seen you since. You've nothing to worry about....' He broke off, then: 'Say ...' he drawled. 'You *didn't* kill her, did you? It's just occurred to me that you might have been framing me.'

'Don't be a fool!' snapped Garth. 'How the hell could I know you'd come here? And I told you the truth.'

'Oh, sure, sure,' said Russi hastily. 'I guess the whole thing's just kinda got on my nerves.' He smiled widely. 'We both know where we stand. Now, I'd better beat it.'

When he had gone, Garth returned to the lounge and examined the carpet where Anne had lain. There was no sign of blood. He crossed to an easy-chair and slumped into it, for the first time realising that his head was aching dully. He felt as if he had just finished a long run; his heart was beating too fast, the blood pounding in his ears.

Anne, he thought, achingly.

He remembered his promise to her lifeless body:

I'll make them pay for it.

And he would.

He was sure Russi knew all about it: and that Ryall was also involved. Bitterness swept over him: partly at his own gullibility, partly grief—but chiefly a desire for vengeance. God knew how, but somehow he would keep that promise to Anne.

He smoked three cigarettes in quick succession, then brewed himself some tea. He didn't want more whisky: he wanted a clear head. Wanted to think. And gradually his thoughts turned to the cousins at the Regent Palace. The death of Anne seemed all too obviously a part of the over-all pattern. He no longer doubted the truth of anything they had told him, and only wished he had not spoken so definitely to Mike on the telephone. He eyed it now, could he possibly contact them?

A bell did ring, making him sit up abruptly. But it was the front door, not the telephone.

His mouth felt suddenly dry. But he got up at once and went to the door, switching on the hall light so he could see the face of his caller.

Two men stood there.

The first was a stranger, and for a split second his heart leapt with fear. Then he recognised 'Mike'—who grinned his engaging grin as he said amiably:

'Sorry we're so late, Garth. Can you spare us a moment?'

'Yes, of course,' Garth stood aside, eyeing the second man.

Ryall had made a deep impression; in a different way this man, although much younger and of only medium height, did the same.

He was dressed in brown; his eyes were brown, and so was his hair. A close-clipped brown moustache covered the whole of his upper lip and beneath it, his smile held a touch of reserve. He was broad and well-knit and moved with an easy, almost cat-like grace. Garth had an impression of quiet authority, of leashed power.

'This is Bruce Hammond,' Mike introduced him. 'And I'll give you the rest of my name now. It's Errol.'

'Thanks,' said Garth, flatly. 'I'm glad we're dispensing with the mystery.'

'Frankness pays,' Errol waved an airy hand.

'Bruce is my chief, so to speak. And he's here to do the talking....'

'I'd like to do some of my own,' Garth told him, as he led the way to the lounge. And as they seated themselves, refusing his gestured offer of drinks, he added abruptly: 'I want to take back what I said on the telephone.'

'Oh!' said Mike, blankly.

Hammond looked as surprised, and shot a humorous glance at Errol before saying, quietly;

'That's good!' His eyes were curiously alive and intent. 'But why the change of heart?'

'Does it matter?'

'A great deal.'

'I've thought it over....' Garth began.

'No,' Hammond cut in. 'That won't do. You can refuse to tell us, and we've no way of compelling you—but evasion isn't necessary. You gave Mike the impression that you were badly upset on the telephone. It's not surprising. People who make contact with Franklin ...'

'The man I met called himself Ryall,' Garth told him.

Hammond raised his eyebrows.

'What was he like? Thickset, bearded—might have stepped out of Dickens?'

'That's the man, all right.'

'Same fellow, different alias,' Hammond shrugged. 'Probably he has others. I was saying—people who make contact with him often get some nasty surprises. You've been told of one meeting that ended tragically.' With no change of tone, he added: 'Has he been blackmailing you?'

'Not yet,' said Garth, only to wish immediately that he had not said so much.

Hammond's manner was disquieting in its very self-assurance; he looked a man whom nothing could shock off-balance. And it had suddenly struck Garth that he might be an official from Scotland Yard.

'Not yet?' echoed Hammond, with a glimmer of a smile. 'By the sound of things, I think perhaps what Mike calls "cards on the table" would be in order. You asked whether he was a secret service agent. He is. So am I.' Hammond took out his wallet, extracted a buff-coloured card, and handed it over: 'My authority.'

Garth scanned the small photograph of Hammond—an exact likeness—and the brief statement signed by both the Chief Constable at Scotland Yard and the Home Secretary. It stated that Hammond had 'full authority under Regulation 118c'. Garth had no idea what regulation that was, but the obvious hand-signatures satisfied him.

'Want to see mine?' offered Mike Errol, engagingly.

'No,' growled Garth. 'But why didn't you tell me before? It might have saved a lot of trouble.'

'Mike didn't tell you because he hadn't the authority,' Hammond told him quietly. 'Since his report of your tele-phone message, I've obtained authority—and also we've had a run-down on your activities in the past three years. You've been given a good character.' He smiled briefly. 'In any case, it would not have been wise to tell you before you saw Fran—Ryall. He might have asked questions without giving you a chance to evade them.'

'Operative word "might",' put in Mike. 'We couldn't be sure.'

'It was all done quickly,' Hammond went on. 'Several people who have returned from America have been approached—their mail, and that of a number of others, has been watched. Yours has been opened: the letter was seen before you had it. Ryall wanted you quickly which meant there was no time for us to check up—no time to do anything more than interest you, without giving you too much information. While, naturally,' he smiled again, 'hoping you'd prove worth getting on the team.'

The fact that his correspondence had been opened seemed amazingly unimportant. Garth simply nodded and waited.

'You say that Ryall hasn't started blackmailing you, "yet",' Hammond continued. 'That means you're afraid he might try. And that suggests that he might be able to find ...'

'A skeleton in the cupboard,' murmured Mike, and Hammond nodded.

'That's right. We're not interested in any skeleton you may have in your cupboard, Garth—provided it isn't even remotely connected with treason. What I'm telling you,' he added quietly, 'is that you've no need to fear any revelation to the police of facts disclosed to us.'

Garth stood up and moved restlessly across the room. Then stopped and said abruptly:

'So many things have happened that I don't know whether I'm on my head or my heels. Although one thing I'm damned sure of ...' He paused, marshalling the factors which had convinced him that Russi had known of Anne: that she had been murdered so that he would be compelled to do exactly what he was told.

Hammond was eyeing him steadily; Mike looked hopeful.

'Well, here goes!' he said wryly, and began to talk.

He kept nothing back.

Another man might have started with the murder of Anne. Garth started with the early days of his visit to America and his conviction that it was a mistake to hide from the American people the fact that public opinion in Britain was sometimes just as incensed by American attitudes as the Americans were by British. He touched on that only briefly, and as briefly on his recall and official reprimand. He spoke incisively, his facts marshalled and presented with a clarity that brooked no misunderstanding.

Then with no outward emotion, he described what had transpired at Wimbledon, and his discovery at the flat. He went into greater detail over Russi's part in what had followed, describing how Russi's manner had altered: the underlying threat in all he had said after Anne's body had been moved.

Quietly, he emphasised:

'I want to try to make myself understood. I haven't had an easy time in the past month. I've felt the strain—and it's obviously rattled me a bit. I think I was looking on Anne as a means of getting back to normal. Do you follow me?'

'I do,' said Hammond, equally serious.

'Her attitude gave me a shock,' Garth went on. 'I hadn't been letting myself admit how much I felt for her—how much I was relying on winning her back. And there she was—treating me like some stranger. Then came the Errols, and Ryall.' He grimaced. 'I suppose one thing on top of the other put me off my stroke. I like to think that in other circumstances, I should have gone to the police without hesitation. I still think given a few more minutes' thought, I'd have done so. But then Russi appeared, and—well, I lost my head. I don't think I shall again.'

'Neither do I,' Hammond told him.

'Thanks,' Garth nodded, wryly. Then frowned. 'I'm sure Russi knows something about Anne's murder. I'm going to try to *make* sure—it's a job to be done, that's all.'

Hammond smiled gently.

'It's one of a series of jobs,' he corrected, 'You've taken us at our own valuation, Now we'll take you at yours. You needn't worry about the police for a start. They may interrogate you but there won't be repercussions. You can see the enormous value of what has happened, can't you?'

'Value!' echoed Garth, bitterly.

'Try to see beyond the personal issues,' Hammond suggested. 'We believe Ryall and Russi are working to sabotage Anglo-American relations. I don't mean war-time unity—they won't try to interfere with that. But post-war understanding is a different matter. Financial and economic interests are at stake and a few individuals would rather lose their right hands than lose the chance of making big profits out of post-war chaos. I can't put it more strongly than that, yet. We don't know what Ryall is after, but we suspect he is working for powerful interests. And as I'm sure you know, if he is and he succeeds there could be some mighty unpleasant repercussions.'

'Yes....' Garth nodded slowly. He was surprised: it was possible to forget the strictly personal issue, even though he knew the full bitterness of it would never leave him.

'Good,' said Hammond. 'Then the value of what's happened is that Russi and Ryall have—in their view—succeeded in forcing you into a corner. The next step, I think, will be an ultimatum.... "do as we tell you or we'll inform the police of what happened". They may not use it yet—may save it for an emergency. Things may take a long time to develop, or they could come to a head very fast. What matters is that you will be in their confidence to some degree. They won't

know you are also in ours, and working for us. That's why
we've been so careful. We came here after dark, remember,
and there is no chance at all that we were seen.'

Garth nodded again, and Hammond went on:

'In the course of finding out what Ryall is after, we'll
discover just why Miss Duval was killed. And …'

He stopped, smiling gently, as Garth stared at him
wide-eyed.

Garth had not mentioned her surname: had called her
'Anne' throughout his narrative.

How did *Hammond* know who she was?

Chapter 6
George Kent

G arth did not put the question into words.

Staring at Hammond, he came to the conclusion that words must often be superfluous, with that man—and Errol, too. They gave him a strange impression of solidity: an unspoken assurance that they know very well indeed, everything whereof they spoke.

From the first, he saw now, they had known more than it was reasonable for them to know. Now, he was hardly surprised when Hammond said quietly:

'You're wondering how we know it's Anne Duval?' He smiled, fleetingly. 'But you'll realise we've *had* to check on you pretty thoroughly, Garth—and we've learned enough to be able to guess that only Miss Duval would affect you so strongly. Then there's another—possibility,' he added thoughtfully.

'What do you mean?' demanded Garth.

Hammond said:

'George Kent, Miss Duval's fiancé, is in your Ministry—and a stickler for the orthodox approach to all matters. You know, of course, that ...'

He spoke quickly and to the point for a minute or two.

None of what he said was news to Garth, although much was presented in a way which surprised—even startled—him. He saw possibilities which he had not dreamed of before.

George Kent—sound, solid, exasperatingly conventional, and, as Hammond said, a stickler for the orthodox approach—was in the American Relations Section. He was not Garth's immediate superior, but was senior to him. There was little doubt that he would strongly disapprove of the speeches which had caused the trouble.

And Hammond thought that Kent might have been approached by Ryall.

'We can't be sure,' he emphasised. 'And it wouldn't be a direct approach. Kent would report that immediately—and Ryall would have the sense to know that he would. But there are ways of getting round the problem. Kent has some influence at the Ministry, and recently Miss Duval worked there as his secretary. Did you know that?'

Garth was astonished.

'I'd no idea!'

'Staff shortage, as you know. Presumably at his request, she took a special course in secretarial training and went to help him. She may have been killed solely to give Ryall a strong hold on you, but there could also have been some other reason.'

'This gets more and more incredible,' Garth protested.

'Why?' asked Hammond quickly, and Garth hesitated a moment before replying.

It was partly because they were discussing *his* Anne so dispassionately: the others had not known her gaiety, the warmth of her smile, the deep joyousness of her laugh. But it was partly, too, the remembered tone of that first greeting on the telephone.

He could still hear that unbelieving: *'David!'*

Was he wrong? No, dammit! There *had* been a note of welcome, almost excitement in her voice. Then why that mercurial change? *Had* she suddenly decided to be discreet? Was he reading more into it than he should?

He explained his uncertainty as best he could.

Hammond looked thoughtful.

'I see … Yes. You think it's possible she had some information affecting you?'

'Well … *just* possible,' Garth said, awkwardly. 'But it was so unlike her—the sudden change, I mean. I couldn't understand it.'

'We'll keep it in mind,' Hammond told him. 'You may have hit on something. Meanwhile, what matters most is—are you with us?'

'Of course!' Garth looked his surprise at the question.

'Hook, line, and sinker?' Errol demanded brightly.

'I'm with you all the way.'

'You don't quite know what it might entail,' Hammond reminded him. 'You've seen something of their methods. I don't think there is the slightest doubt that they murdered Miss Duval—and if they had any idea you were working with us, they would kill you without compunction.'

'I might do a little violence myself,' said Garth, grimly—and was aware at once of a subtle change in the atmosphere. Hammond's eyes had narrowed and Errol raised an eyebrow and contemplated the ceiling.

'Well, what's the matter with that?' he demanded, gruffly, and Hammond said:

'The point is, Garth, you may frequently feel like murder—but you mustn't give way to it.' He smiled widely. 'An odd kind of moralising! What I mean is: you may be fully justified in wanting to kill Ryall or Russi in self-defence, but until we know about their activities we must not allow them to be killed. We want to keep in touch with what they're doing—and you will be able to help us a great deal. On the other hand, if they discovered what you were doing....' He shrugged. 'Someone else would have to take your place.'

Garth stared at him, slowly comprehending.

'No matter what the provocation,' Hammond added. 'You've got to remember that. At the risk of embarrassing you, I'll say that we've reached the conclusion that you've considerable moral courage. That's why we selected you as the most likely man to help us—and why we've investigated your past so thoroughly. As the position stands now, you're able to tell Ryall and Russi something about us. They might want to know it....'

'I shan't talk!' Garth said sharply. 'What do you think I am?'

Hammond eyed him steadily.

'Very good men—brave men, strong men—have talked, under pressure. It's no shame to them. Pressure can be excessive. There aren't many who can stand up against every kind of persuasion.'

'What are you trying to do?' Garth demanded. 'Scare me out of it?'

'No,' said Hammond. 'I'm doing what Mike did at the Regent Palace—trying to make sure that you do understand all the dangers. I'm not justified in asking you to help when you know only half a story. I don't think I need go into any further detail.' He paused. 'Are you with us?'

'What do I do next?' asked Garth.

Hammond and Errol had gone.

The flat was very quiet. It was nearly one o'clock and no sound came in from the street. Garth could near the ticking of his wrist-watch as he sat back, staring through narrowed lids at the ceiling. The only movement in the room was when he raised a cigarette to his lips, or took it away.

His instructions had been simple: he had to wait until he heard from Russi and Ryall—and then to do whatever they wanted. He would hear from Hammond, or the Errols, as and when he had information to impart: they had not volunteered how they would know when such moments arose. But oddly enough, he believed that they would. And they would see that he was watched, and if possible aided, whenever action threatened. He himself had no means of making contact with them, or the Department for which they worked.

He did not even know, yet, that it was known to the *cognoscenti* of Whitehall simply as 'Department Z'.

Bruce Hammond left Mike Errol at the corner of Parliament Street, searching for that rarest of war-time birds, a late-night taxi. Hammond, himself, crossed the road and reached Whitehall. There was a narrow turning not far from Scotland Yard, which many people passed unnoticing by day and night because it was so insignificant-looking. Many of those who did use the little alley as a short cut also passed a small doorway, piled high with sandbags, for the same reason.

Hammond found his way past the sandbags and, guided by a handrail, climbed a narrow flight of stone steps. He climbed another, stood listening a moment, then returned to the first landing. There, he ran his fingers along beneath the handrail, he touched a small nodule, and carefully manipulated it.

In the room beyond, Gordon Craigie, Chief of Department Z was seated in an old but obviously comfortable winged armchair. Opposite him, lolling back with his eyes closed and a smile on his heavy face, was his deputy and second-in-command, Bill Loftus. In some moods, Loftus was inclined to be bitter about his 'inactive executive' position in the Department. His active share in its operations had been curtailed after one such affair had robbed him of his right leg.

Behind Craigie was a large cupboard, built into the wall. The door was open, revealing a miscellany of oddments from tinned food and tobacco to spare collars and socks. Gordon Craigie's hair was thin and very grey, his long face deeply-lined, his drooping lips had an expression and his hooded grey eyes could turn from grave to gay in a flash. He was personally the untidiest man in the Department, but his records—for which he was responsible—were scrupulously kept.

At the moment, as indeed at most times, there was an elderly meerschaum in his mouth: and within easy reach were a dozen others, all ornately carved and all darkened with constant use.

Loftus—a very large, apparently ungainly man, until he moved—smoked a big conventional pipe.

A few embers glowed in the fireplace and the eyes of both men were closed, as if they were dozing. But the moment a button of green light glowed beneath the mantelpiece, Craigie opened his eyes and took the meerschaum from his lips.

'Here he is,' he said, as a small bulb suddenly glowed green and a section of the wall near the fire-place slid open to admit Bruce Hammond. Craigie pressed a button, and the door slid to.

'What-ho, my hearty!' greeted Loftus, opening one eye.

'Hallo, Bruce!' nodded Craigie: 'Pull up that chair.'

'Thanks,' said Hammond, doing so.

It was like them not to ask questions. Hammond some-times felt that to people outside their little circle, they must present an exasperating front. He had been part of the cir-cle for many years; but for much of that time he had worked abroad—and even he was not yet fully accustomed to regu-lar contact with the Whitehall office.

'And how is the Operations Commander tonight?' boomed Loftus, opening the other eye.

Hammond smiled.

'I'm all right.' He understood very well what it must mean to a man the same age as himself and essentially a man of action, to be compelled through no fault of his own to hold a watching brief—particularly on cases where experi-ence could mean the difference between life and death. Yet Loftus, who had been the Operations Commander imme-diately before him, had given his successor every possible help; and Hammond knew he would continue to do so.

'I think Garth's all right,' he went on, coming straight to the point. 'He's taken the death of the girl very hard.'

Loftus frowned.

'Like that is it? Pity.'

'I don't know,' murmured Craigie. 'Might quicken his interest—give him greater staying-power. I don't like bring-ing in outsiders, but ...' He shrugged. 'We needn't go into that again. You've told him just what we arranged, Bruce?'

'Exactly,' said Hammond. 'And ...'

For fifteen minutes he reported in detail on their conver-sation, the gist of which he had telephoned to Craigie right after leaving Garth's flat. Another fifteen minutes passed before they had finished discussing that angle of the case.

Finally, Craigie went to his desk, pulled out a drawer, and selected a manila folder.

The part of the long room at the fire-place end was homely and comfortable. The larger part, furnished as an office, held three steel filing-cabinets, one large steel desk—on which stood five telephones, all of different colours—two smaller desks, a typewriter, a dictaphone and several chairs.

Craigie came back to the fire-place and passed the manila folder to Hammond.

'Kent's file,' he explained.

Hammond opened it. The first thing he saw was the photograph of a plumpish but good-looking man, with meticulously-parted dark hair and a rather petulant expression. There were two other photographs—George Kent's profile, taken from right and left. If anything, he was more handsome in profile than full face, for the querulous expression was not apparent.

Hammond ran through the reports. They were of a man who had entered the diplomatic service straight from Oxford and whose career had been exemplary but unexceptional. His transfer to the Ministry of Propaganda had come in the second year of the war; and there again, his record was unblemished.

On the last page relating to his professional career, Craigie's neat hand had appended a note:

Thorough, careful, unimaginative.

Kent belonged to three clubs: the Carilon, the Carlton and the Junior Conservative. All of his known friends, as recorded in the dossier, could be found in *Debrett* and *Who's Who*. He had no known hobby, but a reputed liking for polo and hunting. He had spent several years in various European capitals and was an excellent linguist.

Hammond finished reading and said mildly:

'Not a lot there for suspect Number 3, is there?'

'Have we got that far, yet?' asked Craigie. 'Ryall—or Franklin—is Number 1, Russi, Number 2. Kent might be in it somewhere. But we can't say more than that, yet.'

Loftus raised an eyebrow.

'Wally Davidson thinks Anne Duval discovered something about Kent that she shouldn't. He warned us that something might happen to her. It's happened. Ought we to look further than that?'

'Well ...' Craigie rubbed his long chin. 'It could also be that she discovered something which Ryall didn't want known. It might be that she discovered he was making an approach to Kent, and so could warn Kent. Or to Garth. It's all too indefinite at the moment.'

'It's all too much in the air, that's for sure,' said Loftus, with some irritation. 'It's going too slowly. We might get results from Garth, but even that is by no means certain. I don't like these shows which hang fire. It always makes me think that a lot we know nothing about is going on. I don't ...'

'Like being kept in the dark?' grinned Hammond.

'Damn your eyes!' Loftus grinned back. 'But are you satisfied? Of course you're not.' He scowled. 'If we're right, Ryall is going to pull something very big. But we haven't the faintest idea when it's to start or what it's about—except that it won't make things very healthy between London and Washington. If we had even a vague idea of what interests are behind him, it would be a help.' He stretched up to grip the mantelpiece and hoisted himself to his feet, then stumped somewhat awkwardly across the room: he was always a bit stiff when he had been sitting for some time. 'We've not had a single report of real interest. Not a single flash of inspiration, or ...'

Craigie's hooded grey eyes twinkled.

'You must be tired, Bill.'

'Tired!' snorted Loftus. 'I'm worried, dammit! It's time we got a move on.'

'We haven't had the sort of chance we've got with Garth before,' Hammond pointed out. 'It won't surprise me if we get some action pretty soon, Bill. And there's another thing to remember—this is the first time we've had approval from Number 10 to concentrate on one job and let the others go hang. The Cabinet is deeply worried about Anglo-American amity now, thank God. Give it a few days, and we'll start breaking it open.'

'I hope you're right,' said Loftus, darkly. 'I certainly hope you're right. I wish ...'

He stopped as a telephone rang, and limped towards the desk.

'It's the red one,' Craigie told him; constant usage had made him able to differentiate in a flash.

Red for danger—and red for Number 10.

All three of them were tense now: it was seldom that there was a call from Downing Street so late at night, although the P.M. was renowned as a 'late-bird' and had been known to ring for information in the early hours of the morning. But it could well be something of exceptional importance.

The big man lifted the receiver, and a moment later heard the unmistakable growling voice of the Prime Minister.

'That you, Loftus? Is Craigie there?'

CHAPTER 7
QUICKENING TEMPO

The Rt. Hon. Graham Hershall, M.P., Prime Minister, was no respecter of persons. All he demanded was that a job should be done well. There were times when he exasperated some large Government departments by holding up as an example a much smaller and little-known one, the work of which was considered unimportant by many, trivial by others. That Department was called Z. In a caustic moment the P.M. had once said that the only Department in Whitehall he could enter without using scissors to cut the red tape was Gordon Craigie's.

'Hallo, Craigie,' he growled now, the tone of his voice telling Craigie at once that this was no minor matter. 'Are you in bed?'

'Not yet,' said Craigie.

'Who's with you?'

'Loftus and Hammond.'

'Good, I'll be there in ten minutes.'

'If you'd rather we came to you, sir ...' began Craigie.

'No, I can do with a breath of fresh air,' said the P.M. 'Ten minutes, then.'

Craigie replaced the receiver with a slight frown.

'He's coming over,' he reported. 'I don't know what it's about but he sounds grimmer than usual.'

The green light glowed, a little more than ten minutes later, and Craigie pressed the push. The door in the wall slid open and Hershall came in: a thick-set man with great, ox-like shoulders, a large, pale face with jutting brows and an aggressive-looking chin. A small, black cheroot stuck out from his pursed lips, and his greenish-grey eyes had an angry glint.

He was dressed formally, suggesting that he had come straight from a function of some consequence.

'Ha!' he growled, surveying the trio with approval. 'At least there are some people around who don't sleep all night. But I can't understand you, Craigie. All these secret buttons and sliding doors—lot of child's play, isn't it?'

Craigie answered the comment—which he had heard often enough before—with a smile:

'It works well enough, sir.'

Hershall grinned.

'So it does! As I seem to remember you've told me before. Sit down, all of you.'

As they obeyed, knowing he preferred them to relax, he strode across to the desk, pushed two telephones aside, and perched on the edge, staring at them. He was ten feet or more away, an impressive man but a worried one: that much was obvious to them all. The quickening tempo for which Loftus had prayed seemed already to have come.

'What have you got to tell me?' he demanded.

'Little enough,' said Craigie. 'We've found a man who's been approached by Franklin—now calling himself Ryall—and I think we shall be able to use him.'

'Who is it?'

'A David Garth,' said Craigie.

'Garth ... Garth?' Hershall scowled. 'Don't remember—
oh, yes, I do! Fellow who talked too much, isn't he? Liked
his spirit, but we can't have that sort of thing. H'mph. Well,
whether you get them through Garth or the Devil himself,
I don't much care—but you must get results. Kearnley was
attacked tonight. He's in hospital—not yet sure whether
he'll recover. You see what that means?'

'Kearnley!' ejaculated Hammond.

'That's who I said,' growled the P.M. 'And when an official visitor from the United States is attacked and nearly
murdered, I want something done about it! Kearnley is a
very good man—I want to make that clear. We see eye to eye
on many things. Most things. Exceptional fellow—and he
was reaching agreement with Scott. Now, it will mean delay.
And even if Washington can send someone else quickly, it
won't be another Kearnley; there's only one of him.'

'Look here, sir,' Loftus interrupted. 'We know all about
Kearnley. But we don't know where he was attacked and
what's been done about it. Shouldn't we?'

The P.M. glared at him. There was a moment of silence
before the button of a mouth relaxed and the stormy eyes
smiled.

'Quite right, Loftus! Not that it'll help much. He was
found badly injured in front of the American Embassy, and
taken to the Central Hospital. And he was there three hours
before he was recognised. I haven't heard from the hospital
since he went on the table—but I've arranged for you to
have word direct, as soon as it's available. Not much you can
do about it, is there?'

'Three hours,' mused Loftus. 'It was dark, then. No, I
suppose there's little ...'

'Listen to me!' Hershall cut in restlessly. His cheroot had
gone out and he took it out and glowered at it, but made no

effort to relight it. 'I know I've often asked you people to do the impossible. I know the difficulties—and your limitations. But I've come to tell you that you must work as you've never worked before. I know you haven't much material—you'll just have to find it! Hang the expense—bring in all the men you need. This is absolutely Number One priority. Is that all clear?'

'Absolutely,' grunted Craigie.

'Good. What have you done about the Franklin fellow?'

'Nothing, except what we've told you about Garth. And until we know more about it, Franklin must be left free. We're agreed on that.'

'H'mph!' The Prime Minister's stare was disconcertingly direct, but he shrugged his massive shoulders as he conceded: 'If you say so. I didn't come here to tell you how to go about it—only that it's to be done. Contrary to belief held in certain quarters,' he added, sardonically, 'I do have some regard for conditions after the war. And, for three months now, on both sides of the Atlantic efforts have been made to sabotage working agreements—this Kearnley business is a case in point. The Federal Bureau is looking after the American side—and they'll probably be sending a man over to see you. Not much doubt that it's starting here, though. It would!' Hershall sounded bitter. 'Well, I suppose we all ought to get some sleep.'

He stood up, his eyes twinkling. 'How's your wife, Loftus?'

'Very well, sir, thank you.'

'Good! And that young woman of yours, Hammond? Still giving you spiritual support and guidance?' He smiled widely. 'Well, I'll be off. Goodnight, all of you—and for all our sakes get some results and get 'em quickly!'

And with a lift of the hand and a fleeting smile he was gone. As the door closed behind him, the three men sank back, sober-faced, into their chairs.

'Kearnley!' Loftus murmured, still shocked, and Craigie said drily:

'Well, you've got what you wanted—something to bite on! They're coming into the open, Bill. Kearnley won't be the only American over here to be attacked, so we've got to have all the likely ones watched. Action stations!' he added, looking positively cheerful. 'We'll take a telephone apiece and get started right now.'

'What about the men we're going to have watched?' asked Hammond, and Loftus grinned.

'What do you think we've been doing all evening?' he demanded. 'We've been listing the people who're likeliest to be affected if things warm up. The Executive does have its uses, my son!'

In the next two hours, they made call after call to agents of Department Z. Most of them were asleep in their beds, but none raised the slightest protest at being wakened. All were given precise details of the job they were to do, and the names of the men who would be their especial charges for the next few days—or weeks.

The dialogue was the same every time. Nothing was said that could have been understood by anyone overhearing the conversation, but the instructions went home and some forty men began at once to dress and prepare themselves for action. And all of them, as one man, having armed themselves with their automatics and various other weapons, went blithely out to challenge whatever unknown dangers Fate—and their jobs—held in store.

Chapter 8
The Errols Strike Lucky

Michael and Marcus Errol, their particular task with David Garth completed, had spent the night at the Regent Palace Hotel, Mark having objected to 'throwing away' the money already paid for the room. So they received the orders from Loftus there, and Mike relayed the gist of the call to Mark as they began to dress.

'You going to shave?' grunted Mark.

'Need we?'

Mark rasped his fingers across his stubble and scowled.

'I should, but you look all right. You go along first—I shan't be ten minutes after you.'

'Right,' nodded Mike, and continued to dress with a speed many an actor might envy. Five minutes later he was on his way, a silenced automatic snug in his pocket.

Mike liked to claim that he was the optimist of the cousins. Mark like to say that he was the steadying influence; the one who made sure Mike did not go into crazy situations as blindly as he otherwise might. The truth was that while they bickered amicably between themselves, when there was criticism of either from third parties they defended each other stoutly.

As Mike went out through the main doors, a ghostly figure loomed up in the gloom.

'Taxi, sir?'

'Taxi?' exclaimed Mike. 'Is the Age of Miracles upon us?'

'Taxi waiting, sir,' said the man, stolidly.

'You are a herald of good tidings,' Mike told him. 'Yes, please! In about ten minutes my cousin will be coming out and he'll want one, too. If you can keep one up your sleeve for him....'

'How shall I know him, sir?'

'Looks like my twin brother—just ask him if he's Mr. Errol.' Silver changed hands and he climbed into the taxi. 'Queen's Gate, this end,' he told the driver.

At 27, Queen's Gate, there lived Mr. Arnold K. Livesey, one of several representatives of the American Farmers Union currently visiting Britain, and one of the Allied Nations Committee discussing post-war food problems. Livesey was an exceptional man inasmuch as he had the ear of the farmers as well as farm-workers in the States and was equally popular with both. Trouble with the Farmers' *bloc* in the Senate had been resolved largely with the assistance of the burly Middle West farmer, whose solution to the problem had satisfied the *bloc* as well as the President.

Mike knew no more about Livesey than he had read in the papers. Since he was often too busy to do more than glance at the headlines, he did not know that at 27, Queen's Gate, there also lived Arnold K. Livesey's daughter. Not that the fact would have interested him greatly. Mike was engaged and currently at the stage where there was only one woman in the whole world to be seen, heard or even thought about. He even spared a few minutes to day-dream of his Regina before the taxi drew up at the end of Queen's Gate.

When the cab had disappeared, he picked his way slowly in the pitch-darkness along the wide pavement. There was no indication that he would see any action that night. His orders were to hold a watching brief with Mark until daylight, when Craigie would send someone else to take over their beat. But Mike, the undying optimist, lived in constant expectation.

When he had walked about a hundred yards, he shone a torch to check his position.

All the houses in Queen's Gate were approached by a flight of five stone steps, and each porch was supported by tall pillars. In front of each house, a railed-off area served by a flight of steps led to the servants' entrance and the semi-basement. Mike knew all of that well.

His torch-beam picked out Roman numerals in gilt on a painted pillar: XXVII.

'Right first go,' he told himself, with some pride.

Somewhere in the distance, a solitary searchlight swept across the sky and then went out abruptly, leaving the darkness suddenly more intense. There were no people about, and no traffic. Well, hardly surprising, he thought, as a clock not far away suddenly struck half past two: he had not realised it was so late. He was glad of his overcoat, for the night was chilly and a fresh wind blew from Kensington Gardens.

'Livesey,' he mused. 'I wonder if ...'

Across his murmured words there came a sound, faint at first but growing louder from inside Number 27! He stared towards the porch. Someone was approaching the door—the footsteps were unmistakable now. Hurrying, light—sharp heels on marble, he thought: or very hard wood. A woman's footsteps. He stepped a little to one side, peering towards the door, catching only a glimpse of polished brass. The tapping sound drew nearer and he fancied he could hear someone breathing heavily.

Then: *crack!*

'Holy smoke!' he breathed.

It was a pistol shot; he had no doubt at all of that, as the sound echoed in his ears. Tensely, he stared towards the door as the footsteps continued: the heavy breathing grew more laboured. He stepped forward as a second *crack* came; nearer, this time, and sounding very loud. Then a crashing noise, as a pane of glass in the door shattered and flew in all directions.

The door opened.

Instinctively, he drew back against the side of the porch and reached for his gun. He could not understand why there was no cry of alarm, no call for help.

Then someone fell headlong down the steps.

The white-clad figure was on a level with Mike before he realised what was happening. He shot out his left arm and something soft struck against it—soft and light and perfumed, but heavy enough to send him momentarily off-balance. He recovered in time to break the worst of her fall—then let her go in a flash, as he saw the shadowy figure on the threshold: a man, his face just visible as he fired again.

This time, a flash of yellowish flame heralded the *crack,* and fast upon the shot, the smack of a bullet hitting a step or pavement. Mike had no idea whether the girl had been hit. She fell to the ground and the man came after her.

He drew level with Mike, who calmly put out a hand.

'Going places?' he murmured.

As he grabbed the man's wrist, he touched the cold steel of the gun. He pushed it sharply downwards and a fourth shot echoed clearly as the bullet wasted itself. Mike had dropped his own gun back in his pocket and now aimed a clenched fist at the other's chin and as he staggered against the opposite wall, the pistol clattered to the steps and bounced down them.

Mike was anxious about the girl, but his first and most important task was to render the man *hors de combat.*

He pulled out his torch and flicked it on.

The dazed face of the sprawling man was caught in the beam of light. The punch had landed squarely and a trickle of blood came from the thickish lips. It was the face of a thug. The forehead low, the face heavy. A hired gunman, at a guess.

Mike bent forward and jerked the man's head up. Vacant eyes peered at him for a moment—then the face suddenly took on an expression of sheer terror and the man tried frantically to get to his feet. Mike let him rise to his knees, then put in an uppercut which rattled his teeth as he reared back and then flopped down in a crumpled, unmoving heap.

'My night out,' murmured Mike, happily. 'I wish ...'

But he was enjoying himself too much. He realised it even as he was turning to the girl. His immediate concern was with Mr. Arnold K. Livesey. He spun round and strode in over the threshold of Number 27.

His torch-beam played over a large but sparsely-furnished hall. For a moment, he stood there, straining to hear some kind of sound, unable to understand the quiet. He thought he heard footsteps in the street and the sound of a car engine as he moved towards the sweeping staircase. Then as he reached the foot, he heard a movement above his head—and looked up to see an evil face staring down and a gun pointing straight towards him. Pressing himself back against the wall, he fired from his pocket. A bullet buried itself in the floor a foot away, but his own shot went equally wide.

Yet it served one purpose, for the gunman turned and ran up another flight of stairs.

Then the footsteps behind him drew nearer, and someone ran into the hall. Voices sounded outside, too: and he swung round, prepared to deal with another attack. He was suddenly blinded by the glare as a huge chandelier was switched on and a voice came urgently:

'What's doing?'

'Mark!' He grinned his relief. 'Strangers upstairs, I think!'

'Upstairs?' echoed Mark, and raced for the staircase.

He had reached the first landing when Mike, a few steps behind him, heard a door slam below and looked down to see a policeman and a warden gaping up at him.

'Look after the girl! and guard that man—he's dangerous!' he yelled, and raced on, pulling out his automatic.

Footsteps came from above him now: the house seemed to be full of noises. He thought he heard the bark of a gun, but could not be sure. He did hear a high-pitched cry.

The landing light was on, and as a brighter light shone from an open door on the far side, Mark came running from the room, his face set and gun in hand. He turned right into a passage and as Mike raced in his wake, he glimpsed through the open door a big man in pyjamas stretched out on the floor, and bedclothes in a heap by his head.

'A night for deserting the injured!' he muttered aloud and ran on.

At the end of the passage, Mark was putting his shoulder to a locked door in a futile effort to force it open. As Mike drew level, they hurled themselves at it together. But it was much too solidly built and they did no more than shake it.

'It's a waste of time,' said Mike and Mark grimaced, rubbing his shoulder.

'Yes, confound it! Did you see him?'

'Not after you arrived.'

'He came out of the room back there and I let him go,' growled Mark. 'I thought I'd better see what damage he'd done, and whether anyone else was there. There was only the man knocked out—no more than knocked out. Our merchant came through this doorway, which probably leads to another staircase.'

'We could find the back door?' Mike suggested, but Mark shook his head.

'Too late,' he said, briefly.

'*Now!*' demanded a heavy voice, behind them: 'What *is* this?'

Mike turned to see the outraged face of a policeman—who glanced with some apprehension at the gun in his hand. Mike promptly put it back in his pocket and as Mark followed suit, the man seemed distinctly relieved.

But Mike's thoughts were in too much of a whirl to attempt an answer. There had been an attack on Livesey and the girl, obviously : but there were other stranger things to be considered. Why had the girl run out without saying a word? Why was the huge house deserted, save for the injured man? It was the headquarters of the Agricultural Committee and be knew that many of those who worked there lived on the premises.

'The quicker,' he said, thinking aloud, 'Bruce knows about this, the better.'

'The quicker *I* know something about it, the better!' growled the policeman, as Mark nodded and went in search of a telephone. 'Who *are* you?'

Mike treated him to the disarming Errol charm.

'Oh, yes. I'm sorry, Constable, but it's been rather a scramble.' He took out a card like the one Hammond had shown to Garth, and the policeman's suspicions melted miraculously.

'I *see*, sir!' He handed it back. 'Then I am of course at your service.'

'Good man,' said Mike. 'Now, did you see to the young lady?'

'Yes, sir. The warden's looking after her—and we've got the man locked in a cloak-room—I picked up his gun, sir.'

'Good! Well, there's a man, also unconscious, in one of the bedrooms. We could do with a doctor—will you send for one, right away?'

'Yes, sir.'

'And how many men can you raise, immediately?'

'Well … if I include firewatchers …?'

'Include all able-bodied men.'

'About a dozen, then, sir.'

'Not bad,' Mike nodded crisply. 'Have the back door watched, will you? And put a sprinkling of chaps in the house—say, two to each landing. Then there'd better be a thorough search of the house. There should be people in residence, surely?'

'There certainly *should* be, sir!' the man said, startled not to have thought of it sooner.

Both he and Mike were relieved by the arrival of the P.C.'s sergeant, who put the work in hand promptly after one glance at Mike's card.

Mark was coming from a room off the big entrance-hall when Mike returned downstairs.

'I've phoned Hammond,' he said.

'Is he coming over?'

'Yes. So is Bill.' Mark frowned. 'Livesey's still out cold, unfortunately. What about his daughter?'

Mike looked puzzled.

'The girl I nearly tripped over, coming in,' said Mark with a touch of impatience. 'I only had a quick glimpse, by torchlight, but I'm sure it's her. She's been pictured with him often enough—and she's his right-hand man, in a manner of speaking. So if she's able to talk....'

The girl had been carried into a small lounge across the hall, and the A.R.P. warden stood guard at the door. Beyond him, the Errols could see her head, propped on a cushion: presumably she was lying on a settee.

As they made to go in, the elderly warden barred their way.

'Where do you think you're going?' he demanded.

'In there,' said Mike, drily.

'Oh, no, you're not!' the man told him. 'Is there another lady in the house, do you know?' And as the Errols stared, he added firmly: 'Because if not, you just go upstairs and fetch a blanket. We'll see about you going in afterwards.'

Mark and Mike exchanged glances as the truth struck them. They could just glimpse one of the girl's shoulders, bare save for the strap of a flimsy nightdress. There was something touching, as well as funny, about the man's concern for the girl who was an utter stranger to him.

'I'll get her something,' Mark assured him, and hurried off.

As the warden pulled the door to and stood square across the front of it, Mike proffered cigarettes and they both lit up. Then the front door suddenly opened and two policemen, more wardens, and half-a-dozen steel-helmeted fire-watchers crowded into the hall, all showing excitement and curiosity. But the police sergeant gave orders and the hall was soon deserted again.

'Is she hurt?' Mike asked.

'Not much,' the warden reassured him, thawing. 'She's been bruised, and cut about a bit but she won't come to no harm. Not that she mightn't have, if I hadn't brought her in,' he added self-righteously. 'What she was doing, lying out on the pavement with nothing on but a night-dress almost torn to ribbons....' Words failed him.

Mark came hurrying down at that moment, carrying a blanket, and the man took it and went in. Then returned almost at once to say that it was all right for them to enter. And as they stepped inside together, the girl on the settee opened her eyes.

CHAPTER 9
OLIVIA

The blanket stretched from her neck to her feet; only her head showed. As she blinked dazedly about her, Mark went across to switch on a softer table-lamp, while Mike switched off the main light.

'Thank ... you,' she murmured, haltingly, and the two words were enough to betray her American accent.

Mike went over to the foot of the settee and smiled down at her.

'So it wasn't too bad?' he said.

Her eyes widened, puzzling.

'Too ... bad? What do you ...' She broke off abruptly, staring at him with sudden fear.

Then suddenly she flung off the blanket and tried to get up. Her short lace night-dress was certainly badly torn, although hardly in a condition to justify the warden's precautions. But the two men gasped, obviously shocked by the display of so much long, bare leg, as Mike stepped forward swiftly and pressed her shoulders back against the cushion.

'It's all right!' he soothed. 'He's not badly hurt.'

'Are ... are you sure?' The fear faded, but not altogether 'My father—Mr. Livesey....'

'He's all right,' Mike assured her. 'He'll take a little while to come round, but he has only superficial injuries—hardly more serious than your own. Mustn't shock grandpa, here,' he added brightly, pulling the blanket over her again.

'Grandpa?' she echoed, glancing about her, and the warden looked away quickly.

'Forget it!' grinned Mike. 'Look, Miss Livesey, I don't like worrying you—but there are one or two questions which should be answered quickly. How many other people should there be in the house?'

'About ... a dozen.'

'Were they in the house, when you went to bed?'

'Yes, surely. Why do you ...?' Her eyes filled with fear again: 'You mean ... they're not, now? But what's *happened* to ...?'

'They're not about now,' said Mike. 'But they'll turn up, all right—a dozen people can't just disappear into the night! Who attacked you, do you know?'

She shook her head—and winced: it was obviously aching.

'I was asleep. Someone came into my room—he'd tied a scarf round my mouth before I could shout.' She shivered. 'I was terrified! And then he locked me in. But I had another key, so I got out. Then—not knowing how many there were, or ...' she shivered again—'what they might do, if they saw me, I tried to get out of the house and find help.'

'Nice work,' approved Mike. 'You found it!' He bent to pick up a silk scarf which lay with a pair of high-heeled slippers beside the settee. 'This it?'

'Yes....' She frowned. 'I couldn't untie the knot—it was still round my neck ...'

The warden cleared his throat self-consciously.

'Begging the lady's pardon, sir—but I took the liberty of removing it.'

'Good man,' said Mark, solemnly. 'Doesn't do to let too much get in the way of a person's breathing.'

Mike grinned at him behind the man's back. But he was reflecting that the girl had answered all his questions with commendable clarity, at the same time explaining why she had not cried out or called for help. But the whereabouts of the missing staff and residents was still a poser.

Well, Loftus and Hammond were on the way....

He nodded towards Mark.

'My cousin,' he introduced him, and Mark inclined his head. 'Mark Errol. I'm Mike.'

'How ... how are you?' Her eyes seemed to be trying to smile. 'I'm ... Olivia Livesey.'

'How many men attacked you, Miss Livesey?' asked Mark.

'One.'

'Did you see him well enough to recognise him?'

'I saw him well enough to know he was a complete stranger to me.' She wrinkled her brow, trying to remember. 'What happened to me? I remember he saw me, and started shooting, and I ... I think I fell down. Didn't ... didn't someone try to catch me?'

'More or less,' Mike told her, and grimaced wryly. 'It was a question of you or the gunman, so I concentrated on the gunman. I wouldn't, another time!' he smiled, then added to the warden: 'Do you think you could get some tea? It would do her a world of good.'

'All these questions won't,' growled the warden. 'Why don't you let her be?'

'We shan't worry her much longer,' Mike assured him. 'And it really is important.'

The man scowled but went out at once, and violet-blue eyes smiled gratefully up at Mike. She was flushed now; and her soft, dark hair was prettily dishevelled. She was quite charming, Mike thought—and almost beautiful, despite a bruise on one cheek and a cut on the other.

'Who *are* you?' she demanded.

'We were looking for the men who attacked your father,' Mike evaded, easily. 'The trail led here. Then we heard the shooting ...'

He broke off at a sudden, noisy clatter of footsteps in the hall—several people hurrying together across the marble floor, by the sound of *it*. Voices were raised: angry, excited, anxious—and all with pronounced American accents. Then the babble grew suddenly louder, as the door shot open to admit a tall, fresh-faced fair-haired man in an almost comically gaudy dressing-gown.

'Livvy!' he cried, and flinging himself towards the settee, he crushed the girl in his arms. Mike could not be sure, but he thought that Olivia hesitated fractionally before she returned the embrace.

He exchanged glances with Mark.

'I think perhaps ...' he began, after a pause, cutting short the newcomer's rain of endearments.

'Livesey!' gasped the young man, jumping to his feet. 'Livesey! Jumping snakes, where is *he*? Livvy, sweetheart, is he all right?'

'He's as well as you are,' Mike told him. 'But Miss Livesey will probably have a relapse if you keep shouting the roof off.' He smiled pleasantly.

The fair-haired young man stared at him, showing no signs of umbrage. He had the clean-cut look common to many Americans and his pleasant face had strength and character.

'Gee, yes—sorry, Livvy! I didn't think. You're sure the Old Man's all right? You can tell me—I'm Catesby. Dick Catesby.'

'Mike Errol—and my cousin Mark, also Errol,' Mike rejoined. 'I've been busy convincing everyone that he's perfectly fit.' He felt just a little uneasy: he could not know how quickly Livesey would recover from the attack, and he would hate to have to tell the girl if he was wrong.

He saw Mark glance towards the open door—and having heard no sound, was astonished to see another man already inside it.

The newcomer, who was fully-dressed in a dark, well-cut suit, was very small: certainly no more than five feet tall, and slimlybuilt. He was olive-skinned and his hair had that peculiarly dull blackness which characterises some American Indian tribes. His nose, large and hooked, dominated his face and his expression as he looked from one Errol to the other was coldly inscrutable. Then his dark gaze found Olivia—and his thin lips parted in a smile that completely transformed him.

'Ben!' she exclaimed. 'Oh, Ben! Is Dad …?'

'He is just fine, Olivia. He sent me down to check that you were not hurt.' The small man's voice was deep-toned but very quiet, yet somehow reached every corner of the room. Over his shoulder, he called: 'Wills—go and tell Mr. Livesey that Olivia is quite safe.'

'O.K.,' answered a man in a nasal voice, and footsteps plodded off across the hall.

There followed a few moments, which, as Mike afterwards put it, 'Ben' let them know by unseen smoke-signals that he considered their presence an unnecessary intrusion. But the Errols were on a job: the only 'messages' they were prepared to receive were the kind that came direct from Craigie. They greeted his frigid hostility with beaming smiles—and stayed.

Olivia, too, had seemed to be expecting them to go. But now she broke the silence:

'Ben, these are the gentlemen who—saved me.'

Once more, the little man's expression altered magically. Clearly, Mike decided, he worshipped the girl. In a flash, he and Mark had become men to whom, in 'Ben's' eyes, gratitude alone could never be enough.

His manner was curiously impressive: despite his stature, there was remarkable dignity in the man.

'I am deeply grateful, gentlemen. And I know Mr. Livesey will wish to signify his own appreciation in person.'

'That's all right,' Mike said easily. 'Our job, when all's said and done. Did I hear a biggish crowd in the hall, just now?'

'Ben' smiled drily.

'My colleagues had been incarcerated in the cellar. They were what might be termed excited, when eventually they were released. You doubtless heard them hurrying to their rooms to learn what was missing. They assumed, I imagine, that he had been robbed.'

'I wonder if he was?' said Mark, and Mike frowned with him, struck by the same new and disturbing idea.

They had no time to brood on it, however. The front door opened suddenly, and they heard the voice of Bill Loftus enquiring for them. A moment later, he appeared in the doorway, moving now with none of the stiffness he had shown at the office. Behind him came Hammond, but it was Loftus who took the eye.

'Hallo, hallo!' he said cheerfully, his glance flicking from the Errols to the two Americans and then lighting on the girl with a broad reassuring smile. 'Everyone alive and kicking, Mike—if I may put it like that?' He beamed again, and 'Ben' asked quietly but firmly:

'May I enquire the identity of you gentlemen?'

'Bruce?' Loftus queried, careful not to usurp any of his successor's responsibilities.

'Go ahead,' Hammond smiled.

'Right!' Loftus turned back to 'Ben': 'You might call us Special Branch agents—the equivalent of Federal Bureau men. May I present—Bruce Hammond, Mike Errol, Mark Errol. My name is Loftus.'

'Ben' inclined his head.

'Thank you, sir. Allow me to introduce Miss Olivia Livesey, Mr. Richard Catesby. And I am Benjamin Roosevelt Washington.' His eyes seemed to anticipate amused astonishment, if not worse. When they all merely nodded acknowledgement, his own smile returned at once. 'My parents,' he murmured, 'were very good Americans.'

'Ah!' said Loftus, and smiled with him.

Then he and Hammond took control.

They did so smoothly, upsetting no one; but in less than an hour every person at Number 27, Queen's Gate, had been questioned. Their stories were almost identical, and nothing, as far as it was possible to ascertain for the moment, had been stolen. The safe in the study next to Livesey's bedroom, Washington assured them, was untouched.

Finally, Hammond and Loftus went with Washington to see Arnold K. Livesey himself, leaving the Errols with Olivia and the youthful Catesby.

Livesey had been more seriously hurt than his daughter, but his injuries were comparatively light.

A doctor had seen him and his head was bandaged. But his face was hardly less ruddy than usual, and his blue eyes were bright and piercingly direct. He sat propped up against his pillows, smoking; his cigarette in a long, black holder jutting out at a jaunty angle, his massive shoulders doubly impressive in royal blue pyjamas which contrasted vividly with the snowy linen.

Arnold K. Livesey was a character: Hammond's first glimpse convinced him of that.

'Is it true Livvy's O.K.?' he demanded of Washington, as soon as they appeared, and the little man said soothingly:

'She's fine, Arnold. She was hardly hurt at all.'

Livesey scowled at the other two.

'She's really all right?'

Hammond nodded easily.

'A few minor cuts and bruises,' he assured him. 'Nothing more.'

Loftus, leaning against the dressing-table, watched with amusement, what amounted to a battle for ascendancy between Livesey and the deceptively quiet-looking Hammond. It was obvious that the American was used to mastery in any situation, although there was nothing aggressive in his manner: it was more an excess of self-confidence.

'Who are you?' he demanded now.

Hammond explained briefly.

'Special agents, huh?' Livesey boomed. 'Too bad you weren't a bit quicker off the mark, son.'

Hammond raised an eyebrow.

'Why do you think you had visitors?' he asked mildly.

'You need me to tell you?' demanded the American. 'I'm not popular around here. There's plenty of folk would like to see me dead and buried!'

'You're alive,' Hammond reminded him.

'I sure am, and I aim to ...' Livesey stared. 'Say! You mean you guys have something to *do* with that?'

'Everything,' nodded Hammond. 'Our men were here on time. Yours ...' he smiled amiably '... were in the cellar. All of them. They were forced there at gunpoint by your assailants—presumably so that you could receive their undivided attentions thereafter.'

Livesey gaped at him. After a long pause, he said:

'That's what happened—the boys fell as easy as that?'

'Just as easily as you did,' Hammond said, pointedly.

Livesey's stare became fixed; it looked as if Hammond had been too blunt. Then the sharp blue eyes creased at the corners and he uttered a great guffaw.

'I like that!' he roared. 'I like it plenty! I guess that puts you and me in our place—eh, Ben? O.K., Hammond—you were on time and we owe you one helluva lot.'

'Our job,' murmured Hammond. 'Now, do you know why you were attacked?'

'Haven't I just told you?'

'You've made a suggestion. What I'd like to know is whether the man who attacked you asked questions—made any statements—that would confirm your suspicions?'

'Oh, sure. He asked questions.'

'Questions about what?'

Livesey said drily: 'I'm allergic to questions.'

Hammond showed a touch of impatience.

'If we don't know what it's about, how can we prevent it from happening again?' he demanded. 'We've full authority to make investigations. You've seen my card.'

'Sure. But *I'd* need full authority to talk freely on this one, son. Sorry—that's the way it is! It'll have to wait.'

'Delay could do a lot of harm,' Hammond told him. And added flatly, as the big man grimaced: 'Kearnley was attacked this evening. He's in hospital and it isn't certain he will recover. It's probable that others were also attacked.

Many Americans are in this country—on one official visit or another. You must know there's been trouble brewing for some time. What are you trying to do—make it worse?'

His voice was still mild, but his manner had stiffened.

Livesey pursed his lips, took the butt from the holder and leaned to a bedside table to fit in another cigarette. Then, abruptly, he said:

'O.K.—you win. He wanted details of what foodstuffs we plan to ship from the States to the Continent as soon as the last shot's fired.'

'Did he get them?'

'Now listen to me, *Mister* Hammond,' Livesey growled. 'I don't give information away like that!'

'No, and they wouldn't have had time to make you,' conceded Hammond. 'Did he particularise what he wanted to know?'

'He did,' said Livesey grimly. 'He wanted to know how much stuff is already stored near the ports for shipment. There's plenty, I'll tell you! And he was mighty keen to know exactly where it's all kept, and just what it is.'

'I see. Had you ever seen him before?'

'I had not.'

'Can you describe him?'

'Well, he was an American.'

Hammond's eyes widened.

'Are you sure of that?'

'Look, son—I guess I know when a man has a real American accent, and when he's putting one on. I'm dead sure! He was American, all right—and from New York or some place near. I didn't see his face: he was masked.'

'A real mask? Or a scarf over his face?'

'A scarf. All I could see were his eyes—but I wouldn't forget them, in a hurry. They were a real pale grey—big, and round. Like a baby's—you know! He was wearing grey, too—some kind of silky-looking stuff. Expensive looking, too. Good cut.'

Livesey's dry smile flashed briefly: 'Good American cut, that is! He was just warming up with the questions when another fellow stuck his head in to say Livvy had gotten out of her room. There was some shooting right after that. Then I got myself hit over the head—with a gun.'

'Ah!' said Hammond.

'Maybe you know why,' growled Livesey, and Hammond smiled.

'I know that if he hit you over the head with a gun instead of shooting you with it, he doesn't want you dead, yet. So at least we've got that—you're more valuable to him alive than dead, Mr. Livesey! There's nothing more, at all?'

'It sounds plenty to me,' growled the American.

'It helps,' Hammond admitted briefly. 'Thank you, sir.'

'Where are you going?' demanded Livesey.

'To report. I'll let you know later what is arranged. Meanwhile, we shall watch the house back and front—and it would be wise if you would let our men know where you are going, any time you leave the house.'

'I don't want a bodyguard!' snapped Livesey.

'I think you'd be safer with one,' said Hammond mildly. 'Goodnight, gentlemen.' He inclined his head to Livesey and Washington in turn, then left the room, and Loftus echoed his 'goodnight' and followed suit.

As the door closed behind him, Livesey was scowling, Washington expressionless.

'He thinks he's smart,' Livesey ground out, at last.

'Perhaps he is,' said Washington, gently. 'Don't you think you should stop worrying about it for tonight, and get to sleep?'

He did not wait for any response but left the room—moving with that remarkably silent, almost stealthy manner which had earlier so astonished Mike.

In the passage, he moved more quickly.

At the foot of the stairs, Hammond and Loftus were talking to Mike Errol. Once he had seen them, he walked sedately down and waited on one side as Hammond continued to give instructions.

'Livesey's to be followed wherever he goes,' Hammond wound up. 'And his daughter. All right, Mike—that's the lot.'

'Right—and I'll take Olivia,' Mike grinned. 'Mark will look after the old man.'

Hammond smiled.

'I'll leave that to you.' He had made no attempt to prevent Washington from overhearing, and now turned with a smile to ask pleasantly: 'Did you want me?'

'I should like a word with you,' Washington nodded, gravely. 'Shall we step in here?' He went towards the small lounge, then stopped. 'Unless Olivia ...?'

'She's gone back to bed,' Mike told him.

'Thank you. In that case....'

Hammond and Loftus followed him into the room, and he went to stand with his back to the mantelpiece. Somehow it was impossible to think of him as a small man. That innate dignity helped, of course: lent him stature. Hammond found it quite impossible even to guess at his age. He wondered if Loftus found him as intriguing a character.

Loftus was leaving this interview to him, too: had perched himself on the high end of the settee. He would have a good chance of studying the man.

'I have served Arnold Livesey for many years,' Washington began, quietly. 'And I know him better than most people. I wish to advise you not to be annoyed by his manner.'

Hammond's eyebrows rose.

'Why should we be?'

'You might well consider it—truculence. It is not—please believe that. He will appreciate all you have done when he has had time to recover from the shock and from the very great anxiety he felt for his daughter. Please understand …' He hesitated, then went on: 'I mean to say, Mr. Hammond, that since the death of his wife, not very long ago, he has depended a great deal on Olivia. Any thought of danger or injury to her affects him far more deeply than anything else ever could.'

'I see,' murmured Hammond.

'Also, he is by nature a very self-assertive man.' Washington smiled briefly. 'He has clear-cut ideas and knows exactly what he wants to do and how it is to be done— perhaps because he is also very able.'

'I'd gathered that,' Hammond murmured drily.

'It would truly be a tragedy if anything were to happen to him,' Washington said, earnestly. 'One hesitates to use the word "irreplaceable". But he has a habit of keeping a great deal to himself. He distrusts others and he distrusts written statements.'

'That has its disadvantages, admittedly. But there's a lot to be said for it. And if he is sensible, nothing will happen to him. Can you make him take the necessary precautions?'

'I think so,' Washington nodded: 'Yes, I think so. But he will probably prefer to have a Federal Bureau man to look after him.' He grimaced ruefully, apologetic: 'You understand, Mr. Hammond, I mean nothing derogatory by that, but …' He spread his right hand a little: 'It is just his way.'

Hammond nodded smilingly then looked a query at Loftus, who shook his head: he had no questions.

'Then we all know where we stand,' said Hammond easily. 'Thank you for filling us in, Mr. Washington.'

A few minutes later, he and Loftus left the house.

There were police outside, now, as well as the fatherly warden. Yet even a dozen yards away from the house, there was complete peace and quiet. Nothing seemed more unlikely than that raid on Number 27.

Hammond's car was parked a few yards further along the road. They made their way to it in silence, climbed in, and started off. Hammond waited until they had turned into the main road, then said a dry:

'Well, Bill?'

'You handled him well, old son,' Loftus said judicially. 'Not the way I would have done it, perhaps,' he grinned. 'But you achieved your object. He doesn't know what to make of you, so he'll be wary—I presume you did want that?'

'Yes....' Hammond seemed very thoughtful. 'What did you make of him?'

'Washington summed him up.'

'M'mm ... Why didn't they kill him?'

'I don't know. But I'd say you were about right—he's of more value alive than dead.'

'It could be that,' Hammond frowned. 'It could also be that it was all a put-up job, Bill. Or am I going haywire? But the whole of the staff pushed into the cellar, everything set for a secret session upstairs—if the girl hadn't broken away, what would have happened? And teetering along on her high heels, in a white nightie,' he added drily, 'against a dark wall—she'd take a bit of missing, even with a pop-gun.'

Loftus said, slowly:

'What are you driving at, Bruce?'

'That I don't trust Arnold K. Livesey,' Hammond told him abruptly.

CHAPTER 10
ALL THROUGH THE NIGHT

Neither man spoke again until they reached Whitehall. Loftus was digesting what Hammond had said: Hammond wondering if he had let personal dislike prejudice him. He admitted freely that he did not like the man—and not merely for that truculence and self-assertiveness Washington had tried so vainly to defend. What he felt was an instinctive and possibly quite irrational distrust. But as both men knew, if he were right and Livesey was not to be trusted, there was no reason for placing reliance in Washington.

Half-way up the stairs to Craigie's office, Loftus said:

'I can't go all the way with you, Bruce.'

Hammond smiled in the darkness.

'I haven't gone all the way with myself, yet. A few hours' sleep will help get it clearer in our minds. I wonder what else has been happening?'

Loftus sounded startled.

'What else are you expecting?'

'I don't know. But we cast our net pretty widely—we may have caught some other fish.' He pressed the button and the door slid open.

As they stepped into the big room, they realised there was something up.

Craigie was hurrying back to his desk—had obviously rushed to the mantelpiece to operate the door—and three telephones were ringing simultaneously.

What was more, Craigie's desk was littered with paper.

Craigie's *desk*, untidy!

Neither man had seen it like that in a very long time. Craigie's precision in his records was a by-word. But now there was paper everywhere. As Craigie lifted one receiver and began making notes, they reached the desk and grabbed one each themselves.

'Hallo,' said a faintly languid voice in Hammond's ear. 'Is there someone about? This is Davidson. N-O-S ...'

The speaker began to spell his name backwards—the simple formula which had served the Department well over many years. But there was only one voice like that one.

'Hammond here, Wally,' he interrupted. 'What is it?'

'Much ado!' drawled Davidson. 'And a Chelsea policeman doesn't like me. I've been to River Walk—remember?'

'Go on,' said Hammond, grimly.

Davidson's sleepy-sounding voice went on.

At 11, River Walk, Chelsea, there were stationed several of the more important members of the United States Post-War Finance Mission, whose task was to devise workable arrangements for the solving of financial and currency problems after the war. The leading member of the mission was one Ernest Cattino, New York banker, millionaire, philanthropist—a man of more than middle age and respected in all countries.

Cattino had been attacked.

Davidson had been at the house with another agent named Graham. The attack had been too powerfully made for them to prevent it altogether, but they had been able to avert the worst consequences. Two members of the staff had been badly injured: Cattino himself had escaped with minor injuries. Hammond gained a distinct impression that Davidson liked Cattino.

'Did you catch anyone?' he asked, crisply.

'Yes. One nasty little roughneck—'no talkee' type. Hence my quarrel with the bobby. He wants to take the little beggar to the station, and I told him I wanted his *corpus*. What shall I do—let them have him?'

Hammond thought for a moment, then:

'Yes. But send Graham with him to the station. I'll call them and make sure they don't give him a chance to get away or injure himself. Right, then, Wally—I've got to go. You stay with Cattino.'

A telephone was ringing in his ear. Loftus was speaking into a third, Craigie replacing a fourth and just about to lift the fifth. Hammond lifted the second and said into it:

'Hold on a moment.'

There was a pad on the desk in front of him. He made a brief note of what Davidson had told him and tore the page off, anchoring it with the telephone before saying:

'Right—fire away!'

'Carruthers here,' said a voice: 'S-R-E …'

As he spelled through his name, Hammond jogged his own memory. Robert Carruthers had been to Hendon, where a leading member of Pan-American Airways, one Joseph Patton, was discussing Civil Aviation development with British Government representatives. Patton was famous chiefly for his fiercely outspoken opposition to the Luce term '*globaloney*'.

Carruthers and another agent, he now learned, had reached Patton's hotel in time to prevent an attack materialising, but too late to catch the two men who had tried to stage it.

Hammond made the necessary notes and rang off.

Loftus was still talking, Craigie scribbling. Another telephone rang.

And so it went on, all through the night.

Of the forty Americans Craigie and Loftus had arranged to have watched, twenty-seven had been 'visited' and twenty-three saved from serious injury; in half of that number of cases, the attacks had been thwarted from the beginning. But three of the Americans had been killed, and there were other, minor casualties. Eleven of the assailants had been caught: all of them, for the moment, were lodged in the relevant local gaols.

It was getting towards dawn, when the telephones stopped ringing at last.

Craigie was looking gaunt and grey, Loftus tight-lipped but generating repressed excitement, and Hammond was frankly tired out. Despite his weariness, Craigie began at once to assemble and summarise their various notes, including Hammond's report on Queen's Gate, recording his findings and conclusions straight into the dictaphone. Loftus lit a gas-ring and brewed tea. Hammond's mind was veering tiredly between all he had heard since reaching the office, and the nagging uncertainty of his grounds for distrusting Livesey.

He forced his mind away from Livesey.

Twenty-seven attacks, needing at least two assailants for each one. Fifty-four men at least—no: fifty-five, for there had been three at Queen's Gate.

Craigie finished dictating and came across to sink into his big winged chair, smiling gratefully as Loftus handed him a cup of steaming tea.

'Thanks, Bill.'

Hammond, already sipping his, murmured:

'The tempo fast enough for you, William?'

'Damn your eyes!' Loftus growled and laughed shortly. 'Yes, it's moving—and proving how much we didn't know. We have the luck in some ways, though.'

Craigie eyed him thoughtfully.

'Luck?' echoed Hammond.

'Luck,' Loftus repeated, emphatically. 'If we hadn't got the thing moving as soon as we heard about Kearnley, there'd have been nothing to stop it. Three American V.I.P.s murdered will cause sensation enough—twenty-seven would have caused the biggest shindy since Munich.' He lit a cigarette; he had long since discarded his pipe.

'The more you think about it, the more you must admit that it's a brilliant conception.' And as Hammond made strangled sounds of protest, he went on: 'Simultaneous attacks on twenty-seven important Anglo-American collaborationists. Even if public opinion in America were persuaded to take it all right, look at the damage it would have done!'

'Need we dwell on that?' demanded Hammond. 'God knows we're all too horribly aware of it.'

Loftus grimaced wryly. 'Yes, I'm talking too much. But you know—I'm only just beginning to realise how much depends on Garth. You caught that link-up, at Queen's Gate?'

Hammond nodded.

'What's this?' asked Craigie.

'You saw Garth's description of Russi? Well, Livesey's description of the man who attacked him, and asked all those questions ...' He began to repeat it, verbatim.

'You think it was Russi?' Craigie interrupted.

'It could be,' said Hammond, quietly.

'It probably was,' murmured Loftus. 'I'd give a lot to know what that man is doing right now.'

Paul Russi was sitting in the Wimbledon House, meeting the hard stare of Ryall, *alias* Franklin. Nothing in the expressions of either suggested pleasure or satisfaction. Russi's round, pale eyes had lost their baby-like clarity. And there was nothing childish about the grim, harsh lines at his mouth.

Ryall was breathing heavily—like a man recovering from a severe shock.

'Three!' he rasped, at last. *'Three!'* he exploded. 'Three, out of twenty-seven! That is the best you could do?'

'It's no use blaming me!' Russi snapped. 'Obviously, they had been warned.'

'They weren't warned—it would not have been possible!'

'I tell you they were waiting for us! It's no use trying to blame me, Ryall—I won't take it, understand? It's your end that went wrong! You said you had everything arranged—that no one could guess what was coming....'

'There was no leakage!' bellowed Ryall. 'You damned fool, what do you think you are? Who do you think you are addressing?' He rose to his full height—a great shaggy figure; terrifying in his rage. He shook a clenched fist close to Russi's face; but the American did not shrink away, and there was hatred in his eyes. 'My arrangements were perfect! A leakage was not possible! You hired men who were useless—fools! You were told to pay for the best—instead, you kept the money yourself, and bought cheap labour!'

'That's a lie,' said Russi, thinly.

'It's the only possible explanation!'

'It is a lie! I hired the best—men who've worked for me for years. You don't have to worry about them!' Abruptly, he added: 'Listen here—you did your best; I did mine. I guess something we didn't expect went wrong.'

Ryall still glowered, but returned to his chair in silence.

It was a little after six o'clock. They had been discussing reports from the attackers for the last hour; had just received the final word on the over-all situation. Each of them was confident of his own part in the venture; each certain the other was responsible for the failure of so many of the attacks. And lurking in the mind of both, was the sobering knowledge that eleven men, at least, had been arrested.

Ryall spoke at last; much more quietly, now.

'You are right, my friend—we are both so worried by what has happened that we cannot think clearly. Something has gone wrong and we must find what it is. It must not be allowed to happen again. There are other things, also. We are in more danger than we have ever been before.'

'None of the men knew me,' Russi told him, flatly.

'Are you sure?'

'Say, listen—I'm not a beginner at this game, Ryall! I know how to fix it so they can't rat on me. The cops might close up two or three contacts....'

'Those contacts know you.'

'Save your breath!' Russi snapped. 'As soon as I knew what was coming, I phoned round. They all know what to expect and will be gone before the cops can get near them. I've told you before—apart from my eight agents in and around London, *none* of them know me. Those eight have always paid the men and passed on the instructions, they've handled all personal contact. And like I said: they've been warned—the police won't get them. We don't have to worry.'

'You're quite sure?' Ryall persisted.

'Damn' right I'm sure,' said Russi. 'I can't afford not to be.'

Ryall nodded gently, now much more self-possessed.

'Of course, I know you would not be careless, my friend. So ... now, our first task is to repair the damage which has already been done. It will not be easy: the police will be on guard, now. So will our victims.' He looked ugly as he uttered that word. 'It will be slower, but ...' he shrugged. 'We are working well ahead of time, at all events.'

'We've got more to do than simply start again, and you know it! We've got to find what went wrong.'

'Yes, yes,' said Ryall. 'And I think perhaps we should leave here until we do know. If there should by any chance be a leakage, it may conceivably lead to us. We will not wait till morning,' he added, decisively. 'We shall go now!'

'Go where?'

'To Kingston, of course—where else?'

'I guess it's wise,' admitted Russi. But he sounded reluctant. 'Do you reckon to come back?'

'When we know what went wrong, we can decide that,' said Ryall. 'We shall take Ethel with us. If she were questioned, she might well break down.'

A little less than an hour later, all three entered a small private guest-house on the outskirts of Kingston, which commanded a view of Richmond Park on one side and the By-pass on the other.

They reached it by taxi—the same taxi which had taken David Garth from the Wimbledon house to Jermyn Street. The driver did not return to his garage but remained at the guest-house, where a loud-voiced woman greeted them with professed delight.

By half-past seven, all four were in bed. Russi and Ryall both slept for three hours before the maid brought them tea, just as if they were in their rooms at The Elms.

With the tea, were the morning papers.

Russi, in a room next to Ryall's, was the first to open his. He did not expect any news of the night's activities for he knew that the papers went to press before the first attack had been staged. But as he read one headline on the front page, he sat up with a jerk. For a moment, his glance flickered over the news-story.

Then he jumped out of bed.

As he grabbed up his dressing-gown, it struck the tray and sent a cup of tea crashing to the floor. He swore viciously as a few drops of scalding tea fell on his bare foot, then snatched up the paper and strode off to the next room.

Ryall was drinking tea and looking pensively out of the window. The newspaper on his bed was still folded.

Russi slammed the door and snapped:

'Take a look at this, will you?' His voice trembled with rage as he pointed a quivering finger at the item which had so startled him.

Ryall shot him an irritable glance, then took the paper and read as directed.

'JUSTIN M. KEARNLEY ATTACKED
American Envoy Badly Injured

Just after dark last night, Mr. Justin M. Kearnley, personal representative of the U.S. President, was the victim of a savage attack near the American Embassy. He is now in the Central Hospital in a dangerous condition. The police ...'

'Just after dark!' breathed Ryall. *Just after dark? The* fools—they started early! They started too early....'

'That's all it was, damn their blasted hides! Someone was too goddam clever and started before zero hour. That's what warned the cops—of course they'd see right off that it could happen to others: it stares you in the face! When I get my hands on the guy that...'

Ryall said shortly:

'Be quiet, Russi!' His eyes were gleaming now. 'Don't you see? That *is* all that happened! Our first attempt failed only because of this trivial thing.' He paused, then went on: 'So at least it is not a leakage, as far as we can judge. Find out who attacked Kearnley and how the mistake occurred. If it was just a mistake, there is nothing we need do about it. In any case we can return to Wimbledon.'

'I'll kill the guy!' muttered Russi.

'Don't be a fool!' snapped Ryall. 'That would only make more trouble. You can watch him and deal with him later—but remember we need all the help we can get, now. Including ...' He smiled widely: 'Mr. David Garth! We shall have even more need of him, now, than we expected.'

Russi nodded, still looking savage.

'He'll do what he's told, that's for sure.'

'I'm sure you are right.' Ryall smiled again. 'It is a thousand pities that so much went wrong. But we have our contact in Livesey's *ménage,* and at the Ministry. Oh, we shall get results in good time, Russi, never fear!'

'When do we have to finish?'

'I don't yet know.'

'When is he going to tell you more?' demanded Russi, edgily.

Ryall said softly:

'We are not in a position to make demands. We shall receive instructions from time to time and carry them out. He is very clever, our friend Brown. But ...' He smiled, mirthlessly. 'We are not fools, Russi—except when we are foolish enough to quarrel. At the moment, we must carry out our instructions and show ourselves as willing servants. We must even expect a sharp rebuke for what happened last night. But later, my friend—*later* we shall be able to make capital!'

Russi was almost himself again, now.

'That's what I like to hear! Well, I'll check up on the Kearnley business and then—are you going to see Garth, today?'

'I think so,' murmured Ryall, gently. 'Yes, I think so.'

Chapter 11
Business as Usual

Most men would have considered that the night's disturbance was excuse enough for a leisurely morning. Not so Arnold K. Livesey. At a quarter past seven, a middle-aged servant awakened him with a glass of cold water and a bottle of fruit salts. Livesey widened one eye—the other was half-hidden by his bandage—and growled:

'What time is it?'

'Why, the usual time, sir. I'm sure I'm never ...'

'I said what time is it?' snapped Livesey. 'I didn't ask if you were late!' He struggled up to a sitting position and forced back a groan as his head throbbed.

'A quarter past seven, sir,' said the woman, coldly.

'That's what I wanted to know. Is Ben up?'

'If you are referring to Mr. Washington, sir, I did see ...'

'Tell him I want him!' roared Livesey.

He glowered at her retreating back; then as the door closed behind her, he shrugged and climbed gingerly out of bed. He was somewhat shaky on his feet, but he managed to mix himself some fruit salts and drank the mixture down, steadying himself against the dressing-table as he regained his breath. Then he stepped to the window, which was wide open, and breathed deeply.

By the time the door opened to admit Benjamin Roosevelt Washington, he was calmly going through the morning exercises he performed every day of his life.

'Are you sure you're wise, Arnold?' asked Washington, gently.

'What are you bellyaching about, now?' demanded Livesey, but his smile robbed the words of any offence. 'How's Olivia?'

'Still asleep.'

'That's bad. I need her this morning....'

'If you will be advised by me, you will rest till this afternoon and allow Olivia to do the same,' said Washington, firmly.

'Sure I would! Only I'm not being advised by you. If she isn't awake by eight o'clock, get someone to ... well, no; don't wake her up. But just—disturb her.'

Washington made no comment. But at all events, there was no need for him to disturb Olivia.

A little before eight, she woke of her own accord and rang the bell for tea. Washington learned of it quickly: little happened at 27, Queen's Gate, that Washington did not know of almost before it took place. He decided to see Olivia and reached the door of her room at the same time as Richard Catesby.

'Good morning, Dick,' he greeted.

'How's Livvy?' asked Catesby, sharply. He still wore the gaudy dressing-gown and he looked tired: his fair hair was awry and he badly needed a shave.

'Haven't you enquired?'

'You know damn' well I haven't!' muttered Catesby. 'Heck! My head feels as if it belongs to somebody else!'

'Perhaps it does,' murmured Washington.

Catesby glanced at him quickly but the little man's smile was unhelpfully obtuse as he opened the door.

Olivia was sitting up and drinking her tea. The adhesive dressings which covered her scratches made her look more badly hurt than she was. Her eyes were bright enough as she smiled at Washington and looked in surprise at the younger man.

'How're you feeling?' demanded Catesby.

'I'm all right, now, thanks,' she told him.

'Well, listen, Livvy—I came to tell you to make sure the Old Man doesn't put you in harness this morning. You're not fit to work after what happened last night. It's crazy,' he growled. 'You'd think there was no one else who'd do his work. Having you running around the way he does—it makes me mad!'

'We've argued about that before!' said Olivia, tartly. 'He doesn't force me to do anything—I do it because I want to. And I'm perfectly able to work this morning.'

'Oh, heck!' Catesby stood in the doorway, Washington near the bed. 'I never came across anyone so stubborn in my life! Livvy, you really should take care of yourself....'

'I can—take care of *myself.*'

He stared at her, then turned on his heel and went, snapping the door shut behind him. Olivia looked at Washington and said a shade too quickly:

'How's father, Ben?'

'Like daughter, like father!' Washington smiled drily. 'He is anxious to get to work, my dear. The man Kent is coming at half past nine and he wants you to be there. Will that be all right?'

'Sure it will,' said Olivia. 'Why not?'

Washington shrugged.

'Why not, indeed. You really are a remarkable family, you know! By the way ...' He hesitated, then asked lightly: 'Does Dick worry you?'

'Why should he?' she demanded, flushing a little, and he shrugged again.

'He is a persistent young man. At all events, my dear, if you do find his attentions troublesome, just advise me. I will deal with him.'

Olivia shook her head.

'He doesn't worry me. If he weren't such a thick-head over father, I think I'd like him.' She smiled suddenly, widely: 'A lot! What does one do in a case like that?'

'Give the situation time to work itself out,' said Washington, promptly. 'Both Dick and your father are wilful men, Olivia. They are bound to have differences.'

'I don't mind their having differences face to face. What I don't like is when they criticise each other to me. Why can't they see that I'm fond of them both?'

'Your father probably finds it hard to see what you see in Catesby, as a prospective husband,' he suggested smoothly. 'And Catesby is a young man in love, which of course is blind.' He smiled. 'But I know I can safely leave you to deal with him—provided you don't find him too persistent.'

'Don't worry about Dick,' said Olivia.

He left her, soon after, and she was thoughtful as she bathed and dressed. Washington had made her think more deliberately about Dick Catesby. It was true that the only reason for her manner towards him was her father's hostility. And she did not think that hostility was in any way personal.

It was a mistake for Dick to have come on this mission. The two men, one with the rude assertiveness of youth, the other with the crusty obstinacy of age, often opposed each other for the sake of opposition. Livesey resented the fact

Catesby was the nominee of certain sections of American farming interests. He would have preferred to handle matters without constant prodding or obstruction from interests he did not particularly like.

Olivia shrugged off the subject, examined herself in the mirror and grimaced at the bruise on her right cheek and the scratch on her left. The more she thought of what had happened the previous night, the more she realised how fortunate she had been. She shivered suddenly, remembering her terror when the shooting had started: she had been very much afraid that she would die.

She thought of the two men who had first interviewed her. They were Englishmen of a type she had not very often met, and she preferred them to the Kent type. George Kent was …

She frowned, seeking the right word. There was something about Kent that aroused her antagonism. His manner was too condescending for one thing. Her father seemed not to notice it, although had Dick done and said half the things that Kent did, it would have precipitated a monumental row. The truth, she had to admit, was that her father was something of a snob. George Kent was the son of an earl—the Honourable George—and Livesey liked it. When she typed his letters to Kent, her father made sure that she added 'The Honourable' before his name—a strange trait in a blunt-speaking man.

Several other members of the staff were already in the breakfast-room. Catesby was not there, but she had hardly seated herself when he came in and sat down beside her. He was morose throughout the meal: his pleasant face spoiled by a scowl. One by one, the others left the room; when they were finally alone, he burst out:

'I don't care what you say, you shouldn't work this morning. It's a lot of nonsense!'

'We're not going into that again,' said Olivia coolly. 'And if you haven't more courtesy than to sit through a meal looking like death and glowering at everyone who asks for the salt, I'd prefer you sat somewhere else.'

Catesby flushed.

'Livvy! You don't mean that!'

'I most certainly do!'

'Aw, gee, sweetheart—don't you understand I'm only thinking of you? It's not fair to …'

'Did you know there was a war on?' she demanded, cuttingly. 'Do you realise that it might end soon and that about 70,000,000 people will desperately want feeding? And that half a day's delay might cause thousands of them to die of starvation?'

Catesby's flush deepened.

'Yeah. I know. Oh, gee, Livvy, I'm sorry! But I can't help it—I can't bear to think that you're in danger.'

'I'm not in danger!' she flashed, and he looked incredulous.

'After what happened last night …'

'Father might be,' she conceded. 'But I asked for what I got. Anyway, I don't think there's much to worry about. These Englishmen who came were pretty smart.'

Catesby's eyes clouded at once.

'The English, huh? Yeah, you like them, don't you? You'd rather risk a relapse and a week in bed, than miss a session with the Honourable George!'

For a moment, she was so angry that she could have slapped his face. Then the absurdity of the statement—plus the knowledge that he was jealous—robbed her of anger, and she laughed.

'Dick, you fool!' she protested. 'Kent is …'

Then Washington came into the room and she changed the subject quickly, and very soon after went to the study-cum-office. Her father always breakfasted there and now he called a gruff: 'Come in!' when she knocked.

He looked paler than usual: much of the ruddiness which had still been there after the attack had now faded. There was an ugly bruise over his right eye, too; but the bandage had now been exchanged for a large square of sticking-plaster at the side of his head.

"Morning, honey,' he greeted, his face lighting up at the sight of her.

'Don't get up,' she said quickly, pressing his shoulder down as he started to rise. She kissed his forehead and stood back to scan his face searchingly, before she nodded, smiling. He had been examining hers with equal intensity, and smiled with her.

'You're okay,' he said, as she said:

'You can teach the young ones something! But shouldn't Kent be here?' she added.

Livesey's mood changed, and he scowled.

'Don't know what the hell's keeping him—he's a man who usually realises time is important.' It was twenty to ten: Kent was already ten minutes late. 'Well, I guess he'll be here pretty soon.'

The Honourable George had not arrived by ten o'clock and Livesey had begun to growl. Had it been anyone else in the world, Olivia thought, he would have been sending caustic messages a long time before.

At five past ten, he nodded to the telephone and said sharply:

'See what's keeping him.'

Olivia put a call through to Kent's office, to be told he had neither been in nor telephoned. She called his Brook Street flat: a suave-voiced servant said that he was out, but had telephoned to say he would be in again by half past ten. He had several urgent personal matters to attend to and was not likely to be at his office until after lunch, if at all. The servant knew nothing of the appointment at Queen's Gate.

'Damn the man!' snapped Livesey, when she passed on the message. He paused. 'What time will he be at his flat—did he say?'

'Half past ten.'

'Go and see him,' said Livesey. She looked startled and he growled: 'I think he's there and won't answer the 'phone—I've been put off by these smooth-voiced English servants before. He'll see you, if you call.'

Olivia protested ineffectually. She saw little point in going and wondered why her father insisted on it. Only when she was getting out of the taxi at Brook Street did a possible explanation strike her—and she stared for a moment at the taxi-driver, till he ventured a smiling:

'Lorst something, Miss?'

'Er—no. No,' said Olivia. 'I'm sorry!'

She paid him quickly and turned towards the house, shaking her head and smiling. The old fox! He was friendly to Kent, made more allowances for the Englishman than most people, to foster *her* acquaintance with him. He wanted *her* to see Kent: that was his sole reason for sending her as a messenger. He did not greatly mind not seeing Kent, himself: he did mind if *she* lost an opportunity for meeting him!

It explained her father's animosity towards Dick, too.

She reached a circular landing on the second floor. Two doors opened from it, and on one, a door marked '5', a small brass frame held one of Kent's visiting cards. She pressed the bell and prepared to be pleasant.

A man opened the door.

This was no servant. He was tall, elegantly-dressed and groomed, and had a distinct air of poised self-assurance. His eyes, very direct, were as vividly blue as her father's and his hair had a flaxen fairness that would have made Dick's look almost brown beside it.

'Good-morning,' he said, and his voice was deep and pleasant.

'Good-morning. Is … is Mr. Kent in?'

'I'm afraid not.'

'Are you sure? It's most important that I should see him.'

'He isn't available,' said the stranger. 'But I can give him a message when I see him, if that will help?'

She hesitated.

She was convinced now that her father's intuition had been right: that George Kent was in the flat.

'I'm sorry—but I really should see him,' she insisted. 'I'm from Mr. Livesey. Mr. Kent had an appointment at Queen's Gate this morning, and …'

'*Good God!*'

The voice was Kent's. It came from well inside the flat. And as George Kent erupted into sight from a room to the left of the small lobby, the stranger inclined his head politely and stepped aside.

Olivia was too astounded to accept the implicit invitation. She was staring in disbelief as Kent approached. She had never seen so great a change in a man.

His plump, usually florid face sagged; it was pasty in patches and there were heavy, dark rings beneath the eyes.

His mouth looked slack and ugly. He was unshaven and his hair was awry. His suit was crumpled and his collar and tie hung loose about his neck. His eyes, usually clear and cold, were red-rimmed and dull.

'Miss … Miss Livesey!' he said, thickly. 'I can't … can't apologise enough! I completely … Garth, you …?'

The tall man smiled gravely as Kent subsided: 'Please do come in, Miss Livesey.' And this time, she did so.

As the door closed, Kent turned to look at her again. He seemed to have made a great effort to regain something of his composure.

'I … I've had … a severe shock. Bowled me over. My … fiancée.' He gulped and looked an appeal at David Garth, who said quietly:

'Mr. Kent's fiancée was murdered last night, Miss Livesey.'

It should have sounded cruel, almost brutal. Somehow, Garth's voice turned the blunt words into a quiet statement of regrettable but tragic fact.

'Apologise … your father,' mumbled Kent, making another effort. 'I shan't be … oh, God!' His voice cracked, as he swung away and fled back to his bedroom.

Olivia was shaken. She could hardly credit the change in him. Kent was one man whom she had believed would put up a good front whatever the circumstances. She could understand how badly he had been shocked and even that he would forget to arrange for the cancelling of his engagements. But that he would crack like this …

Garth was regarding her gravely.

'My name is Garth, Miss Livesey—David Garth. If there is any way I can help …? I'm afraid we'll have to avoid worrying Mr. Kent for the next day or two.'

'I ... I can't believe ...!' she stammered, then stopped abruptly. This man's quiet composure was not only in striking contrast to George Kent's utter lack of it: it also made her conscious of her own.

'Yes, it has been a severe blow to him,' he murmured, and Olivia said without thinking:

'I didn't even know he was engaged. I still can't really ...'

She stopped again as she saw the glimmer of a smile on his face. And she had a strange feeling that although he was amused by her gaucheness, he found it difficult to smile—that this man was labouring under an emotion every bit as deep as George's.

'I'm sure the Department will be sending someone to see your father, in Mr. Kent's place,' he said gently; reminding her of the excuse for her visit, tacitly ending it.

She hesitated. 'Isn't there anything I can do?'

The truth, as she later admitted to herself, was that she did not want to go. But as soon as they were out, the words seemed the crowning absurdity. And colouring, she murmured an apology and turned to the door.

'If there is, I will let you know,' Garth promised quietly, somehow giving her offer credibility, lending her exit more dignity; winning her completely, had he but known it....

George had sent an urgent message for him, late the previous night, and he had come at once, and stayed. Why George had turned to him he did not know. The wicked irony of the situation was a constant hurt: almost unbearable. Yet above it all, he was chiefly conscious of a sense of incredulity—shared, he knew, by the American girl.

It was difficult to believe that the death of Anne would affect George so deeply. He would have bet on George never to give way to his emotions. Nor could he convince himself that this was proof of an overwhelming love for Anne, an inconsolable grief. He was struck with a conviction that there was something deeper behind it all: something he did not understand.

He could not rid himself of an impression that George Kent was a frightened man.

He wandered restlessly into the sitting-room and went to stand at the window—staring at, without really seeing, the passers-by in Brook Street below.

Then he was suddenly jolted by the sight of Mike Errol, strolling casually along. The girl appeared a moment later. Walking fairly briskly, she passed Errol, who sauntered nonchalantly in her wake.

It did not occur to Garth that Errol could be shadowing Olivia. He took it for granted the man was watching him—and was not sure whether he liked it or not. Then as he watched, it struck him that while Errol appeared to be meandering aimlessly, he remained a steady ten yards or so behind Olivia. There were quite a few people about, although not much traffic: only two or three cars had passed as she neared the first side-street.

Garth frowned in puzzlement as he saw her stop short—and saw Errol stop, almost in the same instant. It was his first indication that Errol might be interested in George Kent's visitor.

Then he saw the girl gesture sharply towards a man who had come out of the side-street and was hurrying along, head down as if walking in a stiff wind. Garth did not hear her exclaim, as Mike Errol did, but he saw the hurrying man pull up, raise his face and stare.

And Garth had no way of knowing what drama he was witnessing—as Mike Errol recognised the man who had fired at him from the staircase at Queen's Gate.

Chapter 12
George Kent Recovers

The man's glance darted from Olivia to Errol. His right hand flashed to his pocket as if for a gun—and as they both ducked instinctively, he turned and fled. Errol pounded after him, while Olivia stood cursing her own helplessness. The man ran into the road and a car pulled up with a squeal of brakes; another swerved on to the pavement.

He reached the far corner, turned, and fired through his pocket at Mike Errol.

Mike had expected it—had seen that furtive hand dive again to the pocket: knew the man was relying on his 'flight' to convince his pursuer he was unarmed. Mike ran on as the bullet whistled past his ear—with the familiar *zutt!* that came with using a silencer. Only Mike and the gunman knew the shot had been fired.

As the gunman raced round the corner, Mike drew closer to the houses and sought his own gun, half-expecting an ambush.

Behind him, unknown to him, the bullet struck the handlebars of a cycle which an unsuspecting errand-boy was pedalling furiously towards the scene, then ricocheted off past Olivia's face. The shocked errand-boy felt the handle-bars knocked from his grip—and quite out of control crashed over the kerb into Olivia, cycle and all.

David Garth reached the street-door in time to see her fall. He had raced down intending to go to Errol's assistance—was instinctively certain that this was all part of the same business, and was on edge to be active against the man who had killed Anne Duval.

But as the girl hit the pavement, he knew what his particular job was, just then. And as Mike Errol raced on towards Piccadilly, in the wake of the gunman, David Garth bent over Olivia Livesey and helped her to her feet.

She was dazed, and the fall had re-opened the small cut on her cheek. Her stockings were torn and one of her knees was bleeding. Her hand, too, was grazed, and she was thoroughly shaken—nor did the stares of the small crowd that quickly gathered help her to regain her poise.

A policeman elbowed his way forward as Garth held her steady, while the scared errand-boy, still thoroughly shaken himself, apologised nervously.

Garth looked into the policeman's face.

'I'll take my friend up to my flat,' he said quickly. 'I don't know if you saw what happened? Two men started to run wildly along the street towards Piccadilly....'

He had not anticipated the success of the red herring. Two motorists, the cyclist and half a dozen passers-by all began talking at once. From their descriptions, there might have been a pitched battle in the middle of Brook Street, and the policeman grew hoarse in his pleas to be told one thing at a time.

Garth claimed that he had been coming out of the flats and had seen Miss Livesey fall. No one appeared to have noticed her part in the affair and he was allowed to help her into the flat without further questions.

As they reached George Kent's door, she smiled wanly up at him.

'That was smart of you, Mr. Garth—thank you.'

'Smart?' He looked surprised. 'It seemed the only thing to do. You didn't want to be mixed up in that, did you?'

'I did not!' said Olivia, fervently.

They went in, and he led her to the bathroom. Olivia caught a glimpse of her face in a mirror as she sank on to a cork-topped stool.

'Heavens—it gets worse every time!' She glanced down at her knee. 'Oh, my stockings!'

'You're clearly feeling better,' Garth said drily. 'Would you rather get cleaned up first, or shall I make some tea?'

'I *would* like some tea,' she admitted.

Neither of them even noticed when George Kent suddenly appeared in the doorway. Garth was searching in a first-aid cabinet. Olivia was watching him with a faintly puzzled air, aware of a feeling of vast contentment: not even remotely aware, yet, of what was occasioning it.

'What's happened?' demanded Kent, heavily.

They glanced round, startled.

He still looked dishevelled, but his voice suggested he had taken a firmer grip on himself. He had brushed and combed his hair, too, and his face was not so haggard.

Garth explained briefly.

'Damned cyclists,' muttered Kent. 'Do you want some iodine? It's in my bedroom—I'll get the box.' He did so and added, returning: 'Did I hear you say something about tea?'

'Yes,' said Garth.

'I'll make some,' he offered, awkwardly. 'Simms won't be back for an hour.' He forced a ghost of a smile and went out.

Garth and Olivia exchanged glances: and as the kitchen door swung to, behind him, they both spoke at the same time:

'He's better,' commented Garth.

'Much improved,' said Olivia.

She gave a little laugh as he grimaced wryly, and with mock-severity he told her that she had to be patched up: that this was no time for frivolity. Olivia allowed him to sponge the abrasions on her face, hand and knee, surprised by and very much aware of the gentleness of his touch, yet in no way embarrassed by it.

His hands were unusually slender and very pale by comparison with her father's, or Dick Catesby's—it did not occur to her, then, to wonder why she should compare them with Dick Catesby's. But the long, tapering fingers were quick and capable, and she could still feel the reassuring warmth and strength of their grip as he had stood there in the street, supporting her.

Garth himself was surprised by the confusion of his own emotions. There was something about this girl which attracted him in a way different from anything he had experienced before.

There was a warmth there: an easy, comfortable, companionship. As if he had known her for years—could communicate without speech. He smiled to himself; that obviously came from the sight of her earlier—as clearly perturbed and embarrassed by the manifestation of the 'new' George Kent as he was.

But the attraction, whatever it was, certainly existed. And that oddly warming feeling. He had a strange certainty that he could talk with this girl—that, indeed he could voice all his confusion and uncertainty, even his thoughts at this moment, and be quite sure of real understanding and sympathy. *Simpatico*—that was the word he was searching for: *simpatico*.

Warmth, sympathy, instinctive mutual liking and understanding; that was it. There was nothing of romantic interest about it: nothing of sex-attraction, he told himself, yet wondered why he suddenly felt more confused and uncertain than ever.

Deliberately, as he tidied away the first-aid paraphernalia, he concentrated on the surprising sight of Olivia and Mike Errol together. Did she know Mike, he wondered? And if so, did she know what sort of 'job' he did? He wanted to question her about the incident itself, too. But if she didn't know Mike—didn't know his job—he would certainly have to be very careful he himself did not say too much.

Then George called out that the tea was ready, and the chance was gone.

George had done more than make tea. He had obviously washed and shaved at the kitchen sink, and had changed the crumpled suit for casual but immaculately-pressed slacks and cashmere cardigan, and the grubby collar and tie for a green open-necked shirt with a pink silk scarf.

Garth suspected that this transformation had been partly inspired by his realisation that he had been seen at his worst by Olivia Livesey—and partly by the obvious fact that in forgetting his appointment, he had openly shown himself to have lost his grip. George was a man to whom 'face' meant much; he would certainly be at pains to retrieve any he might have lost with people of the Liveseys' calibre.

Olivia was surprised, but pleasantly so, when she learned that Garth would be seeing her home. She protested, not very firmly, that it was not necessary. But Kent, too, insisted she should be escorted and apologised for not taking her himself. She already conveyed his apologies—and assurances of a fresh appointment in the very near future—to her father, whom she had suddenly remembered to telephone.

Garth had taken the opportunity for a quiet word with their host.

'You're sure you're all right?' he had urged, and Kent had managed a strained smile.

'Yes—thanks. You've been very good, Garth ... Felt I had to have a word with you. I mean ...' He mumbled the words: 'Anne was fond of you.... I suppose we'll find the swine who did it.' He spoke without much feeling or hope.

Garth felt sure that the man had recovered from the worst, but equally sure that he would never be quite the same again. He could not rid himself of a feeling that the man was afraid. And he had also been struck by the thought that Kent's behaviour almost suggested that he blamed himself, in some measure, for Anne's death. He seemed anxious, now, however, to be left alone at the flat.

Garth was lucky enough to find a taxi almost at once. Olivia told him the address and he relayed it to the driver:

'And go through the park, will you?' he added.

'Yessir.' The cab started off and Garth sank back in his corner. That last-minute instruction had been quite unpremeditated: had almost surprised himself. The park drive would take longer than by the main roads, in the thin traffic of war-time London. But as he glanced at Olivia, beside him, he realised that it had been an instinctive reaction: he had no desire to part company with this girl, in fact he had subconsciously wanted to make the journey last as long as possible.

She met his gaze gravely.

'Do you think Mr. Kent will be all right now?'

'Oh, yes,' Garth nodded. 'It was just the shock—he'll be much more himself in a day or two. Do you know him well?'

'We met him in New York,' Olivia said. 'I don't know that I'd say we knew him well.' She gave a quick little smile: 'The funny thing is—I *seem* to remember *you!* We *haven't* met, have we? I can't imagine that I'd forget …' She broke off in confusion and Garth laughed aloud.

'Bless you! I take that as a real compliment—and no, I don't think we've met. But I was in America for a few weeks—recently.'

'Were you?' She eyed him again for a moment, puzzling. Then suddenly her face cleared: 'Of course! *That* David Garth! I remember I kept seeing pictures of you in the papers, after you'd shaken everyone up at Ligham Hall. *That* Garth!' she repeated, and now her eyes were shining.

'I'm afraid so,' Garth said, drily.

'Afraid? Why?'

'I wasn't exactly popular.'

'Oh, hooey!' Her spontaneity was too real to be insincere. 'You didn't make many enemies in the States, through plain speaking—except those who were your enemies, anyhow. My father liked all you said—he was there! He came back and talked about it for an hour. Would you mind coming in and meeting him? He'd be tickled pink. He's always impressed by people who can express themselves really cleverly, in public.'

Garth smiled, in no way self-conscious:

'I'd be delighted to meet him.'

No one was in the hall at Number 27. But as they reached the landing, a door opened along the passage and Dick Catesby came striding out. His face was flushed and his eyes looked angry.

'And if you argue with me again, my lad, I'll have you recalled!' Livesey's voice boomed after him.

'Damned old idiot!' muttered Catesby and then saw them both. He pulled up short, seemed about to speak, scowled, and strode on without another word.

Olivia glanced sideways at Garth, wondering what impression her father's outburst would have on him—or indeed, Dick's ungracious behaviour. Garth gave no sign that he felt he had heard or seen anything untoward.

Livesey was sitting back in a vast, inclining swivel-chair, behind a desk littered with papers. He was reading some typewritten material with obvious absorption: his argument with Catesby seemed to have gone completely from his mind.

'Dad....' Olivia greeted him, and he looked up.

He caught a glimpse of a man's figure on the landing behind her, and said: 'So you've brought him, have you? Good. We can ...' He broke off as Garth came further into the room. 'Now what?' he demanded, aggressively. 'I haven't a lot of time, Livvy.'

'Dad!' Olivia protested, colouring. 'This is Mr. David Garth—you remember? The speaker at Ligham Hall you talked so much about.'

'Never had much time for speechifying.' growled Livesey. 'Actions speak louder than words—always did. Every time a sheep bleats, it misses a bite!' He grinned; partly at his own joke; partly, Garth suspected, in tacit admission that his daughter had won that particular round.

'But I remember you, young man! You talked straight— I'll say that for you. Where'd you pick him up, Livvy?'

'Really, Dad!' Olivia remonstrated. 'Mr. Garth was with Mr. Kent at the flat.'

'Oh, I...' He stared at her, suddenly. 'Say ... what have you done to your face? And ...' His sharp eyes flicked over her; reached her torn stockings; 'Say, what *is* this? Isn't once enough for you?'

'You mean ...?' Garth darted a glance at Olivia.

'I'll tell you what I mean, son!' said Livesey. And in a few graphic sentences he described what had happened the previous night.

Perched on a chair-arm, Olivia sat silently approving the innately elegant young man who was so completely untroubled—and, she was sure, completely undeceived—by her father's outward show of brusque aggressiveness.

Garth, for his part, found himself warming to the blunt American. The man said what he thought, ignoring the niceties: it occurred to Garth that a discussion between Livesey and George Kent must be a highly diverting affair....

His attention was suddenly caught by Livesey's description of one of the men who had interviewed him. The big American was amused:

'I guess he had a mighty poor opinion of me, the time he left. Didn't trouble to hide it, either!' He chuckled. 'Reckon that fellow's gonna find out who came here, if anyone does. Even if it's only to show me!' He chuckled again.

'What was his name?' asked Garth, as casually as he could.

'Yeah. What was it, now?' Livesey scowled. 'Ham ... Hampton? No. Ham ... Hammer ... *Hammond!* That's it.' He shot a quick, shrewd glance at Garth: 'You know him?'

'I'm not sure,' Garth lied.

He was quite sure. The Hammond who had charged him with the task which even now seemed fantastic and unreal was the Hammond who had been at Queen's Gate—had sent Mike Errol to keep an eye on Olivia. That last disturbed him: it suggested there was real danger for the girl. He had a sudden urge to talk to Hammond, find out more of what was happening. But he contrived to maintain an easy flow of talk on Anglo-American problems, finding Livesey's forcibly-expressed views very similar to his own.

And now, when his thoughts wandered, Russi and Ryall kept coming into his mind.

Chiefly on that account, he regretfully declined an invitation to stay to lunch and returned to Jermyn Street.

He felt surprisingly fit, for the night hours had been trying. After Hammond and Errol had gone, he had stayed for a long time slumped in his chair. Thoughts of Anne had alternated with thoughts of what the two secret service agents had told him—and the fact that at any time, now, he might be called upon for much more than had yet been required of him. He had faced that with equanimity: at least he would be doing something towards avenging Anne's death, he had reflected, as he fell into a troubled sleep.

The telephone had wakened him. He had lifted the receiver, drowsily—to hear George Kent say, tense-voiced:

'Garth, I must see you! About Anne. I must!'

There had been only one thing to do but Garth had gone reluctantly. Kent had poured out the story. Anne's body had been discovered, and the police had called to break the news to him. He had clearly been in a dreadful state of nerves—and thus had begun Garth's feeling that he was afraid: that something more than the shock of the murder had affected him....

The one advantage of having so many things on his mind, Garth thought wryly, pouring himself a drink back at the flat, was that he could forget a great deal. The danger, he warned himself almost in the same breath, was that he could forget too much.

He was still shaken by the realisation that Livesey and his daughter were implicated in the same labyrinthine business.

He took his drink over to his favourite chair and sinking into it, looked at a paper for the first time that day; and for the first time read of the attack on Kearnley....

He lunched at his club, and was returning to the flat when a newsboy's cries caught his ear. He bought a paper and scanned the front page—and stopped in his tracks. Two or three people knocked into him and made surly comments, but he hardly heard them.

He was reading a story which was not in heavy black type, and which the Ministry must obviously have insisted was to be played down. But even the bare facts were shocking enough:

A number of attacks were made during the night on prominent Americans currently resident in this country. Many men were arrested and the police are interrogating them this morning. Among the victims of the assaults were...

He read the list quickly and then turned to the back page. In the stop press column was the bare statement:

Attacks on Americans—see Front Page

Three of the victims of last night's attacks have since succumbed to their injuries.

He raised his eyes at last, but still hardly able to believe what he had read. He stared blankly at men who were casually scanning the same front page as they bought their newspapers and waited for change. None of them seemed even to have noticed that starkly-worded little paragraph. Or perhaps they simply had no way of knowing those names—and so the implicit dangers of this suddenly and delicately contrived assault on the unity of two great nations.

Sick at heart, Garth knew all too well what it could mean; saw all too clearly the vast possibilities for Anglo-American estrangement and for unthinkable delays in vital agreements. It was desperate—and must not be allowed to go on.

He made his way back to the flat in a daze.

At the door, he glanced again at the paper, then pushed the key in the lock and went in.

The lounge door was standing open—just as it had been when he had found Anne. In his dazed state, he had reached it before he realised that—as then—it should have been locked. Then before the fact had fully registered on his mind, a suave voice spoke.

'Come in, Garth—come in!'

He went in. There, sitting in one of the big armchairs, was Ryall; the white cylinder of a cigarette vivid against his dark beard and moustache.

Chapter 13
Ryall Takes off the Gloves

Ryall's voice held a very different note from that Garth had heard on the previous evening.

Garth stared at him, not bothering to hide his anger and suspicion.

'What are you doing here?' he demanded, coldly.

'I am here.' The massive shoulders lifted in a shrug. 'That is all that matters.'

'It certainly is not!' Garth's voice was sharp, incisive. 'The last time that door was opened, I found a woman dead in the room. There is only my key—and the one you used. Why, you …!'

'Be quiet!' snapped Ryall.

His tone, like his gaze, was imperious. There was no doubt—he had taken off the gloves. Garth stared at him, a searing anger in his mind. Then slowly, caution asserted itself—he was no longer responsible to himself alone. He had a job to do: instructions to carry out. It would be senseless to antagonise Ryall—yet.

He licked his lips.

'Now close that door,' said Ryall, in a quieter voice. And added, as he obeyed: 'Come and sit down.'

Garth drew a deep breath.

'I'm not used to being ordered about in my own home.'

'I am not used to a great number of things, my friend. Nevertheless, I have to adjust myself to them. You will have to do the same. I have been told what happened here last night—Russi gave me the full story. So you think you can shelter behind me, to save yourself from the gallows?'

'I didn't kill …!' Garth snapped, but Ryall cut him short.

'Now come!' he said, softly. 'Russi pretended to believe you, but of course he knew the truth. You killed that poor girl. Russi thought he was doing the right thing by helping you—he knows how deeply I have the cause of Anglo-American friendship at heart and believes that you will be of great help in furthering that cause. He gave you an opportunity. Provided you are amenable, I shall help you also.'

Garth snapped: 'I didn't kill Anne! And I still want to know how you got in here.'

'The door was open.' Ryall did nothing to suggest that he thought it necessary to bolster the lie. Except to add a casual: 'Obviously your guilt has affected you so much, you hardly know what you are doing.' His eyes hardened. 'But I wish to know! What are you going to do for us, Garth, to *deserve* the help we are prepared to give you?'

Garth thought: *I mustn't give in too easily. I must make him think I'm fighting.* Aloud, he said in a low-pitched, angry voice:

'I've done some thinking since I saw Russi. And I'm damned sure he knows who killed …'

'Garth,' Ryall interrupted, in that suave, dangerous voice. 'I advise you to listen, very carefully. Russi *may* have to go away—and no one will know where. If that should happen, he will make a written statement describing what he found here last night, and how he helped you. He will state that on reflection, he could not be a party to aiding a murderer to escape justice. The statement will be sent to the police—and you, of course, will hang for that poor woman's murder.'

Had it not been for Hammond's assurances, the effect of Ryall's words on Garth would have been devastating. As it was, he had to fight hard to remember that he, too, was acting a part—that, in fact, Ryall was completely without power to undermine his true position. But he would need to let the man believe him frightened.

'You ... you wouldn't do that!' he muttered. 'You can't ...'

'*Can't* I?' purred Ryall.' *Wouldn't* I? You'll see, my friend, that I can and will do a lot more than that—unless you do as I tell you.'

Garth licked his lips; his fingers trembled when he took out a cigarette, and twice the end of it put out the flame of his lighter.

'What ... what do you want with me?' His voice was barely audible: 'I thought you wanted help in ... in improving relations between ...'

'I *do* want help, my friend—and that *is* my object. Your conscience ...' Ryall sneered the word '... might convince you that some of my methods are not justified. Last night the situation was different. Today ...' He paused, then asked abruptly: 'Have you seen a mid-day paper?'

'Yes,' muttered Garth.

'So you know what has happened to certain Americans in this country?'

Garth stared at him.

Only a fool, he thought, would fail to realise that there was at least a chance Ryall knew something about those attacks. Ryall would expect him to say so. Ryall was counting on fear ... fear of his inability to convince the police of his innocence, in the face of his actions ... to make him obedient. But he would not believe Garth a fool.

'Well?' snapped Ryall

Garth said, slowly and in a low-pitched voice:

'What do you know about that? Is this part of your ...?'

'You crazy fool! Do you think I would play any part in such madness? Free your mind once and for all of any such idea!' He glared, daring Garth to argue. Then went on, suave again: 'It *is* possible, however, that I know who allowed these attacks to be made, and it will be part of my task ... our task, my friend ... to bring retribution upon them. But that is by the way. I want you to understand this, Garth. Unless you do *exactly* what I tell you, that statement of Russi's will be sent to the police.'

Garth continued to stare at him in mutinous silence.

'I believe you are acquainted with George Kent?' Ryall added abruptly.

He startled Garth, who did not bother to hide the fact.

'*Kent?* Why, he ... the girl...'

'The woman you murdered was Kent's fiancée and private secretary,' nodded Ryall. 'At the moment, Kent has possession of certain Government proposals which are to be made to Washington. He has them in his capacity as a member of the Ministry of Propaganda staff advising on what is to be published and what kept secret. And I, my friend, want a copy of all those proposals.'

'But good God, man!' Garth exploded. 'I can't possibly ...'

Ryall heaved himself from his chair, took three long strides across the room and gripping him by the coat with both hands, shook him like a rag doll. The physical strength of the man was terrifying. His eyes glittered with a rage which might have been assumed but had a frightening effect.

'You'll learn not to argue with me, you fool!' he rasped, flinging him away so that he staggered back against the wall.

'You'll learn to do what I tell you ... or else. Don't make any mistake, Garth. I can *prove* that you murdered the woman. I can provide the evidence.'

Garth stared. 'But ... but that's impossible! You ...'

'All right!' snapped Ryall. 'I will ring the police now.'

Garth watched him, fascinated. He knew quite well the man would not telephone Scotland Yard, yet he was acting with sublime confidence. Garth wondered what his reaction would be if he had actually killed Anne—or even indeed if he had not had Hammond's assurances that he would be in no way suspect.

'No ... no, don't ...!' he began, unsteadily.

Ryall glared at him and began to dial a number.

'Don't!' cried Garth. 'Please!' He gripped Ryall's arm, trying to pull his hand away. 'I'll try!' he promised. 'I'll try to get them!'

'*That's* better,' said Ryall, heavily. 'That's very much better, my friend!' And apparently quite satisfied that he need have no more fear of disobedience from Garth, he replaced the receiver and calmly proceeded to issue his instructions in more detail.

He did not bother, now, to hide the fact that he knew Garth had spent a long time with George Kent since the murder. And, to Garth's considerable interest, he made a shrewd guess at Kent's reaction to the news....

'See that you get them quickly!' he warned as he was leaving. 'There's no time to be lost.' At the door, he paused to add: 'Remember just what I can do to you, Garth! Don't be fool enough to try to cross me. You will be closely watched.'

'I ... I'm not a fool!' muttered Garth, and Ryall reached for the door-knob.

Then the telephone rang. Before Garth could think whether or not he should answer it, with Ryall still there, the huge man had pushed him roughly aside and was back in the room and lifting the receiver.

Garth went cold with apprehension.

It might be Hammond, or Errol; or some message from them. If Ryall heard anything remotely suspicious, the whole plan would be destroyed. His mouth felt suddenly dry as Ryall spoke into the mouthpiece.

'Yes, who is that?'

Garth went forward slowly, wondering whether he should make a show of resentment—whether he should, perhaps, have snatched the instrument from Ryall's hand. Then suddenly realised: the call was *for* the big man—had obviously been expected.

'Yes, *go* on!' Ryall was saying. And as he listened his eyes turned to Garth, and his expression would have daunted most men. 'Are you sure?' he demanded. 'All right … What's that? … Yes, I will. I will indeed!'

He replaced the receiver slowly, his eyes glittering as he held Garth's gaze.

'So, Mr. David Garth, you dare to cross *me?* You dare to pry into my concerns.…'

'What the devil are you talking about?' Garth snapped. But his forehead was suddenly clammy. Had the man learned the truth?

'You know!' said Ryall. 'You know very well, my friend!'

'I don't know! I've done nothing at all!'

'You call it nothing, do you?' Ryall said softly. Then snarled: 'What were you doing with Livesey? What do you know about his daughter? How much do you know about 27, Queen's Gate? I warn you, my friend—I shall find out! It will be simpler and less painful for you to tell me.'

Indignation welled up in Garth's breast: half genuine, half assumed. There was a sense of shock, too, because the Liveseys mattered to this evil man.

'Don't talk nonsense!' he rasped angrily. 'I was at Kent's flat when Miss Livesey called—I had never seen her before! She went out and was knocked over by a cyclist. I took her back to the flat to give her first-aid and then saw her home at Kent's request. And why the devil shouldn't I?'

'*Very* plausible!' sneered Ryall.

'It's the truth, I tell you!' Garth gripped the back of a chair as he faced the man, and his knuckles showed whitely. It was time, he decided, for a show of spirit. 'Look here, Ryall, you've got me in a corner. I know that, and within limits I'll help you—although if I thought there was more behind this than you say I'd be damned if I would! But I won't have my private affairs dragged in. I won't be talked to as if I were a school-boy. I won't be told that I'm a liar when I tell the simple truth.'

His voice was quiet, but steely hard. 'If you don't want to believe me, get to hell out of here! Tell the police if you must—Russi will be in a spot, as well as I, however he puts it! I've had enough of being treated like a crook or a bloody fool!'

He was quivering now—a trick he had learned, and very simple to achieve by continued, enforced tension: 'I'm warning *you*, Ryall ... there *are* limits!'

Had he convinced Ryall? The man eyed him steadily for a long moment.

'Yes ...' he said, at last. 'If the explanation is indeed as simple as that....' He narrowed his eyes thoughtfully. 'Yes ... It is even possible that we may be able to make capital out of your newfound acquaintance with the Liveseys. Arnold Livesey has some very interesting data. Of course, the fellow is a dangerous reactionary and we may have to clip his claws. M'mmm, a friend at court might well be useful. I'll see. Meanwhile, Garth—get that stuff from Kent!'

When Ryall had gone, Garth returned to the lounge and watched from the window until he saw him reach the pavement and step into a waiting taxi. He waited till the cab moved off, then drawing a hand across his brow, he dropped into an easy chair. God, he was tired!

It had been a ghastly interview. Yet reassuring, in its way, he realised, wearily.

There was no doubt whatever now. Ryall was utterly ruthless; would be deadly, if he ever learned the truth. And power-obsessed. A dangerous megalomaniac, Garth summed him up. And there was no longer the slightest doubt that Ryall was deeply involved in the affairs of the previous night—that the Secret Service men were on the right trail. He was making real progress: needed no telling that they would wish to hear all that he had learned.

How and when would they get in touch with him. They could hardly come here again, Ryall had said he would be watched. He went cold at the realisation: how could he warn them? And he needed—urgently—to know what he was to do, in respect of Ryall's demand for those proposals.

He went out to buy another newspaper. But although it was a later edition, there was little in it he did not already know. He returned to the flat so much on edge that he had to check every room before he felt able to sit down again.

He had just done so and was lighting a cigarette, when there was a rat-tat-tat at the door. The sound brought him straight to his feet: rings and knocks were beginning to jar on his nerves. He steeled himself to meet Ryall again— or even Russi. It certainly could not be Hammond or the Errols, in broad daylight.

It was a diminutive telegraph-boy, with a shiny red face and an impudent smile.

'Telegram, sir! Will there be a reply?'

'Er ... I'll see.' Garth took out the folded sheet and opened it with something like reluctance. Then relaxed as he read:

IF POSSIBLE SEE ME AT MRS. PARMITTERS SEVEN O'CLOCK. AUNT MABEL.

'Any reply?' repeated the lad, eager to be off.

'No,' said Garth. 'No, thanks.' He tipped the lad almost absent-mindedly and closed the door.

He had no Aunt Mabel and he knew no Mrs. Parmitter. But that name was familiar, he thought, tiredly. Where the devil had he heard it before?

CHAPTER 14
DISCUSSIONS AT WHITEHALL

H e stared at the telegram again: *Mrs. Parmitter?*
Then remembered, suddenly. Of course, Mike Errol
had mentioned the name on the telephone. But only mentioned it, he remembered. He had given no address. Did
Mike himself imagine that he *had?*

Oh, hell! he thought, suddenly irritated by the lack of
communication, of any real guide-line to his proper course
of action over Ryall's demands—at the whole, continuous
disruption of his pattern of life.

What had he let himself in for? He would never be sure
what might come out of the blue. Scowling moodily, he
returned to the lounge and slumped into his chair. Assailed
by Ryall and prodded by Hammond, it was going to be no
picnic....

He was just beginning to doze off, when the absurdity of
that 'no picnic' struck him, and he laughed aloud. This job
was going to demand every reserve of energy and ingenuity
he possessed. It was the kind of work he would ordinarily
have leapt at the chance to do.

'It's time I took myself in hand,' he said aloud. 'Now:
where do I find Mrs. Parmitter?'

He looked in the telephone directory. There were several Parmitters listed, and three of them had the prefix 'Mrs.' One was at Barking; he discounted her. Another was at Hendon; possibly she might be the one, But a Mrs. Adelaide Parmitter of Greek Square, London, S.W.1. seemed far more likely.

He rang her number.

'Mrs. Parmitter's residence,' said an impersonal feminine voice.

'My name is Garth,' he said. And added, feeling a bit of an ass: 'I think my aunt ... Aunt Mabel ... is staying with Mrs. Parmitter.'

Then was vastly relieved as the woman said, simply:

'I shall enquire, sir.'

He was kept waiting for what seemed a long time before she spoke again.

'Yes, that is right, sir. Lady Grey is out, at the moment, but is expected back by seven o'clock. Could you ring again then?'

'No,' Garth decided, quickly. 'I'll call in person.'

'Thank you, sir. Good afternoon.'

So an Aunt Mabel had been wished upon him and her name was Grey. His mild amusement quickly gave place to a dawning and impressed awareness of the size and scale of the organisation to which the Errols belonged. Ryall would have worthy opposition, he thought with grim satisfaction.

It was then half past four: he had two hours at least before he need start for Mrs. Parmitter's. He set his alarm for six and stretched out on his bed. He needed some sleep, if he was going to be any real use to himself or anyone else. And the interview at Mrs. Parmitter's, he was sure, would be very important.

Mike Errol did not consider it had been a satisfactory day.

After following Olivia to Kent's flat and waiting outside for nearly twenty minutes, he had allowed himself to be so so off-guard that he had been taken by surprise when she had drawn his attention to the man who had fired at him at Queen's Gate. It would have been all right if he had managed to trace the man to his quarters, or even to catch him; he had succeeded in neither. He reported morosely to Craigie, then went home to the Mayfair flat he shared with his cousin.

Mark, relieved by two other agents at the Livesey abode, had just fallen into bed. He opened one eye and grunted, as his cousin came in. Mike, in no mood for talking, grunted back. Mark took that to mean there was nothing to report, and went straight to sleep—an ability all Craigie's men learned to develop very fast. Sleep was a luxury, in the course of a job: they grabbed it whenever they could.

Mike's dissatisfaction with himself was not enough to keep him awake, either. The shrilling of the telephone finally awoke them both. The instrument was nearer Mark, who stretched out an arm, pulled the receiver on to his pillow, and muttered:

'Mark Errol.'

'Wake up, old man!' Bill Loftus chided, obviously amused.

'I *am* awake!' Mark protested.

'I should hope so,' said Loftus, amiably. 'It's been ringing for thirty seconds! Not to worry—you haven't missed anything. But both of you be at Mrs. Parmitter's just after seven, will you?'

'What's on?' Mark could see from a bedside clock that it was nearly six already.

'Garth will be there,' Loftus told him. 'Bruce hopes to get there, too, but may not manage it.'

In the office at Whitehall, Loftus hung up and grinned across at Hammond, who was lying back in an easy chair and apparently communing with himself.

'Pleasant dream?' the big man prompted.

'No ...' Hammond, like Loftus, had managed to get a few hours' sleep since the all-night session, and was clear-eyed and very alert, now.

He knew that Craigie was making a report to Hershall and other senior Ministers at a special Cabinet meeting convened to discuss the American affair, and could imagine the consternation it was causing. The Department's New York representative had come through on the radio-telephone to report that the American Press was 'creating hell's delight' over the attacks. There had been many hurried consultations in the Foreign Office and the American Embassy.

The fact that only their early knowledge of the assault on Kearnley had prevented much graver consequences from the subsequent attacks, was apt to be overlooked. Although God knew they were grave enough. And the full repercussions would not be felt until the pundits of Whitehall and Washington—as well as public opinion in both countries—had had time to assess the situation.

Loftus began to fill his pipe.

'What's on your mind, Bruce?' he asked, more seriously.

'Ryall,' said Hammond.

'What about him?'

'Ought we to allow him to remain free? We can pick him up if we want to, while I think we can find Russi.'

The big man's eyebrows rose.

'No direct connection has yet been proved between Ryall, Russi and last night's schemozzles,' he pointed out, mildly.

'No ... But the connection's there, all right. Are we really wise to let him remain at large?'

'There's nothing else we can do, for the time being,' Loftus objected. 'We can haul that pair in any time. But we want 'em all.'

'Yes ...' Hammond frowned. 'Oh, I don't know! But perhaps if we were to give Ryall a scare—get him on the run—he might make a slip. I mean: he's back at Wimbledon. He must feel pretty sure of himself, or he wouldn't have left Kingston as quickly as he did. And he doesn't know that we've spotted the Kingston place, which suggests that he's either kidded himself or that someone's convinced him he's a lot safer than he is.'

'That really what's nagging you, old son?' Loftus asked sceptically. 'It's hardly ...'

He broke off as the sliding-door opened: only Craigie, Loftus and Hammond knew how to open that door from the outside.

Craigie greeted them with a tired smile, and Loftus noted with carefully-concealed concern that he was looking singularly weary, even for him.

It was a constant if secret source of anxiety to the big man that he had not seen Gordon Craigie looking truly fresh and rested for years—almost since the beginning of the war.

Like Hammond and every other member of the Department, Loftus revered Craigie, but he had always been conscious of the existence in the man of some indefinite quality which separated him from the rest, far more surely than the authority of his position, *per se,* could ever do. A sort of reserve—perhaps unconscious, but nevertheless making itself felt.

Since he had become his chief *aide,* Loftus had seen something of the reason for it. Reports reached Craigie constantly, from all over the world. All of them had to be attended to without delay: analysed, sifted, assessed, until the true importance of each item could be estimated. And like his unique grasp on world affairs Craigie's grasp on any situation affecting the work, of the Department or its members, was positively uncanny.

He was not only aware of what they were working on in any given part of the world: at a moment's notice, he could call to mind every individual agent, and the point of his progress in the job on which he was engaged. Although the Department might, as in this case, drop everything to concentrate on a single matter of outstanding importance, Craigie could not.

The reports never ceased: from occupied Europe and occupied Asia, from neutral as well as from Allied countries, they arrived in a constant flow. And Craigie wrestled in person with them all. There were other leaders of Intelligence Departments, but Craigie's men reported only to Craigie. When he reached his conclusions on any matter, they were passed on for comparison with reports from the other Departments.

Hershall's undisguised admiration for and faith in Craigie and his men was wholly deserved, as some of the very few in a position to know were well aware. But there were always the dissenters: the few either wilfully blind or crassly unimaginative.

Loftus drew slowly at his pipe as Craigie seated himself wearily in the winged armchair.

'Bad session?' he queried, sympathetically, and Craigie gave another tired smile.

'No worse than we had to expect, Bill. Hershall was with us, as usual—which counts for a lot. But he had to agree with the others: this mustn't go on.'

'And C-A-T spells cat,' said Loftus, sardonically.

Hammond put a kettle on the gas-ring and demanded:

'What's the chief trouble, Gordon?'

'There's a sharp division of opinion as to whether we should allow Ryall to stay free, or bring him in. At one time they looked like saying "bring him in" without further delay, but we have a reprieve. It won't last long, though—especially if anything else goes wrong.'

'Wrong!' exclaimed Loftus. 'Last night's shows went as well as any reasonable human could hope!'

'As Hershall convinced them.' Craigie smiled with more spirit. 'Thank the Lord for that man! But convincing them that Ryall is acting for someone else was a pretty sticky job.'

'M'mm …' Hammond murmured.

'*Is* he, Gordon?'

'Bruce has been bitten by the bug of doubt,' said Loftus, drily. 'His sixth sense is working overtime.'

'Don't be an ass!' Hammond smiled equably. 'It's an obvious possibility that we're looking too hard for something or someone who doesn't exist.'

Craigie pursed his lips thoughtfully, but said nothing, and Hammond busied himself making the tea. He had poured three cups and successfully foraged in the untidy cupboard for a tin of biscuits, when Craigie said, slowly:

'We've been watching Ryall and Russi for a month, now, and we've a complete dossier on each of them. Russi has no background earlier than 1940, when he appeared over here working for Ryall. Ryall is an importer of American produce in a comparatively small way. I can't believe they're the only men concerned—and if there's someone else, I don't believe we will get the result we want by detaining Ryall and Russi under 18B.' He regarded Hammond thoughtfully. 'Don't you see it that way, Bruce?'

'Well ... put like that.... But ...' He frowned. 'We took eleven prisoners, last night. So far, not one of them has cracked. That shows how well it's being handled.'

Loftus shrugged his vast shoulders.

'Either that, or not one of them is in a position to know anything worth divulging. Anyway, we're further on than we were, and I'm pinning my hopes on Garth. The man's no fool. He had contacted Mrs. Parmitter within minutes of getting that telegram.'

'Yes ... Question is—is he strong enough? I don't think there's much doubt that he's reliable, but he's had no training at all. Oh, hell!' Hammond grimaced. 'I'm talking a lot of nonsense—I know that! But it's time we were further on than we are.'

'Last night, you were grousing at me for saying the same thing,' grinned Loftus. 'I think it's breaking open now.'

'Then it's got self-sealing tanks,' growled Hammond.

'You know,' Craigie cut in, mildly, 'this isn't getting us anywhere. Let's take up a new angle. You weren't well impressed by Livesey, Bruce?'

'No,' admitted Hammond, frankly. 'I know on the face of things that it's absurd to suspect the man. But I can't get over the fact that he was left alive. *Why?* Kearnley was left for dead, three others were killed, there's no doubt of the murderous intent of the other attacks. Yet they didn't kill Livesey. It could be that he was attacked like the others to give everything a "Livesey's-on-the-spot-too" appearance, but that his daughter threw a spanner into the works.'

He frowned. 'I don't know that I liked Washington, either. And following up your own reasoning, Gordon ...

Livesey is a far more likely man than Ryall. Livesey's a producer, in a big way—he controls one of the biggest farming trusts in the States. He *is* a man who is going to be affected if the prices at which food is sold are to be kept low, by agreement.'

'More than low,' Craigie corrected. 'Given away.'

'We're not sure that it's food,' Loftus cautioned.

'No....' Hammond shrugged, wryly. 'When all's said and done, what *do* we know for certain?'

There was a long pause. Then Craigie took a meerschaum from the rack by his side and said, very quietly:

'We know for certain that there is a concerted effort on our own part, and America's, to provide some working agreement on international prices of food-stuffs and essential commodities, after the war. We know that it's going to mean a lot of give and take—more give than take—in America. We know that on such an understanding, a great deal depends: prompt assistance to the freed countries once the armistice is signed for one thing. We know that the system has to be ready and operable on the day of, if not some time before, that armistice. We know that if we and America can reach agreement on all points, then the other Allied countries will probably come in. As far as supplies are concerned, the South American countries and the Dominions are the largest factors. And we know that the Dominions have already agreed all material points with us.'

He paused.

Neither of the others spoke, but Hammond lit a cigarette, without moving his gaze from Craigie as the dispassionate voice resumed:

'We know that there are missions from practically every existing commerical and producer interest in America and this country, and that a formula designed to cover every problem is being drawn up. We know there is, and should be, reasonable hope of a successful agreement, but ... *some* private interests are trying to sabotage it. Perhaps here, perhaps in America, perhaps both.'

Craigie's hooded grey eyes were bleak. 'We have reactionary politicians here, as well as in America. And if there's no reason to suspect that they're anything worse than unthinking bigots, they're actually playing the game of the saboteurs and playing it well. *That,*' he wound up, solemnly, 'is what we know, for certain.'

His dry smile came again, as he looked at Hammond.

'I do *not* know for certain, but I do not *believe* that Ryall and Russi are more than agents. Important agents, if you like, but *only* agents. We have to get beyond them. And as I say—judging from the temper of the meeting I've just left, we shan't have long. So what we need is some way of forcing the issue quickly.' He frowned. 'I wish I knew why the attempts were made last night.'

'Could it be that general agreement appears to be getting too close?' suggested Loftus.

It could be ... but there is a month or more of work to be done yet. No doubt about that. There's no visible urgency.'

Hammond said slowly:

'If they'd succeeded in getting rid of all the men they attacked last night ... what would it have meant? I've been trying without much luck to make my own guess. What's yours?'

Craigie considered for a moment.

'Is it a guess we have to make?' he demurred. 'Isn't it certain that the key men in all industries were attacked—and that if they'd gone, a great deal of knowledge would have gone with them? And that ...'

'Good God, Gordon!' Hammond sat up with a start.

Craigie and Loftus stared at him, suddenly alert.

Until then, a stranger might have fancied him to be the odd man out—unnecessarily argumentative, disgruntled because the others would not agree with him. They had known better than that: something had been puzzling and worrying him, they knew ... something about the situation simply hadn't 'gelled' for him. Something still just out of his mind's sight had been taunting with its obviousness.

He had gnawed at the question of Ryall's freedom simply because that was one tangible thing they were doing: one deliberate course of action they were taking. And instinct told him they were going wrong, somewhere—were missing some obvious danger. The same instinct that had made him, in effect, force one or other of them to paint the whole, known picture for him—give him the chance to see if he could spot the flaw: the missing piece of the jig-saw. Now, his compact, brown-clad figure seemed suddenly to grow in stature. His eyes glowed as he stared at Craigie.

'Key men!' he echoed. *'American* key men! What about *ours?* We've been side-tracked, Gordon, or I miss my guess! We've been made to concentrate on the American missions—all the signs would obviously drive us to watch them like hawks believing theirs was the only danger. But what about *our* key men? What are we doing to protect *them?* And who *are* they?'

He stopped, and the atmosphere in the room was now electric. There was a long pause; then Loftus drawled a quiet:

'My God, Bruce, I think you've got something.... Work to do, Gordon?'

Chapter 15
The Home of Mrs. Parmitter

Number 11, Greek Square, Westminster, was an anachronism. The other houses in the select little square were all of Victorian design: tall, greyfaced, and—by modern standards—ugly. A small grass plot in the centre, its iron railings long since gone to aid 'the war effort', was these days part children's playground, part vegetable-patch.

Number 11, situated half-way along the south side of the square, was Elizabethan.

It was surrounded by a perfectly-trimmed yew hedge, nearly five feet high. The pathway meandered towards it from the gate: natural enough in the quiet of rural England, but strikingly eccentric in the administrative heart of modern London. The reddish tiles of its roof were moss-covered and uneven, its chimney stacks had a decided list to westward. The charm of its gabled windows with their leaded panes, was all the greater for their contrast with its neighbours.

In Greek Square, Mrs. Parmitter was what might be called 'an institution'.

Parmitters had lived in that house for three centuries and it was Mrs. Parmitter's one—and very deep—regret that she was the last of her line.

Despite her snow-white hair—and at the age, now, of nearly seventy—her trim, erect figure was the envy of many women twenty years her junior.

To either side of Mrs. Parmitter's house there were empty shells of others which had been blasted to pieces during the London blitz. No one was really surprised that Number 11 was barely affected: a few panes of glass had gone and a few tiles been broken, but if the replacements were a far cry from the perfect match she would have liked, at least they did not offend the eye.

Mrs. Parmitter had been a widow for twenty-one years before the war. Her husband had been killed in 1918 when the destroyer he commanded was sunk on convoy duty. She had lost her two elder sons in that same war and her two younger in this. She had mourned them, but had never doubted that they had died that others might live, and that certainty had made her grief bearable. She had found great solace, too, in the love and companionship of her only daughter and her son-in-law, whose name was Oundle.

Ned Oundle was one of Craigie's men and a close friend of Loftus. He had many surprising characteristics, and as many unexpected accomplishments. Amongst them, a knowledge of Chinese.

Not long after the war had started, Ned Oundle had been sent by Craigie to Chungking. Just before going, he had met Fay Parmitter. He had known Mrs. Parmitter but somehow always missed meeting Fay. Then on one of the worst nights of the blitz, they had met while both were help-ing to put out incendiaries. Three weeks later, they had been married. Two weeks after that, Ned had been on his way to China.

Fay did not know a word of Chinese so she had not gone with him. They had had no choice: Department Z obeyed Craigie without questions and Craigie had not seen how a wife would be helpful to Oundle in the circumstances: rather the contrary, in fact. It had been a general practice that Department agents resigned on marriage, but the war had brought the suspension of that rule—and there were signs that it would eventually be abolished altogether.

At all events, Fay had remained at home with her mother. Craigie, too, was an old acquaintance of Mrs. Parmitter, for whom he had a very real admiration. He had been greatly interested to learn what a regular rendezvous her home had become for Ned's friends, who—calling at his request to cheer Fay up or take her out, had one and all forthwith 'adopted' her mother and become her devoted slaves.

Craigie had not been slow in suggesting that the house might be an excellent meeting-place for men whom he did not want to meet in his office or his own flat. Mrs. Parmitter had been more than willing, and indeed very proud and deeply grateful: she felt that it kept her, somehow, in closer contact with Ned. And so 'Mrs. Parmitter's' had become a byword in Department Z.

An old manservant opened the door to David Garth, took his hat and gloves and card, then announced him. Mrs. Parmitter was seated with an air of almost regal dignity on a high-backed chair near the window of a long, low-ceilinged room which—as he recalled it afterwards—was full of age-darkened panelling, period funiture, and charm. The charm was the first and so the most lasting impression—and was to no small degree occasioned by the sweetness and friendliness of Mrs. Parmitter herself.

She was not alone.

Fay was sitting at a table, a pen in her hand. Garth had an impression of a tall, dark-eyed girl with shining, jet-black hair and a pale, almost translucent complexion. She was wearing black, with a single strand of pearls at her neck.

Comfortably ensconced among the cushions on a low-built sofa, with two small dogs—Cairns—nestling against her ample bosom, was a third woman. She was wearing casual but beautifully-cut tweeds and somehow contrived to look untidy while giving an impression of innate breeding and dignity.

Fay stood up as Garth entered, but the two other women just smiled at him. Mrs. Parmitter greeted him quietly and declared herself delighted to see him. Then before she could make introductions, the untidy woman seized his hand and declared in deep, throaty voice:

'I'm your Aunt Mabel!'

Garth smiled, his eyes twinkling.

'How have you been, Aunty?' he asked amiably.

A roar of approving laughter greeted him; and echoed as Mrs. Parmitter introduced her daughter. Garth found himself instinctively liking all three; which made polite small-talk easier than it might have been, as he hid his dis-appointment at seeing three women where he had hoped to see the Errols or Hammond. He was in no mood for social visiting however pleasant the company.

The Cairns after sniffing at his trousers, yapped their way back to the sofa to coil themselves up again, while keep-ing watchful eyes on him the whole time.

'Little dears, aren't they?' boomed Aunt Mabel.

'Friendly little chaps,' murmured Garth.

'Your friends will be here soon,' Mrs. Parmitter told him.

She batted a chair beside her as Fay asked to be excused and returned to her writing and Aunt Mabel rustled paper on a bar of chocolate, bringing yaps of delight from the dogs.

Garth took the indicated chair at Mrs. Parmitter's side—
and promptly came under the spell of her china-blue eyes.
Her complexion, he noted, was unbelievably fine: it rivalled
her daughter's.

'You haven't worked for Mr. Craigie long, have you,
Mr. Garth?' She smiled gently, her eyes searching his for a
brief moment: 'He told me a little about it. I'm so sorry.'

Garth smiled back, oddly affected.

'At least I'm being kept busy.'

'You always will be, while you're associated with Mr. Craigie.
It's been very distressing for you ... but you're feeling more on
top of yourself now, are you not?'

'I am,' smiled Garth.

'I'm so glad,' she said, and glanced absently for a
moment at the window. 'I wish ...'

She broke off, and he followed her gaze. A man was
coming up the path.

Hammond! Garth's heart leapt, and Mrs. Parmitter's
smile suggested that she understood exactly how he felt.
Then Hammond came in and she made it equally clear
that she expected them to waste no time in getting down
to business. And with brief but warm greetings all round,
Hammond led Garth up the stairs to a book-lined room in
which the last rays of the evening sun were shining with surprising warmth through the open windows.

Hammond's smile was friendly and reassuring.

'Well, old chap, how are things going?'

'I don't quite know,' Garth said, cautiously.

'What did Ryall want this afternoon?'

Garth stared. 'So you knew he'd seen me?'

'Oh, yes,' Hammond smiled again. 'We have to know
these things.'

Nothing else was said about that but it increased Garth's feeling of confidence. Indeed, the house itself gave him an odd sense of timelessness and peace. He remembered his peevish reaction to the telegram: and could hardly believe it of himself, now. His normal attitude would have been—as it was now—a feeling of pleasure, perhaps even of pride, that Hammond had taken it for granted that he would have no difficulty in following whatever clue they could safely give him. He was particularly pleased that it plainly did not strike Hammond as worthy of comment that he had done so.

'What was he after?' Hammond said, now, and Garth grimaced wryly.

'Looking back, it's hard to believe that he actually talked as he did,' he began. 'But here goes! I'll start with the main thing: he wants a copy of a report which George Kent is vetting for the M.O.P.—Livesey's agricultural report.'

Hammond nodded slowly.

'H'mm … Nothing else?'

'Not yet,' said Garth, ironically. Then plunged into his story.

He told it graphically and in accurate detail and Hammond sat in absolute silence until he had finished. Then nodding again, he said:

'Good. Very good, so far! What do you make of it all?'

'I don't quite follow you?' Garth countered.

'What ideas have you got, about what they're up to?'

'Well …' Garth contemplated him steadily: 'It's somehow connected with last night's attacks. Ryall is interested in the Liveseys and I don't see why he shouldn't be interested in the other victims as well. Or am I jumping to conclusions?'

'You're not far out,' Hammond assured him. 'Did he say anything else at all?'

'No.'

'Did he mention any other names? Any old name, it doesn't matter which! No? Did he give you the impression, say, that he had anything else up his sleeve?'

Garth said slowly:

'I don't think he mentioned anyone but Russi, the Liveseys, and George Kent.... I did get the impression that he's very sure of himself. I mean ... I don't think he was particularly worried that anything went wrong last night.'

'Indeed!'

'But wait a minute!' Garth recalled suddenly. 'Something that happened at Wimbledon: I forgot to tell you. He was going into further details after dinner, and then he had a telephone call. The maid said that a "Mr. Brown" wanted to speak to him. He went out to take the call—and then suddenly drove off, without even coming to make his excuses.'

'Brown....' Hammond mused. 'H'mm ... It might lead us somewhere, but it sounds suspiciously like an *alias.'* He paused then went on: 'The Errols were to have been here tonight but they've gone off on another job. But you'll want that report for Ryall....'

'*What!'*

Hammond looked amused.

'Well, won't you? It wouldn't do to disappoint Ryall the first time. I think ...' He sat back and looked at the ceiling, then spoke quietly: 'I think you'd better go to Kent's flat at ten o'clock. Then, or thereabouts, I'll arrange that Kent's not there, and that you can get in. I'll make sure the report will be at hand. Grab it and get away, as fast as you can.'

Garth protested, bewilderedly:

'But you can't mean ... you can't give him the real thing!'

'Don't worry so much.' Hammond leaned forward. 'We've decided on a policy for this business ... and we'll stick to it while there seems the remotest chance of success.

You needn't worry about anything ... except Ryall. We want to know whom Ryall contacts. It might be this Mr. Brown, or someone else. Ryall is an agent, not a principal. Do you understand?'

'Yes.'

'Good! Then we want that, from you. And we also want to know how Russi works. He has a number of agents in this country and it would be useful to find out who they are and where they live. Any kind of a clue that will help ... you get the idea? Don't worry too much about it ... just use your own judgement, and remember you're most use to us in one piece!'

He grinned drily, then rose with a brisk: 'Right! You're having dinner here, but I'm going off. Oh, by the way: just in case.' He took out a card and scribbled a telephone number on it: 'There—for use in emergency, or if you've anything to pass on that's really vital.'

Garth rising too, grimaced wryly: 'How do I know what is or isn't?'

'Oh, just use your own discretion, old son—marvellous how the instinct tends to develop, as one trusts it! Well, then: Kent's flat at ten or just after. All right?'

'All right,' promised Garth. 'But...'

Hammond eyed him keenly:

'Well?'

'I wish I knew more about this,' Garth said quietly. 'It's a bit breath-taking, you know. I mean, sudden orders from both sides and no attempt at explanation....'

Hammond nodded.

'I know. And we'll explain all we can when we can—don't worry about that. The less you know the better—we made clear why, earlier, didn't we? Once you've passed that report over to Ryall, he'll probably be even more domineering than he is now. He thinks he has you cornered over the murder—but when you've "stolen" that report, he'll know he can get you for treason. The small beginnings—the way they all start! He'll be able to threaten disclosure on two counts, and I *hope* he'll then feel he can use you for bigger things.'

He gave a dry smile: 'Your angle is fear—honest-to-god fear—and not enough guts to break away from it, although you know you should. All right?'

Garth stared at him, then gave a bark of a laugh.

'All right!' he promised.

'Good man!' said Hammond warmly, and went to take his farewell of the ladies.

Garth expected the next two hours to drag: instead, they flew. He was the only man at the little dinner-party, but talk flowed quickly and easily. The more Garth saw of Fay Oundle, the more he appreciated her quick intelligence. He was amused, too, by the hearty eccentricity of his newly-acquired 'aunt'. But it was Mrs. Parmitter's words, when she accompanied him to the door just after nine-thirty, which lingered in his mind :

'The more you think of others,' she told him, 'the less you'll be troubled for yourself. Good luck, Mr. Garth!'

'Thank you,' said Garth, warmly. 'Good night!'

The words might have seemed banal, from anyone else. From her, somehow, they gave him heart.

He went straight to Kent's flat, catching a cruising taxi to take him as far as Berkeley Square, then walking the rest.

He had a queer feeling of repugnance, as he finally arrived at that familiar door. He turned the handle, wondering drily what he would do if it were locked; then found that it was locked, and he was faced with his first emergency.

He could not believe it. Hammond had been so confident—and he had come to rely on everything the man promised. But the door was locked; he shook it, thumped it with his shoulder, tried the handle several times; all unavailingly. He stood back for a moment, surveying it angrily.

A soft blue light shone from the single lamp above the landing. And something was jutting out a little, above the lintel of the door.

He stretched up—and found a key.

His fingers trembled as he tried it in the lock. It turned and he opened the door an inch. No light shone through. He closed the door behind him and took out a torch, shining it in the direction of George's small study. The door was closed—but he switched off at once as he saw that the next, to the dining room, was standing ajar.

And a light was on.

It was a dim light and he saw it only through the crack at the door-hinge. A moment later, it went out: he thought he heard a faint click, just preceding it.

His heart was pumping as he tried to decide his best move. If he went to the dining room, he might meet serious trouble—be overpowered. But he could hardly go to the study to look for the report with someone else there in the flat with him.

He thought swiftly.

He could hear no breathing and detect no movement. But for that light, he would not have dreamed that anyone was there. As a momentary near-panic subsided, he stood staring at the door ...

Then his lips curved. George Kent always left his keys in the locks—on the hall side of the doors, so that he would remember to secure them against cat-burglars, whenever he was out of town.

He moved forward on tip-toe, soundless on the carpet. Near the door he flicked on the torch. There was no key in the lock! So whoever was in there, it was hardly likely to be George Kent himself.

Still no sound came from the room. He reached a hand round, felt the key sticking out on the inside, and took it out quickly.

He heard an exclamation, muffled but distinct, in the split second before he slammed the door and locked it.

His heart was pounding again as the significance struck him: the other had no more right there than he. He moved quickly, half-expecting to hear the prisoner trying to break out. But there was no sound as he entered the study.

It was tidier than it had been that morning, he noted, as he made straight for the small wall-safe he knew to be behind George's favourite Wimparis water-colour. Removing the picture, he pulled at the handle of the safe; it opened without trouble.

Almost the first thing he saw was a heavily-sealed envelope inscribed with George's name and marked 'PRIVATE'. It had been opened: the end was slit across. He pulled out the contents and glanced at the first typewritten sheet. It was headed: *'Agricultural—3. Confidential'*.

He stuffed the lot in his pocket and turned thankfully to the door. Then felt himself go hot with the shock of realising that in those few brief seconds, he had actually forgotten there was anyone else in the flat.

Steady! he told himself. What mattered now was to get safely out of the flat and away. He had what Ryall wanted, and Hammond had assured him he need worry about nothing but carrying out his orders.

He had reached the front door but not opened it when the light was switched on from behind him. He swung round—then stood dead still. A man was pointing an automatic pistol straight at him. But the shock of that was not so great as the shock of recognition—which was obviously mutual.

It was Olivia's friend, Dick Catesby.

Chapter 16

Mr. Ryall Shows His Pleasure

The gun in Catesby's hand was enough to make Garth stay where he was, but his mind worked desperately to find some way out of the situation. Catesby's square chin was thrust forward and his lips set tightly as he rasped:

'So you're the spy, are you?'

The words seemed so ludicrous that Garth literally gaped at the man. Then it struck him that Catesby was probably accusing him in an effort to justify his own presence. Which would take some doing, he thought grimly.

'I don't know what you mean!' he began. 'I came for something I left here this morning.'

'Like hell you did!' sneered Catesby. 'Hand it over!' He held out his left hand, thrusting the gun forward threateningly with his right. 'Don't waste time, Garth ... gimme!'

Garth countered: 'What right have *you* got here?'

'A damn sight more than you! Are you going to hand it over—or do I have to drill lead into you?'

'Don't be a fool!' snapped Garth. 'If ...'

It was then that another door in the flat opened—one which Catesby could not see. But as Garth's eyes flickered towards it, the younger man half-turned. As he did so, something curved though the air towards him—and Garth stared in disbelief at the missile: a kitchen jug. Catesby dodged to avoid it, off-guard in his blank astonishment—and in a flash, Garth had turned, pulled open the door and darted out, slamming it behind him.

He heard the crash of the breaking jug, as he raced down the stairs and out into the street. He had gone some fifty yards when he realised that he was behaving in a manner which was bound to arouse the suspicions of any patrolling bobby. He stopped, breathing heavily as he peered through the darkness. He could hear foot-steps, but they were some distance off and he turned with considerable relief towards Piccadilly.

Moments later, he *knew* that he was being followed.

The footsteps were behind him all the time, soft and padding: reminding him of Ryall. He crossed the road. So did his follower. He reached Piccadilly feeling a strong desire to break into a run, but refrained for fear of missing his footing. He walked all the way, several times thinking that he had shaken off his pursuer—only to find after a few seconds that he was still being followed.

By the time he turned into his own street, the menace in those padding footsteps had reached a high peak.

A figure loomed out of the darkness of the porch of his house. He stood still, and as his heart turned over a soft, hissing voice behind him said:

'It's okay!'

The footsteps passed, still padding softly: a figure loomed vaguely for a moment, then disappeared. He was still straining his eyes to follow the other's progress, when a more familiar voice spoke from the porch.

'Have you got it?' demanded Russi.

'Yes ...' stammered Garth. 'Yes ... but ...'

'Take it to Wimbledon,' said Russi, flatly. 'There's a car along the street. Make it snappy!'

Garth made no rejoinder, but turned to where the rear-lights of a parked car showed a few yards along the road. It was not until a man had opened the door for him, that he realised it was the 'taxi' which had brought him from Wimbledon, the previous night. He could not see the driver clearly but recognised the voice.

'Wimbledon, sir?'

'Please,' grunted Garth, and climbed in. He chain-smoked throughout the journey, deeply-conscious of the envelope in his pocket. The nearer they drew to Wimbledon, the more dubious he became about the wisdom of handing the thing over to Ryall. He had to force himself to accept Hammond's assurances that this was a deliberate and there-fore presumably a tactically valuable move. And by the time the car turned into the drive of The Elms, he had reached a decision to demand more evidence of Hammond's *bona fides* before he accepted further orders.

Ryall was in the upstairs room, sitting at his vast desk. He was expressionless as Garth was shown in by the maid.

'Well?' Ryall demanded, heavily.

I … I've got it,' Garth muttered.

'I hope you have!' growled Ryall, stretching out his hand.

Garth took out the envelope and as the huge man snatched it from him and extracted the papers, he felt as if he were standing on the edge of a precipice. If he had not got what Ryall wanted, this man might well kill him. Why the devil hadn't he checked those papers more thoroughly? His throat contracted as he watched him: it was suddenly difficult to breathe. He had a sudden, vivid recollection of that photograph the Errols had shown him. And another, of

Anne's body—lying huddled there in his flat, with the knife sticking out...

It was not difficult to act as if he were afraid.

Slowly Ryall's expression changed.

The transformation was a remarkable thing. The shaggy beard and moustache parted and he smiled broadly, nodding his head in deep satisfaction. There was nothing forbidding or dangerous about his appearance, now. He was a benevolent, amiable man.

'My dear Garth ... remarkable! Remarkable!'

'Is ... is it ... what you wanted?' Garth spoke as if with an effort, but allowing some slight display of his relief.

'It is ... it is indeed! I was very much afraid that your first mission might not succeed. Tell me, how did you get it?'

Garth said slowly:

'I knew Kent kept a key of his flat above the door. I phoned and made sure he was out, then went round there.' He nodded at the envelope: 'That was in the safe.'

'And you said *"hey presto"*, and the safe opened?'

In spite of the big man's obvious good humour, the question had a barb in it, Garth realised. He had to be careful.

'Unfortunately, no,' he said, stiffly. 'I've known Kent a long time, and I've seen his safe often enough. It's an old one, the same sort as my own ... and one of the keys in his desk was the same as mine, except for the cut. So ...' He shrugged.

'As easy as that?' murmured Ryall. 'Yes, of course. I am apt to forget sometimes, how easy some things are. I am very satisfied with you, Garth. This will be *most* useful. I will send for you when I want you again, and meanwhile you will cultivate the acquaintance of the charming Miss Livesey. *That* will be no great hardship, I am sure! You ...'

He broke off, staring.

'Good evening,' said a voice.

It was a man's, but so soft that it might have been a woman's. Ryall had started to his feet at the sound, and Garth was amazed that the big man was so obviously taken by surprise. More, that *Ryall* was afraid now: the self-assurance had suddenly quite gone. He looked like a man caught red-handed in a crime and aware that he would have to answer for it.

'What is it that you have received?' asked the newcomer, gently, Garth himself swivelled round to see him.

'I ... I was going to ... ring you, Brown,' he heard Ryall bluster. 'I ... I've had a remarkable piece of luck! Nothing less than ...'

But Garth hardly heard him: he was staring in amazement at the newcomer.

'Come, my friend, you will not dismiss it as luck?' chided that soft voice. 'Surely everything you obtain is contrived by your remarkable brilliance ... one might also say genius ... for doing the impossible? I congratulate you ... but what is it? Come, now! Don't be nervous, my friend ... it is a simple question!'

He was small. The top of his head did not rise above Ryall's shoulder as he came forward slowly with his hand outstretched. It was a black-gloved hand: he was dressed in black from head to foot. But what had so startled Garth was that *even his face was black.*

Not the 'black' of racial pigmentation ... although his striking eyes, the whites of which seemed to be luminous, had for a split second fooled Garth into thinking he was looking at a singularly dark-skinned negro. But almost in the same moment, he realised that in fact the strange visitor wore a mask which fitted his features like a glove: almost as if pasted on, like some second skin. The lips of the mask moved when the man spoke: it was an uncanny, creepy thing.

'The … the Agricultural Report.' Ryall's tongue flicked nervously along his lips. 'You remember … I … I told you that I hoped to get it.'

'No, I don't remember,' said the newcomer, softly. 'But I have a careless habit of forgetting, I'm afraid. Of course, you know that, don't you, Ryall? You wouldn't be catching the habit, would you? You haven't forgotten who it is that you work for?'

'Really, even to say such a thing in jest …! I have done very well for you, have I not?'

'Fairly well,' allowed the man called Brown. 'Although you made a remarkably abortive attempt last night, didn't you. That is what I have come to talk to you about.'

'I can explain everything,' Ryall assured him, quickly. 'There is nothing to worry about … it makes no serious difference. The people who matter are …'

Then he seemed to remember Garth.

He glared round at him, obviously furious to suddenly realise that his humiliation had been witnessed by another. And the expression in his eyes boded ill for their future relations as he snarled:

'Get out, Garth!'

'Just a moment,' 'Brown' checked him. 'I am interested in the members of your staff, Ryall. I like to know on whom I rely for the success of my efforts. David Garth. Yes … A somewhat hotheaded young man. I hardly expected to find you in our ranks, my friend!'

'I arranged that to …' began Ryall.

'Are you happy in your work?' 'Brown' asked softly, silencing him with a gesture. 'Are you, Mr. Garth?'

'I … I know I've … it's got to be done,' muttered Garth.

'Let me explain!' cried the big man. 'Garth needn't be here … he's finished what he came for!'

'My dear Ryall!' 'Brown' sounded shocked. 'I do believe you are afraid that I shall tell our young friend more than he should hear? Believe me, I am every whit as discreet as yourself. All right, Garth ... you may go. Tell me if anything troubles you, won't you?'

Garth rose, and mumbled a goodbye.

The luminous, almost colourless eyes of the man were turned towards him and the voice suggested a sardonic smile on the grotesque lips. He was glad to get out of the room, and as the door closed behind him, he stood for a moment in the passage; his mouth dry and perspiration on his forehead.

Ryall was bad enough, but the second man...!

He started; as he suddenly realised that the maid was looking at him from the head of the stairs. She was expressionless and quite motionless, and he had to force himself to go forward. As he did so, she turned and led the way down the stairs. Opening the front door, she stood aside for him to pass and as he went by, said a quiet:

'Good night, sir.'

'G ... good night,' mumbled Garth.

The evening air was cool and he was glad of it. He felt as if he had just been rescued from some stifling nightmare, and was breathing the air of sanity and reality again. He had an impulse to walk all the way home. But the big limousine was waiting, the driver holding the rear door open for him.

He wondered vaguely what the man would do if he walked on.

Then, like a man in a dream, he climbed in and was driven back to Jermyn Street.

No one was waiting for him.

For the second time that day, he checked the whole flat before going to his bedroom to lie full-length on the bed, staring towards the ceiling. He had not yet recovered from the effect of the black-clad man.

The whole affair grew more fantastic by the moment. He had a brief flash of his earlier panic as it struck him again that this wasn't a task for which one could summon up one's reserves of strength in one supreme effort.

There was no end to it. It was a job that called for all one's reserves—mental and physical—all the time; the unknown—the dangerous unknown—was the norm.

But that was the whole point, he reminded himself, with a sudden return of his usual humour. It was a job—and he had accepted it, and was making reasonable progress.

But, my God, when did these Secret Service fellows ever sleep he wondered.

And slept.

Once, towards morning, he grew aware of the light coming through at the edge of the black-out curtains, but he rolled off again and it was nearly nine o'clock when he finally came properly awake.

A cold bath and a shave refreshed him.

He made himself some toast and coffee, and glanced through his morning paper. There was little in it about the American V.I.P. attacks and he guessed that an edict had gone out to play down the whole thing. The bare facts were there, and treated sensationally enough: but there was no attempt at explanation or theory.

He felt on edge about it all, again, and wondered if perhaps this might be the time to telephone Hammond.

Then the flat door-bell rang.

He was tensed-up despite himself, as he went to answer it: prepared for anything.

George Kent stood there. And his plump form nearly hid a second figure, behind him: Olivia Livesey. One look at her face told Garth that she was troubled.

There was also, plainly, something seriously amiss with George. He had evidently recovered from the worst of his shock. He looked fresher, more composed: and he was dressed immaculately, as was his normal wont.

'Good morning, David,' he said, portentously, as he followed Olivia in.

'Why, hallo!' Garth forced a smile for each in turn. 'This is a surprise! How are you?'

George did not answer him. Olivia began to, then looked away as if she could not meet his eye. Shepherding them into the lounge, he warned himself to be on his toes. Catesby, after all, had seen him at Kent's flat.

He managed to retain an amiable smile as George, solemnly pompous, said:

'David, this is a most distasteful task for me, and I must impress upon you that it concerns a matter of an extremely serious nature. I have a single question which I am obliged to put to you and which I hope you will answer promptly and frankly. If you fail to do so, it may lead to most unpleasant developments.'

Garth raised a drily-sceptical eyebrow and shot an amused glance at Olivia.

'It can't be as serious as all that, George!'

'I cannot impress its seriousness upon you too much.' Kent eyed him with owlish gravity. 'But for the fact that we have been friends for a long time, and my warm appreciation of your ... kindness ... yesterday, I should not have given you this opportunity. In the circumstances, I feel bound to do so; but I *must* know the truth.'

Garth began to frown, as if striving not to be offended by this tacit impugning of his honour.

'Just what is this all about, George?' he asked, coolly.

'Were you, or were you not ...' began George.

Dick Catesby had talked, Garth decided. Right: he knew what question was coming—the only problem was in not knowing what would follow, if his necessary denial was not believed. But at best, it could only be a matter of Catesby's word against his, and ...

There was a thunderous knocking on the front door.

Garth was too relieved by the interruption to be worried by the urgency of the knock. With a murmured excuse, he strode again to the front door. He did not know why he was so dumbfounded to see Dick Catesby standing there ... with Arnold K. Livesey at his side.

Olivia was visible through the lounge doorway.

'I *thought* so!' shouted Catesby. 'I *thought* they'd come to warn him! But you won't get away with it, Garth ... I've told the police!'

Garth forced himself to say, with an air of restrained anger:

'What exactly have you told the police? What's got into you all? First, George with some damned unpleasant innu-endos ...'

Livesey's piercing blue gaze was fixed on him.

'You be quiet, fella!' he snapped. 'Don't let him get away, Dick.'

If that 'Dick' was surprising to Garth, remembering that bellowed finale to their row, it was positively startling to Olivia. She stared at him as he strode into the room, his weather-beaten face set as he demanded: 'Livvy ... what are you doing in this man's flat? What do you mean by coming here without telling me what you were up to?'

'Mr. Livesey, I must accept full ...' George began, and the big American turned on him so fiercely that he backed away.

'Hold your fool tongue! Livvy answer me! *What are you doing here?'*

Her face was flushed as she silently returned her father's gaze. Garth watched her, only half-conscious of gratified relief that the deeper significance of this visit did not trouble him. He was far more interested in Olivia's reason for coming with George to warn him of impending danger. Why should *she* be anxious for him?

And while he asked himself the question, Olivia gave the answer.

CHAPTER 17
DEEPER IN THE MIRE

'I came because I disbelieved Dick,' said Olivia. 'Because I thought Mr. Garth should have an opportunity to speak for himself. And I think …'

Catesby moved towards her, hands clenched and eyes blazing.

'Are you saying you think I lied?'

'Oh, don't be a goop, Dick!' she snapped. 'I mean I think you were mistaken. You admitted you didn't see him well, and that someone else was in the flat.'

'I saw enough,' said Catesby, partially mollified.

Garth raised his eyebrows. He hoped he was putting up a good show, but the gaze of Arnold K. Livesey was disconcertingly shrewd. He met it with a smile, drawling his words:

'It looks as though there's been a case of mistaken identity,' he said easily. 'Whatever my misdeeds, I've done nothing that could create a situation like this.' He glanced at Olivia: 'What is it … does someone think I was mixed up in that attack on you?' Then swung round to Catesby: 'Good Lord … is *that* why you snarled in my face this morning?'

'You *see?*' cried Olivia, to the others.

'I can see you're under the spell of this smooth-tongued rascal,' Livesey told her flatly. 'I'm not. It's time you went back home, my girl!'

Olivia flushed but said nothing. Garth sent her a communicating smile, shrugging slightly in well-simulated bafflement: letting her know that he did not include her in his growing resentment.

'Now, if anyone would care to inform me ...' he began, his voice quiet but much harder, now.

'Kindly allow me to discuss this with Garth,' George Kent said pontifically. 'David, my flat was burgled last night, while I was out. A set of papers ... highly important papers ... to do with Mr. Livesey's mission here ... was stolen. Catesby declares that he saw you at the flat.'

'Oh?' Garth glanced at Catesby as at a specimen on a slide, then back at George. 'I was not at your flat last night, of course. Since Catesby was, and the papers are missing, perhaps he can tell you something about it?'

'I had given him permission to go to the flat,' said George stiffly. 'I am afraid that counter-accusation won't get you anywhere, David.'

Garth's jaw set.

'Let me impress upon you, George, just how little taste I have for these kangaroo court tactics! Suppose we leave police matters to the police?' He turned a bleak gaze on the younger man. 'You did say you had called them? I hope that, at least, can be relied upon! And now, suppose you all get out?' He glared from one to the other until his gaze reached Olivia. His expression relaxed at once and he said quickly: 'Miss Livesey, you're the only one who has been reasonably decent about this ... and probably you're the last to have reason to be. I appreciate it very much indeed.'

"That's ... oh!' She flushed again. *'Can't* you convince them?'

'I'm staying around till the police come,' Catesby announced. 'You're not getting any chances to clear out, Garth. I'm not as dumb as that!'

'There's plenty of room on the landing,' Garth told him, moving sharply towards him.

Catesby backed, raising his fists ... and was clearly baffled when Garth merely crowded him, his hands by his sides, and he found himself jostled towards the door while the others looked on.

'Now see here ...!' he began, angrily.

Garth shot out his right hand, taking him by surprise and getting his right wrist in a vice-like grip. Catesby swung a powerful left, but Garth shifted his head and as the punch missed, opened the door with his free hand and propelled him out of the room.

He held the door open.

'Next, please!' he said, ironically. 'Unless, of course, you are prepared to discuss this matter like reasonable people?'

He was not sure how they would react. If the powerfully-built Livesey refused to leave peacefully, he would have problems: Catesby would clearly come to his aid. George he discounted.

'Well, gentlemen?' he invited. Then heard footsteps start up the stairs. They were heavy and deliberate and belonged to at least two men.

Catesby beamed triumphantly as they appeared.

'You're late!' he greeted them.

A very large man in a grey suit, with white-flecked sandy hair and moustache ... a man who looked as if he had been in a flour-mill and hadn't managed to get rid of the last faint dusting of flour ... ignored the young American and advanced into the room. Behind him, a second man, in police uniform, took up a stance by the door.

'Which is Mr. Garth?' demanded the dusty-looking man.

'I am,' said Garth, stiffly, 'But …'

'I am Superintendent Miller, of Scotland Yard,' declared the large man. He took a card from his waistcoat pocket and handed it over. 'I have a warrant for your arrest, sir, and a warrant to search this flat.'

Garth felt his heart-beat quicken.

'You can't be serious?' he demanded incredulously. The card bore out the man's statement of identity and the second man took folded papers from his pocket: the warrants, obviously. In a sudden panic, Garth thought that Hammond and his colleagues had failed him. Sudden anger was succeeded swiftly by cold fear.

'It isn't a joking matter,' said Miller stolidly. 'It is my duty to warn you that anything you …'

Garth stared.

'But this is outrageous!' he exploded. 'You've charged me with nothing … I am guilty of nothing which would possibly justify an arrest!'

'The detention order has been issued under Regulation 18B,' Miller explained, laconically. 'Come along, sir, please!'

Garth clenched his fist. Catesby was grinning over the superintendent's shoulder and Livesey looked complacent. George seemed troubled … a picture of a man doing a duty he found repugnant. Olivia….

Olivia was looking at Garth as if no one else were in the room. Garth found the intensity of her gaze very comforting; it was all that was. He drew a deep breath and spoke quietly and with greater composure.

'If you've paid attention to absurd charges by a hot-headed young fool, I suppose there's nothing I can do about it, yet. But I insist these people are removed from my premises, before I go. Miss Livesey will doubtless be glad to leave. The others ...'

Livesey shrugged his massive shoulders and strode to the door.

'I've seen all I want to see,' he snapped. 'Livvy!'

Olivia stared mutinously at him as he turned his head, impatient. Catesby was still grinning ... Garth longed to knock the smile off his silly face. Then the girl moved, reluctantly. Near Garth, she paused; and her smile was very warm and friendly.

'I'm sure it won't be too long before you get everything put to rights,' she told him. *'Au revoir,* Mr. Garth!'

Garth found himself shaking a small hand; felt the warming pressure of it, and smiled at her as Livesey muttered under his breath, and the grin disappeared from Catesby's face. He felt suddenly very much better.

And when George approached, with an awkward: 'David, I can't say how ...' he smiled and interrupted him.

'It's all right, old man ... none of your doing! As soon as I get it cleared up, we'll have a chat ... find out what's at the back of it all.'

'Good,' George nodded. 'Good!' And went out swiftly in the wake of the others.

When their footsteps had faded, the uniformed policeman glanced a query at the superintendent, then nodded and closed the door, leaving the two of them alone in the flat.

Garth somehow stayed silent and proffered his case: he did not know quite how to take Miller, whose expression was enigmatic as he accepted a cigarette.

'Thank you, sir,' he said, equably. 'I'm sorry I had to act like that.'

Garth stared, uncomprehending.

'What do you mean?'

Miller chuckled.

'Well, it must have been well done! I thought you'd prob-ably guess. I'm the liasion officer between Scotland Yard and Department Z, Mr. Garth. The information was lodged against you, and ostensibly it had to be investigated. As soon as it was realised that Mr. Livesey was coming here, it was decided to act quickly ... convince him that action *had* been taken. You'll be released for lack of evidence, of course.'

Miller beamed, obviously enjoying himself, and Garth said:

'Well, I'm damned!'

'Meanwhile, if you'll come with me to Cannon Row, sir, I think Mr. Hammond would like a word with you there. Er ... do you think that you can look angry with me? We may well be watched and it would be advisable to maintain appearances.'

He chuckled again as Garth assured him:

'I shall look positively fiendish towards you!'

Garth laughed with him: the relief was a tremendous tonic. So was the sense of his strange new job's importance. He would hardly want any further proof of Hammond's cre-dentials after this!

As they emerged into Jermyn Street, he glared at Miller, who had gone down one step in front of him. He saw Catesby standing on the other side of the road; obviously waiting to enjoy his discomfiture. There was no sign of Olivia or her father—but further along from Catesby, was the unmistak-able figure of Russi.

Garth stared involuntarily.

Russi stared at him with no sign of recognition. But Garth was suddenly aware of an unpleasant feeling of insecurity. The knowledge that he was under such constant surveillance from all sides was a chilling thought. Hammond and his associates were one thing: the fact that there was no move he could make that Russi and Ryall would not also know about, was something else again.

The eager anticipation he had felt at the prospect of seeing Hammond and reporting the advent of the little man in black, faded. He felt a presentiment of danger ... Russi's flat expressionless stare had somehow chilled him: left him tense and apprehensive.

He stumbled, suddenly ... and clutched at Miller for support as he lost his balance. The uniformed policeman put out a hand to steady him and then gasped: a strange gasp more like a choking rattle in his throat.

Garth straightened up, staring in utter disbelief at the small hole which had suddenly appeared in the man's temple, just beneath his helmet. The steadying grip on his arm slackened, and the policeman slumped to the ground. But not before Garth had seen a trickle of blood coming from that small hole....

'*What the ...!*' Miller exclaimed. Then in almost the same split-second, put one huge hand to Garth's shoulder and sent him flying backwards.

Something small and black flashed in front of Garth's eyes as he fell. He was being shot at!

Miller had probably saved his life, he knew: had certainly thrust him out of immediate danger. At the Wellington Street end of the road, a small man stood by a car, the gun in his right hand held well into his waist.

Garth caught a glimpse of him as he fell: no one not looking towards him could have seen the gun, and there was no one between him and the man. He saw a flash of flame, pale in the bright sunlight, and a bullet thudded into the pavement by his side. Sparks flew and stone chippings stung his face, and he rolled across the pavement ... all he could do, to make him a less vulnerable target. Miller put a whistle to his lips and as a piercing note echoed up and down the street, Russi began to walk swiftly away from the scene.

The man with the gun, realising he could do little more, vainly fired twice more at Garth's moving figure. Then he jumped into the car. As he did so, two men came pounding into the street their footsteps like thunder in Garth's ears ... and he recognised Mike and Mark Errol. They were on the right side of the road and closing on the gunman, as he started up and began to drive away.

Mike Errol was nearer than his cousin. And as the gunman took a hand off the wheel and turned to fire point blank at him, Mike simply ducked, then made a flying leap and reached the running-board.

Then Mark reached the car's other side as it began to skid across the road. All Garth could see, now, were Mike's legs and behind as he leaned into the car.

Across the road, Catesby was staring wide-eyed at the scene. Then he went forward, his square chin thrust out: an 'i'll-put-this-right' expression on his face. Garth saw him reach the car, and then heard Miller rasp to a constable who came running in response to that piercing summons:

'Get a doctor, man!' Anxiety and outrage cut through his stolid-seeming calm: '*Now*, damn you!'

He was down on his knees, examining the wound in the side of the first policeman's head. The bleeding was very free now, and the man's eyes were closed. Obviously, he had lost consciousness: but his lips were still twisted in pain.

Scrambling to his feet, Garth called, pointing directions: 'There's a Dr. Williams ... fifty yards along. On the right.'

'Thank you, sir!' The P.C. hurried off and Garth fumbled suddenly for cigarettes. He felt badly shaken and had to fight back a wave of nausea as the reaction hit him.

That could … and perhaps should, he felt bleakly … have been him lying there. It had been a cold-blooded attempt to murder him … and that Russi knew something about it, he had no doubt at all. As yet, his mind could not even begin to work out just why he should have been the intended victim….

Miller got to his feet and spoke gruffly:

'There won't be much a doctor can do.' But he was looking impatiently along the street, in the direction the doctor should come.

Garth eyed the injured man helplessly, for a moment, then turned his attention to the Errols, the small car and Catesby. Catesby, at this moment, was helping Mike to lift the driver from the car. The man was kicking and struggling and once Garth saw him try to bite at Catesby's nose. The American smacked him, flat-handed and his struggles grew quieter.

Garth thought: *I must remember not to show that I know the Errols.*

Because he would go on with this, he knew. The reason for his attempted murder was beginning to dawn on him, then: and he felt stiff with cold.

Miller, despite his bitterness at the P.C.'s fate, was methodically searching along the ground. Suddenly, he bent down and retrieved something.

'What is it?' Garth queried, as he held it up.

'One of the bullets,' said Miller. 'The ruddy swine.' He spoke dispassionately, but his face was flushed as he glanced away, along the street.

Then his expression suddenly changed—and he began to sprint towards the Errols.

Staring after him, Garth saw that the little gunman was kicking and struggling far more violently than before, and heard him crying out—shrieking as if in pain, rather than shouting. Mark Errol had not been touched by the man's hands or feet, yet now Garth saw him reel back against the window of a shop, his hands at his face. Catesby was bending over the gunman, who was writhing on the pavement.

'Get back, you fool!' Mike shouted, pulling at him. 'Get back!'

Catesby straightened up. 'Why? What ...?' he began, indignantly.

The two words travelled clearly along the street, before Catesby gasped and like Mark Errol, clapped his hands to his face. And as Mike pulled him further away the gunman's struggles, which had reached a terrible crescendo, grew noticeably weaker.

Miller reached the scene, and this time Garth could not hear what was said. But he did see Mike Errol put a restraining hand on the superintendent's arm.

Then the gunman's body was suddenly quite still.

CHAPTER 18
HOW THE GUNMAN DIED

Garth sat on a wooden bench in a cell at Cannon Row: the police station adjoining Scotland Yard.

An hour had passed since he had left Jermyn Street. Miller, strangely pale, had told him that he would be taken to a cell to ensure that none could say he had received preferential treatment.

The attack on him, and the reason for it, loomed large in his mind, and it was no kind of solace to realise that his life had been saved at the expense of the policeman's.

He remembered with chilling clarity exactly how it had happened.

The shock of seeing Russi had made him miss a step—and so that first bullet had struck the constable as he moved to steady him. His lips twisted bitterly at that thought: Russi had been at hand to see him killed—and had been responsible for saving him from the first bullet. Miller had saved him from the second.

Russi, clearly, had learnt that the police were on the way to detain him. The reason for the attempt at murdering him was to prevent him from making a statement to the police....

Along the passage from his cell, a man was plaintively protesting his innocence of the begging charge on which he was being held. A policeman was arguing with him good-humouredly.

Then a sergeant arrived, unlocked Garth's door, and said: 'Come with me, please.'

He was led out of Cannon Row towards Scotland Yard. Dazedly, Garth followed the sergeant up the long flight of steps to the reception hall, another uniformed man behind him. There followed a long walk through high-ceilinged corridors, their footsteps echoing on the stone floor. Men bustled in and out of doorways as they passed, but Garth hardly noticed them. Then finally:

'Here we are!' said the sergeant, and opened a door.

The familiar, brown-clad figure of Bruce Hammond stood there. He nodded brief thanks to the sergeant; then as the door closed behind Garth, came forward with hand outstretched.

'All right?' he asked, with a dry smile.

'I will be, in a minute,' Garth said, wryly. 'Have you a cigarette? I've run out.'

Hammond proffered his gold case, then turned to press a bell-push. Their cigarettes were barely alight before the door opened and a uniformed policeman put his head round it.

'Did you ring, sir?'

'Send out for a box of Sobrani Virginian, will you?' Hammond handed him a ten shilling note, and the man nodded and went out.

That little incident did Garth more good than anything else could have done, just then. His lips curved.

'How did you know that I smoke Sobrani?'

'Haven't I smoked with you?' countered Hammond, with his slow smile. 'Sit down, old son. I suppose you've guessed what's happened?'

Garth nodded.

'They meant to kill me in case I talked.' It was surprisingly easy to sound calm.

'Good man!' Hammond drew on his cigarette, then went on: 'Yes … That's it.' His eyes narrowed. 'And they weren't exactly slow off the mark, were they?'

Garth nodded again, frowning.

'It's beyond me how they *could* have known so fast!'

'Is it?' Hammond asked drily. And when Garth looked blank, he went on: 'There are two possible explanations, Garth. One, that they foresaw the possibility that you would be visited by the police after getting the papers, and meant to take no chances. The other,' he said, quietly, 'is that they were advised that the police had been informed.'

Garth stared at him, waiting for him to spell that one out. Then realised that Hammond was tacitly inviting him to do so. Hesitantly, almost incredulous, he protested:

'You seriously think that … that someone at Queen's Gate might have told Russi?'

'I certainly think it's possible,' agreed Hammond.

'Whom … whom do you suspect?' Garth made himself ask.

'Livesey … his daughter … Catesby. Although he is almost ruled out. Conceivably, George Kent … who was there when Catesby made his statement and called the police. But of course, there are several others on the premises. Benjamin Roosevelt Washington,' Hammond grinned drily at the name, 'for one. He obviously knows everything that goes on there. You didn't meet him, I suppose?'

Garth shook his head.

'Pity. I don't know what to make of that one at all. Can't even make out what his job is. He seems to be something between a glorified valet and a personal assistant on a high level… calls Livesey Arnold, and whatnot. American Indian, at a guess.…'

If Garth had known Hammond as Craigie and Loftus knew him, he would have recognised the signs: Hammond was gnawing at one of his 'bones'.

'Wish I knew the background, there,' he went on. 'Of course, we'll be getting some of it.…' He shrugged, wryly. 'Don't know why he made such an impression … although there's a point: he is impressive.' He was obviously thinking aloud, now: 'It's pretty rare … a small man, with so much "presence".'

'By Jove, Hammond!' Garth interrupted, and Hammond's eyes glittered.

'Got something?'

'Could well have!' Garth told him, and plunged into an account of what had transpired at The Elms.

He presented the facts calmly and with vivid clarity. Hammond, although he had listened to such an account from Garth before, was as amazed at the orderliness and detail of his statement as at the way he could conjure up a scene, by word alone, so vividly that his listeners seemed to re-live it with him.

Hammond saw in his mind's eye Ryall's gratified reaction to the successful theft … Could almost feel the electrifying change of mood and atmosphere when the little man in black had come in … Was struck, with Garth, by the contrast between the maid's strange, silent stare and her model-servant behaviour.…

'There isn't much else,' Garth finished. 'Washington sounds about the same size as the man in black. The mask covered the face and obviously it could have hidden his beak of a nose. The only real difference seems to be in the voice … and God knows that's the easiest thing to fake.'

Hammond nodded slowly.

'So now we can bring Washington higher up the list of suspects....'

'It would certainly seem so,' Garth agreed. Then frowned, remembering: 'Why did you say Catesby was almost ruled out?'

'Because of the way the gunman died. Cyanic acid ... prussic acid. He popped a cyanic acid crystal in his mouth. The saliva moistens it enough to create the gas to kill a person,' Hammond explained, flatly. 'He didn't mean to be caught alive.'

Garth stuck to the point.

'How does that affect Catesby?'

'Well, as the fellow died and the acid took more and more effect, he'd breathe out the gas. Mark had a whiff of it but he's all right, now ... he realised what it was, in time. Mike was quicker off the mark ... saw what was up, and stayed clear....'

Garth nodded.

'And pulled Catesby away ... I saw him.'

'Yes. And if Catesby were in it, you'd think he would know what was likely to happen to the lesser fry. By his deeds shall ye condemn him!' grinned Hammond. 'You don't like Catesby, do you?' he added, shrewdly.

'He hasn't done much to encourage me to like him.'

'No ...' Hammond shrugged. 'Well, you've made a damned good report, old son ... it's a real help. Now, I think the best thing is for you to stay here a couple of days ... they'll make it comfortable for you! ... and then be released for lack of evidence. After that ...' His expression was suddenly sombre: 'You can please yourself what you do.'

'Exactly what does that mean?' Garth asked him, and he shrugged again, grimacing.

'Well, we can't reasonably expect you to go on, can we? It hasn't worked out as we wanted it to ... but these affairs rarely do. You might get away with it again, of course, but the probability is that you'll be a marked man. I can't imagine Ryall using you again. He'll be suspicious because you've been released and ...'

He stopped abruptly.

A gleam entered his eyes. He looked at Garth, seemed about to go on, then shook his head.

'No ... we've put you through enough! We'll get you away to the country somewhere; you can do with a rest, I'm sure. You're not likely to be a great deal of use to us, anyway, and I don't see the point of letting you stick your head out just for the sake of getting it knocked off.'

There was a tap at the door, and the policeman came in with Garth's cigarettes. He opened the box and offered it, when the man had gone. Hammond shook his head, and Garth himself lit up, before saying:

'You just thought of a way that I *could* help, didn't you?'

Hammond smiled wryly. 'A possible way, but ...'

'What is it?'

'You mean you'd be prepared to go on? Knowing the odds?'

Garth said quietly: 'I mean to go on.'

Hammond regarded him appraisingly for several seconds; then suddenly grinned, the gleam back in his eyes.

'Good man! Well, now. The thing is: if you're released for lack of evidence, Ryall will think there's at least a chance you've talked and that we've released you to act as a spy. That wouldn't do. But if you escape ...' He broke off, and his lift of the shoulders said everything.

Garth asked, thoughtfully:

'Will it look plausible enough, do you think?'

'I don't see why not. We can stage it pretty well … and make sure Ryall gets the full story. In fact …' The smile faded again: 'Garth, there's a chance that by releasing you … or letting you escape … you can help us to find out whether there *is* a leakage of information from Livesey's headquarters.'

'I don't see how?'

'Well, we can tell Livesey—and the others: they're often in conference and I can go to see them—exactly how you escaped. Then you'll get to Ryall. And if Ryall knows just how …'

Garth's own eyes lit up.

'My God, yes! If only that particular group are told, and Ryall gets to know …'

'We shall know where his information came from,' nodded Hammond. He pondered for a moment. 'There's one thing you may not have realised, mind you.…'

'What's that?'

'If we do it that way, we can't allow a story to go out through the Press. In other words, Ryall won't know that you escaped … since he certainly won't take a chance on your word … unless there *is* a leakage at Queen's Gate. You'll be banking on that. And if there isn't one …'

Garth spoke slowly into the pregnant pause.

'There won't be much chance for me … Yes, I see that. On the other hand, you'll then know that you needn't waste time concentrating on the Liveseys and their friends.'

'Precisely,' Hammond raised an eyebrow. 'Are you still game?'

'Yes,' said Garth, briefly.

'Good man!' Hammond rose. 'Do you think you can stand a night and day here before you get away? I mean will anything be bothering you?'

'Not enough to matter,' said Garth, drily, and Hammond nodded his thanks.

They talked for a few moments, Garth learning what progress had been made in other directions. Hammond said nothing of the suspicion that British as well as American representatives might be on the spot. But he did give a general outline of the situation and a summary of the reactions in America.

America, he told Garth, was apparently pretty well divided. One section was clamouring for the return of the missions, declaring it scandalous that American citizens should be exposed to such danger, and claiming that the discussions could just as easily … and indeed more conveniently … take place in America. The other, more realistic, section were convinced there was an attempt to sabotage the agreements by delaying them, and held that no American worthy of the name would let personal danger stop him from carrying on in the quickest possible way.

Thus, controversy was sweeping the United States. And the German and Italian radio was capitalising on it in foreign broadcasts, seizing what seemed an excellent opportunity for sowing discord between the Allied nations.

'And that's about all,' Hammond wound up, at last.

'You're assuming that the interest directing these attacks is financial … commercial?'

'That possibility is high on our list … nothing more. Why?'

Garth hesitated, then said: 'It's just … well, it struck me that it might be a Nazi effort to start discord.' He grinned, suddenly. 'But that's probably on the list as well?'

'Yes, it is,' Hammond nodded. 'But it's a good point, old chap.' He smiled: 'All that M.O.P. training, I expect! Well,

I'll get away. Ask for anything you want—and if anything strikes you that we haven't talked about, ask Miller to call me. If I don't come myself, one of the others will. Miller will vouch for their *bona fides.*'

Hammond went, and alone again, Garth tried to analyse what it was that had prompted his determination to go on with this dangerous work. He could find no real reason—certainly he could see all the risks: Hammond had not tried to minimise them. All he could think of—or really care about—was that it was a job that had to be done.

And everything, apparently, depended on whether or not there was a traitor at 27, Queen's Gate.

Hammond went straight from the Yard to Craigie's office. Both Craigie and Loftus were at the desk, but the telephones were silent.

'The more I see of Garth, the more I like him,' Hammond remarked, as they looked up. 'And he's no fool. He realised what had been done—and the consequences of it.'

'And then what?' asked Loftus, drily.

Hammond reported what he had arranged and although the big man smiled a little and Craigie nodded from time to time, neither man interrupted. When he had finished, Loftus pursed his lips in a soundless whistle.

'Very nice, Bruce!'

Hammond, who was looking at Craigie, emphasised:

'It should tell us once and for all whether we're right in suspecting the Livesey household.'

'We?' Loftus murmured. 'I thought that was your preserve.'

'If you haven't started suspecting 'em yet, you should have done,' Hammond told him equably. 'Is it all right, Gordon?'

'Of course,' said Craigie. 'Garth wasn't questioned, then, about his visit to Mrs. Parmitter....'

Neither of the others was surprised at this seeming irrelevancy: Craigie was probably looking much further ahead than either of them. They waited expectantly, and he went on:

'Ryall will go more deeply into Garth's background, if he continues to use him. Mrs. Parmitter's connection with us won't cause any trouble, because she knows everyone. But Aunt Mabel ...' He smiled, drily: 'She could do with some additional background.'

'Aunt Mabel', they knew, was the widow of Sir Herbert Grey, who had died in an air crash in America.

'I wanted her on this job,' Craigie explained, 'because she has a good many American acquaintances If her husband were alive, he'd be in the thick of all this, of course.'

Loftus nodded: 'Yes ... anyway, we'll leave that to you. The thing is, you want to use her again?'

'We might find it a help. I don't know, yet, We'll bolster up that part of Garth's past, anyhow! And we've good reason now for getting a thorough check on little Mr. Washington. We've a message due from New York in an hour, by the way, Bruce. If there isn't a full dossier, we'll phone Dickson.'

'Also about Catesby?'

Craigie nodded.

'We know Catesby pretty well, but we'll certainly check up. You left Garth quite cheerful?'

'Well ... quite determined!' smiled Hammond.

'That's probably better,' said Craigie, slowly. 'What are you going to do now?'

'See Mike and Mark. The gunman may have given something away while they were having their set-to. It isn't likely, but we'd better cover the possibility. Unless you've anything else in mind?'

Craigie shook his head.

'Have you heard anything from Number 10?' Hammond asked, as he rose to leave.

'Nothing new,' Craigie smiled briefly: 'There'll be trouble unless we do get results quickly.'

As he left the office, Hammond was thinking that there was one thing they had not tried to discuss too thoroughly, because they disliked running before they could walk. Yet it mattered a great deal: if they knew the exact motive behind it all, it could well help them find out who was the guiding intelligence.

His thoughts turned to the little man in black. If indeed this should be Benjamin Roosevelt Washington, confidential P.A. to Livesey, it would solve many problems. He thought of that smooth, controlled voice, those piercing eyes, that strangely compelling presence.

Washington was very friendly with Livesey and their association was of many years' standing. It would be a clever move if he were sidetracking the Department: forcing attention first on Livesey himself and then on Catesby, deliberately making them look like obvious suspects....

Hammond was walking along Whitehall when he saw a plainclothes sergeant he knew as one of Miller's chief *aides*. He smiled, greeting him:

'Hallo, Drew! Where are you off to?'

'Mr. Miller said I might find you, sir. He thought you ought to know that Mr. Washington has called at the Yard to enquire about David Garth.' As Hammond stared at him, Drew added: 'He phoned the office and they said you'd just left. Will you want a word with Washington, sir?'

Hammond frowned thoughtfully.

'No ... No, I don't think so. I'll wait for him and see where he goes. Exactly what did he want?'

'He said he had heard of Mr. Garth's arrest and came to enquire whether he could be of any assistance.' Drew smiled drily. 'Not very convincing, sir, is it?'

'No, it's pretty weak. Just a little too weak, I think. Thanks, Drew. Oh … have you seen Mr. Davidson?'

'He's just along by the gates,' said the sergeant.

'Good. I'll come with you.'

Outside the gates of Scotland Yard lounged a tall man who would have been good-looking but for a long, thin nose which veered first to the right and then to the left. He was immaculately dressed and there was about him an air of affluent indolence. Large grey eyes watched lazily as Hammond approached and Drew went in through the gates.

Wally Davidson had been detailed to watch Washington that morning. With any luck, Hammond thought, he might have much of interest to report.

CHAPTER 19

BENJAMIN ROOSEVELT WASHINGTON AND AUNT MABEL

Davidson's report was negative and Hammond looked disappointed.

Washington had left the Queen's Gate house not long after Livesey and his daughter had returned and almost immediately after young Catesby had arrived by taxi, looking washed-out but excited. Apparently oblivious of the fact that he was being followed Washington had left without haste and gone straight to Scotland Yard.

'And that's my story,' said Davidson. 'Anything your end, Bruce?'

Hammond nodded.

'Plenty, one way and the other. Afraid you'll have to wait for it though.'

'I am patience personified,' Davidson grinned lazily. 'What happened to the Errols? They left the house after the Liveseys—Mike after Olivia and Mark after her old man. They didn't come back.'

'They were held up,' Hammond told him, briefly. 'Will you go round the back, Wally? I'll keep an eye open this side. I don't want Washington to get out without being followed.'

Davidson gave a resigned shrug.

'Confound you!' he said, mildly. 'You want to make sure you get the cake. One day, my son, your conscience will smite you hard.'

Hammond grinned at his departing back as he ambled off across the courtyard to the Embankment entrance. Then he himself went up the small turning which led to Parliament Street and watched the main gates closely.

He did not see Washington for some time. But he did see a large, mannish-looking woman in tweeds striding along from Parliament Square, her good-natured face set hard. There was a distinctly purposeful air about her, as if she was prepared to make an issue of anything with any man. Hammond was at first surprised; but when Garth's 'Aunt Mabel' turned into Cannon Row instead of the Yard he thought he understood.

Probably Craigie had telephoned Mrs. Parmitter, suggesting that Aunt Mabel took an interest in her nephew's incarceration. Aunt Mabel was probably going to raise hell's delight with the police for being so woolly-headed as to arrest her beloved David.

After she had disappeared into the police-station, he lit a cigarette and smoked it. Then another. He was beginning to feel hungry. Big Ben chimed one o'clock as he glanced at his watch. No wonder!

He strolled across the entrance to the side-street—and his interest quickened. Washington was coming sedately down the steps of the Yard. He was so intent on the man that he did not at first see Aunt Mabel, who had emerged from Cannon Row at the same time. But he could not avoid seeing her as she and the little American drew nearer each other.

Hammond watched with sudden amusement. She and Washington indeed, were on a collision course. Then, just when they would have knocked into each other, Aunt Mabel raised indignant eyes from the ground and stepped aside.

Hammond drew a sharp breath.

As Washington drew back, Aunt Mabel looked at him— no longer in annoyance, *but in recognition!* Obviously, she was astonished to see him there. And as obviously, the recognition was mutual.

Washington recovered first. Raising his neat black Homburg, he inclined his head politely and waited for her to proceed. She looked away quickly and flushing, marched towards the gates and turned in the direction of Parliament Square. Washington appeared to take no further interest in her, but Aunt Mabel stopped not far from Hammond and looked round.

The American was heading towards Trafalgar Square and from the woman's expression, Hammond judged that she was tempted to follow Washington. If so, she conquered the temptation and went on, striding purposefully along as before, apparently ready to do battle.

Hammond turned in Washington's wake.

In his eagerness to see what transpired between the two he had lagged too far behind. The American's short figure was already lost among the people crowding the pavement. He quickened his pace and caught a glimpse of the black Homburg; Washington was walking fairly rapidly.

Then two women, with three children in tow, got in Hammond's way. He moved to one side as the women tugged the children in the same direction. Swallowing his annoyance, he apologised briefly, broke through the cordon and hurried on.

He was just in time to see Washington step into a taxi.

There was another coming behind and Hammond hailed it, but the driver shook his head: the flag was down. And Washington's cab was already moving by then.

Hammond swore roundly—then was suddenly cut short in mid-breath, as he saw Wally Davidson's lugubrious face at the window of the second cab. Wally raised a languidly disdainful hand to indicate that he, at least, had the little man in his sights, then permitted himself a deliberate wink. Hammond chuckled aloud.

Not bad at all! he thought. Obviously, Wally had seen Washington reach the gates near Parliament Street and had grabbed a passing cab to come and check that Hammond was on his trail, before reporting to Craigie. He chuckled again: *The beggar won't let me forget this in a hurry!*

Another cab came along, this time an empty one. Hammond decided against going to see the Errols at this moment. He told the man to drive to Greek Square, then sat back to smoke another cigarette and conclude that Wally's move had been singularly fortuitous. He was very anxious indeed to learn why Aunt Mabel had been so affected by the chance encounter with the little American....

He passed her on the way to Greek Square.

He preferred it that way. He would reach Number 11 first and she would not suspect that her encounter with Washington had been observed. He had no doubt of his welcome at Mrs. Parmitter's even though it would be in the middle of lunch: meals were always punctual at Number 11. The white-haired servant admitted him and he was shown straight into the dining room.

Mrs. Parmitter sat at the head of the gleaming refectory table Fay Oundle was on her left, and there were two other places laid.

'Good afternoon, Bruce!' Mrs. Parmitter smiled up at him: he was an old favourite of hers. I'm so glad you're in time for lunch. Marshall, tell cook Mr. Hammond has arrived, will you?'

'Sure I'm not making a nuisance of myself?' Hammond demurred, as Fay patted a chair next to her.

'Don't be foolish,' said the old lady. 'Whatever else is rationed, we refuse to deny ourselves the pleasure of good company. Mabel is late,' she added to Fay. 'She did say she would be in to lunch, did she not?'

'She did,' Fay agreed, smiling. 'But have you ever known her punctual?'

'I'm afraid dear Mabel hasn't a tidy mind,' admitted Mrs. Parmitter.

'I passed her striding along the street,' Hammond told them. And lied unashamedly: 'I didn't realise who it was until I was too far away to offer a lift. She looked, by the way, as if she were at loggerheads with the world.'

Mrs. Parmitter smiled.

'Doesn't she always? You know, Bruce, she is absolutely *delighted* at being able to help you, even in so small a way. It has irked her for a long time that she could do nothing—or next to nothing. She is one of the *really* live wires in the W.V.S., you know. To look at her you wouldn't think that a year ago she was given up as an incurable case, would you?'

'Incurable?' Hammond looked his surprise.

'Consumption,' murmured Mrs. Parmitter. 'And now she is back in England and as fit as you or I. Thank you, Marshall,' she added, as the butler came in with a generous helping of game pie and piping-hot vegetables.

'Where was she, at the time?' asked Hammond, as the man retired.

'In America. She was having treatment in that wonder-ful valley of the sun, where all the sanatoria are. I can never remember what state.

'Arizona,' supplied Fay.

'Oh, yes. She was absolutely *furious* that she couldn't get back to England during the worst of the blitz. And then when she finally did manage to get back, the ship she was on was torpedoed. She spent three days in an open boat.' Mrs. Parmitter's eyes danced : 'And instead of having a relapse, she positively thrived on it!'

They dropped the subject at that point as they heard her let herself in, stride past the door, and stamp up the stairs. When she reached the landing, she appeared to realise that she was late and called down to say she would not be long.

Mrs. Parmitter turned the talk to her surprise at hear-ing that the charming Mr. Garth had been arrested, and Hammond dissembled skilfully.

The household was a convenient rendezvous but none of its members knew much of what went on or in what they were helping, although Craigie, he knew, had made it clear from the start that there was a measure of danger in what they were doing. The fact had been accepted placidly by Mrs. Parmitter and with actual eagerness by Ned Oundle's dark-haired wife.

As he ate, Hammond pondered on the fact that Aunt Mabel had spent so much of the war—and so recently—in America. Craigie had not mentioned that, but doubtless he knew it. Which meant that he had kept the fact to himself for some good reason. Possibly because he wished his agents to consider her without any kind of bias.

Craigie himself had 'discovered' her, and had called upon her to pose as Garth's aunt.

Hammond felt a vague disquiet, which did not fade when Aunt Mabel came in, glowered about her, then stared at him with obvious anger.

Her forehead, he noted, was damp with perspiration.

'Did you see him, my dear?' asked Mrs. Parmitter.

'Yes!' Aunt Mabel glowered at Hammond. 'What fool trick are you up to, *now?* First you want me to help Garth, then you turn round and arrest him—it's absurd! The poor boy doesn't know what he *is*doing. He says he thought you were his friend. A fine friend, I must say!'

Hammond smiled at her soothingly: Garth had clearly done well.

'Not I, Aunt Mabel! The police did the arresting.'

'Haven't *you* any influence?' she demanded, hotly. 'What are you *doing* about it—that's what I'd like to know? I always thought you had some kind of standing at Scotland Yard....'

'Mabel, dear ...' began Mrs. Parmitter.

'I won't be shushed!' snapped the big woman. 'It's intolerable! I know I promised to do what I was asked and raise no questions—there *are* limits. I just can't understand it!' She glared at him. 'A charming young man like Garth, kept in a miserable cell—and a positive *scoundrel* walking away from Scotland Yard as if he *owned* the place!'

Hammond, adjusting his mind to the apparent fact that Aunt Mabel had not been sent to the Yard by Craigie but had learned of Garth's arrest and gone of her own free will—and, what was more, succeeded in interviewing him—contemplated her without any great show of interest. But the emphasis on that *'scoundrel'* showed, he thought, the real reason for her bad temper: she was coming to the subject of Washington. And what she knew of the American clearly did not please her.

'Mabel, my dear....' Mrs. Parmitter tried again.

'I said scoundrel and I mean it!' snapped Aunt Mabel.

'Who is this dreadful fellow?'

'It isn't funny!' she snorted. 'I came out of the police station—and there was this awful little man, coming from Scotland Yard! I met him in America—three years ago. And Herbert said he was the trickiest customer *in* America. Why, Herbert was sure he was deliberately trying to stop deliveries on lease-lend!'

So Sir Herbert Grey had thought that, had he, mused Hammond.

'Perhaps he took too much for granted,' suggested Mrs. Parmitter, placidly. 'I liked Herbert very much indeed—but he did rather jump to conclusions at times, my dear, you must admit! *Do* get on with your lunch, Mabel: it's quite cold and spoiled.'

'Herbert was a fine judge of a man,' declared Aunt Mabel, defensively. 'This little ... *tick!* ... visited him a number of times. Raising all manner of difficulties.' She swung round, her earlier abuse apparently forgotten: 'Before he died, Mr. Hammond, my husband was in America, making arrangements for lease-lend materials. Mostly food. And ... I *never* believed that he died by accident! It was all so wicked. Nine of them ...' She grew a little incoherent and there were suddenly tears in her eyes. Sniffing them back, she dug savagely at her food, already trying to regain her composure.

There was an uncomfortable silence; then she went on, quietly and stubbornly:

'I always did say it and I always shall. That plane was *sabotaged!* And the fire ...'

She dropped her knife and fork and pushed back her chair, no longer able to control her sobs. Fay Oundle sent a strained, commiserating glance at Hammond, and

Mrs. Parmitter touched her lips with a table-napkin as Aunt Mabel stumbled through the door on her way upstairs.

'I know you'll forgive me,' said Mrs. Parmitter, and Hammond half-rose as she followed Aunt Mabel out.

He sat down again, his mind automatically supplying the relevant data. Sir Herbert Grey, an important member of the British Lease-Lend commission, had been killed, along with seven or eight fellow-members of the commission and the crew, when their aircraft had crashed near Colorado Springs after a long conference with farmers of the Middle West.

Fay Oundle was plainly embarrassed, and to break the tension he asked:

'Does she often break down like this?'

'I've never known it happen before,' said Fay. 'Of course, she hasn't been here long, you know. Only about four months.'

'And how long has her husband been dead?' he enquired, solicitously.

He knew quite well: the crash had been in May, 1941. And he had tremendous difficulty in disguising his excitement as a mental file snapped open and he was seeing again one of the mass of reports he had studied away back when the Department had first interested itself in this business.

Only one member of the crew had escaped alive—and he had died before the Court of Inquiry was held. But two people had just missed the plane—owed their lives to their too-late arrival. And now, he was seeing again with vivid clarity the two names written on that report:

Arnold K. Livesey and Benjamin Roosevelt Washington!

'Getting on for three years, I think,' Fay was saying.

Hammond guessed how she must be feeling. She, too, had given an undertaking to ask no questions and make no attempt to discover what Craigie and his men were doing. But her curiosity then, must have been overwhelming.

With a quiet smile, he said;

'I can't tell you much, Fay. But you might be able to tell me something ... not now. After you've seen her again when she's more composed. If I ask questions, she'll probably either jump to the wrong conclusions or else refuse to answer me.' He grimaced drily: 'As a Roland for the Garth Oliver! Anyway ... will you remember all she says about the crash and what her husband thought of the little man? And tell me—word-for-word, if you can—what she says?'

Fay nodded quickly:

'Of course! Is it important?'

'It might be. Very.' Hammond pushed back his own chair. 'And now I must be off.'

'You haven't had your sweet,' she protested.

'Sorry! But I mustn't stop. This gives a new lead—and possibly extra urgency—to the job. Apologise to your mother for me, won't you?'

'Yes, of course.'

'And encourage Aunt Mabel to talk very freely,' he urged. 'Thanks, Fay!' He smiled briefly and went out. And a moment later all else was forgotten as his mind gnawed at that fascinating item from the crash report: the fortuitous tardiness of Arnold K. Livesey and Benjamin Roosevelt Washington.

It struck him suddenly that very possibly, this whole affair had started right then. And that Craigie, suspecting the truth, had for that reason decided to get in touch with the widowed Lady Grey.

CHAPTER 20
GARTH 'ESCAPES'

Hammond went first to see the Errols; only to learn that the dead gunman had said nothing which might give any clue to his associates. And, the cousins protested, *had* he said anything of value, they would certainly have reported it.

'Yes. Sorry!' Hammond smiled. 'I'm trying to do too many things at once, as usual.'

'As usual is right,' Mike dropped the mock-reproach and was unusually solicitous. 'You look as if you haven't slept for a week, old son. What's the matter?' he added, easily. 'Conscience troubling you?'

'No more than usual,' grinned Hammond.

But as he left the flat, he reflected grimly that he was losing his grip; if the Errols could see he was so tensed-up, it would be obvious to others, also. The affair was on his mind; much more than most of the Department's cases. The twin facts, that they still had no real idea of the men responsible for the campaign and could not be sure where the next blow would fall, worried him greatly.

Loftus and Craigie felt the same. Back at the office, he searched their faces: they, too, were showing signs of the strain. There had been too long a period without any definite step forward. The saving of so many of the American

V.I.P.s had been defensive: they were chafing to get on the offensive.

Loftus said casually:

'Back already, Bruce? Any luck?'

'One or two odd things,' Hammond dropped into an easy chair and leaned back. 'Nothing from the Errols, but ... what do you know about Aunt Mabel, Gordon?'

Craigie looked up from the desk.

'Why?'

'She's been to see Garth in prison. Most upset! Did you ring her?'

'I rang Mrs. Parmitter, I told her what had happened and asked her to let Aunt Mabel know. The indirect method,' Craigie gave his slow, dry smile. 'No mystery there, Bruce, although I'm surprised she went to see Garth off her own bat. Perhaps she's developed a fondness for him.'

Loftus said flatly: 'They've met only once.'

Craigie made no comment on that.

'Anything else?' he asked Hammond.

'Yes ...' Hammond considered for a moment, then plunged into his story. He described, with new insight, the expression on Aunt Mabel's face when she had seen Washington—and the way, later, she had broken down as she talked of her husband. Her conviction that Washington was a rogue impressed him even more in retrospect.

When he had finished, Loftus said slowly:

'We knew all about her American contacts, of course....'

And Hammond looked from one to the other, baffled at choosing such a woman to be openly linked with Garth.

Craigie rose absently from the desk, wandered across to the old winged armchair, and sat down again.

'Lady Grey,' he told them, answering their unspoken query, 'is a close friend of Mrs. Parmitter's—and therefore conveniently placed. And I liked her American connections: it was always possible that she would come across something which we couldn't know.' He smiled. 'Sorry, Bruce—I should have told you before. I've had her in mind for some time, but this was the first opportunity we've had of using her.'

'She knows nothing about what we're using her *for*, does she?' asked Hammond.

'We've told her nothing. Her only connection with the affair is through Mrs. Parmitter and Garth—as far as we know. Putting Aunt Mabel aside for the moment,' Craigie added: 'Garth is our major hope, for the time being.'

'Obviously,' murmured Loftus.

'Is it so obvious? Hammond objected. 'I don't know. If it comes off and Ryall takes him back he'll have a chance. But I wish we had another way of getting at it. Something's brewing—and a positive hell's broth, by the smell of it! But ...'

'Steady!' Loftus grinned, and Craigie's dry smile echoed the protest.

'We know it's bad, Bruce. But there it is: we've no indica-tion of what's coming. We've got the Americans covered—and their English counterparts. We've brought in some of the Special Branch to help us and we're all working at stretch. Ryall hasn't made many mistakes yet, but...'

'Gordon,' Hammond interrupted, quietly. 'I may be wrong, but if Garth doesn't succeed, then I think we should detain Ryall and Russi.'

'M'mm ... You're probably right. It won't stop it, though ... at best, it will postpone decisive action. Still, we'd gain time.... When is Garth going free?'

'I thought perhaps in the morning?'

'Good! And if we're wise, we'll all take it as easy as we can today and get a good night's rest. We'll get cracking

in every way we can, of course.' Craigie looked thoughtful: 'That report of the air crash findings won't tell us *why*
Livesey and Washington happened to miss the plane.'

'Newspaper files will help us there,' Hammond offered:
'I'll go over and see what the M.O.P. can dig out for us.
Which reminds me ... what's Kent doing?'

'Nothing. At least, he's not been back to the office since
the murder. He cracked badly then, of course, but he seems
to be on the mend.'

'Was it just the shock?' asked Hammond.

'Who knows?' Craigie shrugged. 'He's being watched.
Don't worry about him.'

Hammond went out, knowing that Craigie's last words
had been in the nature of an assurance that none of the
obvious things were being neglected. He hardly needed telling that, but knew he must have created the impression that
he did. He knew that no one even remotely connected with
the affair would be unwatched—and that some, like the
Liveseys and their close associates, would be under strictest
surveillance.

Russi and Ryall, too. But Russi in particular was a slip-
pery customer who had twice evaded his followers—once,
on the occasion of the shooting at Garth.

Everything reverted to Garth.

Too much, indeed, thought Hammond, depended on
David Garth and on the mood Ryall would be in when he
learned of Garth's escape. Or rather—if he learned of it.

Russi returned to Wimbledon by a circuitous route,
confident that he had not been followed. In fact, one of
Craigie's men was on hand to observe his return, but Russi's
self-assurance was not affected by the sight of a man on the
roof of a nearby house, stolidly fitting new slates.

Ryall was in the study.

His bearded face was inscrutable as he looked up at Russi's entrance, and he did not speak. Russi, who had telephoned earlier with a report of what had happened, dropped into a chair and moodily fished a cigarette-case from his pocket.

After a long pause, Ryall said:

'*Another* failure, Russi?'

'It was luck—just a bad break!' snapped Russi. 'I've never known Paul miss.'

'He *did* miss.'

'Well, what about it? Why pick on me? *I* didn't do it!'

Ryall's voice was quiet but steely-hard:

'Garth is in the hands of the police. He has been there for two or three hours. He is being questioned. He is a frightened man—and the only question is whether his fear of committing an act of treachery is greater than his fear of being suspected of the Duval woman's murder. And if Garth talks of us …'

'He won't talk!' Russi protested sharply. But his voice lacked conviction. 'He's too yellow to talk!'

'I see,' said Ryall, with heavy sarcasm. 'You have such remarkable foresight, of course, my friend. You can tell what will happen with a man as highly-strung as Garth. *I* have not such remarkable powers!'

'He won't talk!' Russi insisted.

'If it were only the police, I might agree with you. But Brown was quite sure last night that Department Z is engaged. Department Z agents do not stop where the police do. They have means of persuasion which could easily break Garth down. Had you thought of that?'

Russi stared, his babyish face suddenly pink, and damp with perspiration.

'Then, then what the hell are we staying here for?' he demanded, his voice rising querulously.

'We are moving very soon,' said Ryall. 'And not to Kingston—it is too close. I have spent the whole morning making the arrangements. Brown is determined that we should make our final effort quickly—he simply cannot listen to reason!' he added, in a snarl of resentment.

Russi licked his lips.

'When do we start?'

'We have started. The letters have gone out already.' Ryall took a small sheet of headed notepaper from his desk and handed it over. Russi glanced quickly through the brief typewritten message: an instruction—unaddressed—to go to The Beacon, Staines, in two days' time, at five p.m.

The letter appeared to be signed by the Foreign Secretary and was marked: *'Highly Confidential'.*

Russi looked up, sceptical: 'Will they buy it?'

'I have little doubt of it. And they *must,* Russi. If they don't ...' Ryall paused, his eyes shadowed. 'But we will not consider failure a possibility. *I* have done my part. The rest is up to you.'

Russi lit a cigarette, studiously casual.

'I can fix it, don't you fret. But I don't like it! If just one of them talks ...'

Ryall cut him short.

'They have instructions in that letter *to* say nothing to anyone. And the signature will satisfy all of them.'

'I hope you're right.' Russi grimaced. 'Anyway, if they get there, I'll sure as hell see that none of them gets away!' He glanced uneasily at his watch. 'How long before we go?'

'Half-an-hour,' Ryall eyed him sardonically. 'I thought you were so confident Garth wouldn't talk?'

'I don't like this talk about Department Z!' Russi snapped. 'Where are we going?'

'Where else but Chertsey. So convenient for Staines! We shall be on hand for the great events and have no difficulty in getting away afterwards,' he smiled. But there was no humour in his expression or in his voice....

Two hours later, in a small house near the river at Chertsey, Ryall, Russi, the maid and the 'taxi' driver were gathered in a small room. The maid and the driver went out when Russi complained that he was hungry and a snack meal was soon forthcoming. They spent the afternoon and early evening in their respective rooms.

There were no alarms during the night.

They did not go to The Beacon: a large house, not far away. Nor did they know that two soldiers and a pretty girl, who paddled downriver in a canoe towards evening, were actually in Craigie's employ. But there was tension at the riverside house; in Ryall's room the light was on into the small hours.

Russi was up early and restless, wandered along the tow-path to fill in the half-an-hour before breakfast. Ryall did not come down to join him for the meal. He was growing increasingly edgy when, at a few minutes after ten, the telephone rang. There were two extensions, but the main instrument was in Ryall's room.

Russi lifted the receiver of the hall extension to hear Ryall say sharply: 'Who is that?'

'Don't worry,' came the soft voice of 'Mr. Brown'. 'It is no one you would not wish to hear from. My friend, I have news of importance for you.'

'What is it?' asked Ryall, and Russi's hand tightened on the receiver.

'Very cheering news, I think you will find,' 'Brown' expanded. 'I have had word—reliable word—that your friend who was so awkwardly situated last night and yester-day morning, has excelled himself. He did not like the place where he was staying and so he—left.'

'You mean ... he *escaped?*' Ryall sounded incredulous.

'From the web of circumstances which surrounded him, yes,' said 'Brown' softly. 'A most fortuitous happening, as I know you will agree. True, he may find it difficult to remain free from certain ... attention. But at the moment, there is no danger at all that he can harm your ... project. Are you satisfied?'

'If you're sure ...' Ryall began, doubtfully.

'I am quite sure!' 'Brown's' voice grew sharper. 'I have satisfied myself completely, as to the manner of his leave-taking. It is not my habit to be vague about such things! Moreover, my friend, he was in no way careless, while he was away from you. He disclosed nothing which might cause concern. A most worthy young man!'

'What ... what do you think we should do with him?'

'Use him,' said 'Brown', promptly. 'Use him to the best advantage. I think he might be most helpful, skilfully han-dled. I don't know, but I imagine that he will be at Brookside, by now. You might care to investigate.'

Then Brown rang off.

Russi banged down his receiver and raced up the stairs. His eyes shining, he burst into Ryall's room. Ryall looked up from his chair by the telephone and smiled: there was deep satisfaction in the expression.

'So you heard that, Russi?'

'I sure as hell did! We're out of that jam!'

'We may not be, if Garth is found at Wimbledon,' Ryall warned him. 'You had better go and fetch him, Russi—or send someone for him. We do not want him recaptured. I wonder,' he added gently, 'how he contrived to get away?'

'Why should we worry?' demanded Russi.

David Garth stood on the porch of The Elms, his finger on the bell-push; but not expecting an answer. No one had answered his knocking and ringing for the last five minutes and he felt sure Ryall and Russi had left the house. A feeling of helplessness surged over him, followed quickly by a mounting tension.

Hammond's voice seemed to echo in his ears.

'A lot depends on this, Garth. Perhaps more than you realise. Remember—they can't know that you've escaped unless they get it from Queen's Gate.' Then had added, easily: 'Would you be happier if you had a gun?'

'No. No!' Garth had repeated, emphatically. 'It's all or nothing. I won't stand a chance if it comes to a shooting-match—I hardly know how to use the things.'

He wondered, now, if he had been right. A gun might well have given him confidence. But good God, a gun, *here*....!

It was a little after eleven o'clock. The perfect Indian summer had continued: the sun was already warm and there was not a cloud in the sky. A little traffic hummed on the road by the common; a few strollers passed the gates, invisible through the mass of shrubbery and trees.

Then someone turned into the drive.

Garth heard him and spun round. It was a cyclist; a short, thickset man who needed a shave. He did not appear to notice Garth until he drew up at the porch. Garth stood quite still.

He would not have been surprised had the man attacked him then. He was expecting an attack. He could not believe that Ryall—even if he had learned the story of his faked escape—would believe it safe to get in touch with him. And if he did not, he would certainly believe him safer dead.

Then the newcomer looked up at him and spoke.

Chapter 21
New Mission

'You Garth?' he demanded, harshly.

Garth spoke calmly with an effort:

'I am, yes.'

'O.K.,' said the cyclist. 'You been followed?'

'I... I've noticed no one.'

'I'll look around,' muttered the other, laconically. 'Here's a key. You're to go to the first room on the right of the right-hand passage upstairs. Got that?'

'The first room on the right of the right-hand passage,' repeated Garth, mechanically. His forehead was beaded with sweat. He still could not be sure what they intended.

'There's a make-up case and some clothes in the wardrobe,' the cyclist told him. 'Use 'em.'

That was all. But it brought first a flood of relief to Garth and then, as he let himself in and climbed the stairs, a realisation of just what it meant. Ryall knew of his escape: here was the proof of treachery at Queen's Gate!

It was what Hammond had hoped to know; but he, Garth, had not. He hated the thought that someone close to Olivia Livesey—perhaps someone for whom she deeply cared—was implicated in an affair which could only end in ignominy and death. During the past few hours, Olivia had been more in his mind than Anne had ever been....

It was strange to be alone in the silent house, to open the wardrobe, search it for suitable clothes, and the make-up case. He was a fugitive ... he had to keep reminding himself of that: so much depended on his ability to act convincingly. As a fugitive, he had to change his clothes and disguise his appearance as much as possible.

He was an utter amateur in such matters and he surveyed an array of chalks and greasepaints helplessly. Then picking up a stick of black, he stared at himself in the mirror, and put the crayon against his skin, just beneath the eyes.

'You have admirable common sense, Garth, haven't you?'

The words came without warning and he swung round, dropping the crayon—as he stared into the eyes of the little man in black.

'C ... common sense?' he stammered.

'Black beneath the eyes is one of the first things,' said 'Brown'. 'But I am surprised that Ryall allowed one so inexpert to attempt this alone. I fear that our friend is getting a little nervous.' He was only a couple of yards away, now. 'Sit down,' he invited. And as Garth obeyed, he came forward and picked up the crayon.

'Don't try to look in the mirror,' he advised, and began to use the crayon deftly. His fingers—the gloves were of black satin Garth noted—were gentle and dexterous. Garth breathed heavily.

Slowly, as Garth recovered from his first shock, he realised that this was almost certainly the man for whom Hammond and the others were taking such big chances. He had twice the man's strength; it would be easy to overpower him.

'Brown' said nothing, until he had finished. Then he stood back and surveyed his work. It was uncanny. Nothing of the man was visible, save those strangely-piercing eyes: everything else was covered in black. Yet he *was* a creature of flesh and blood; and very vulnerable, in that moment.

Garth thought: *Not yet: it isn't time. Not yet!*

'You may look at yourself now,' 'Brown' told him, and he looked.

The mirror showed a face which was Garth's, yet did not seem to belong to him. It looked wider: the expression at his lips was one of petulance. His eyes looked narrow and there were dark shadows beneath them.

'It... it's incredible!' he muttered.

'It is perfectly simple,' said 'Brown'. 'It will deceive no one, Garth, who is well-acquainted with you. But it will deceive anyone who knows you only from a photograph. Have you seen this?' He drew something from a coat pocket: a cabinet-size photograph ... *of Garth.*

'Where ... where did you get it?' he faltered.

'From a very good friend.' 'Brown' laughed softly. 'It is one which the police took yesterday ... perhaps you did not know they had done so? It is now widely-circulated and I think every police-station in the south of England is in possession of one. But look at it and then into the mirror. Are you frightened that anyone will recognise you from it?'

Garth was amazed at the difference.

'You are satisfied?' murmured 'Brown'. 'I am so glad! Now I do not know exactly what Ryall has in mind for you to do. I think I have convinced him of your sincerity in wanting to help us ... and of course, of the manner of your escape from the police. That was very clever of you, Garth.'

'There was half a chance, and I took it.'

'They would not expect you to do so, of course! And you did not mention Ryall or Russi to them ... I have that on the very best authority. You are to be congratulated, my friend'

'How the devil do you know all this,' Garth demanded.

'Through a very good friend.' The little man in black laughed again: an eerie sound. 'You know, Garth, I have quite an affection for you. I like the way you behaved and the way you withstood what must have been a most unpleasant police interrogation. You are a man of parts—I should not like to think you were to hang.'

Garth stared at him, his hands clenched.

'Ryall's methods are sometimes clumsy but they are usually effective,' 'Brown' murmured, reflectively. 'I must admit he is a good worker—but there are times when I am concerned about him. Is he, do you think, entirely trustworthy?'

'I don't know what you mean,' Garth said stiffly.

'Let me explain a little more, my friend. Ryall and Russi work for me—and you will not be foolish enough to inquire who I am; that will never be known! But to proceed: I have at times wondered whether either ... or each ... of them feels that working for me is a little ... humiliating. They are clever men and they have interests of their own. I have to consider the possibility that they will use the assistance I am able to give them for their own ends. That would be most unpleasant, don't you think?'

'What ends are they?' demanded Garth, in a stronger voice.

'Come, come! You do not seriously expect me to answer that question. There may be some people who would not approve of what I'm doing ... but believe me, it is for the best. Very much for the best, Garth, both for this country and America! But let us consider the possibility that Ryall and Russi may be planning to ... er... doublecross me. You can understand my doubts, I think?'

'They're capable of anything!' Garth snapped, bitterly.

'Precisely,' nodded 'Brown'. 'They are capable of anything ... and naturally, I do not wish them to betray me. So I am charging you with a new mission, my friend. You may find an opportunity, in the next day or two, to learn whether they are planning disloyalty. If they are, Garth ... and you advise me, you will *greatly* benefit. I guarantee it!'

His eyes were not brown, as Hammond had told him Washington's were. And the nose seemed flat, beneath the mask. Obviously this could not be Washington. This man's eyes were grey ... almost colourless ... and strangely compelling. They robbed the words of their softness, making them sound harsh and ugly ... making Garth shiver ... as he went on:

'Of course, my friend, if *you* were to side with them, it would be most ... unfortunate ... I have them under constant observation, you see. At the first sign of treachery, I shall act. But ...' He shrugged lightly: 'You will be loyal, I know ... you have no love for either of them. The fools! Had I known they were going to try to kill you....!' He laughed softly. 'But there ... they do not realise your future value, do they?'

'I'm of no value to anyone,' Garth said bitterly. 'I'm wanted by the police ... hunted, helpless. What value can I be?'

'Come!' exclaimed 'Brown'. 'Why so dejected?'

'Russi... Ryall ... that ... that murder!' Garth licked his lips: he was feeling the strain of acting a part; beginning to fear that 'Brown' was deliberately baiting him. 'Somebody has made the police think I know something about it! And I'm sure they didn't believe me ... about Kent's flat!'

'You denied it, of course?'

'Of course I denied it!' Garth snarled. 'And the murder! But they aren't satisfied about the murder.' It was the story Hammond had told him to tell and he prayed he was making it sound convincing. 'How the hell did they even *start* to tie me up with it?' he said, bitterly. 'One of them must have told the police ... deliberately told them! The rotten swine! I did all they wanted, and they ... oh, what the hell does it matter! What can I do? They'll never believe me, now! And all because of those two rotten ...'

'One of Russi's men killed Miss Duval,' said 'Brown', softly. 'I can prove that, Garth. I can clear your name, I assure you. Be faithful to me, and you need have no fears!'

Garth leapt to his feet, clutching him by the arm.

'You mean that? Will you swear it?'

'I mean it, my friend. Ryall and Russi made this unenviable position for you ... I can unmake it. You will be restored to favour with your Ministry, too ... have no fear of that. Just be loyal to me, Garth. That is all.' 'Brown's' curiously pale eyes did not change their expression; yet Garth found himself believing that the man could do what he promised.

'Just what do you want me to do?' he urged.

'Watch and report to me,' murmured 'Brown'. 'That is all, my friend! I shall get in touch with you, from time to time. You will not tell anyone that you saw me here, of course.'

'I'm not *that* kind of a fool!' Garth protested.

'I hope you're not any kind of a fool,' said 'Brown', gently. 'Good-bye, Garth.'

He left the room silently, without closing the door, and turned towards the stairs. But he made no sound, and Garth did not know whether he had gone up or down them, or into another room. He lit a cigarette, then went out himself, going slowly down the stairs and out to the porch.

The thickset man was near the shrubbery; he looked at Garth with narrowed eyes, drew nearer, and nodded.

'You took your time, but you did a good job,' he admitted, grudgingly.

'I've done enough making-up for television,' said Garth offhandedly, as if with a touch of vanity. 'There's not all that much difference. What do we do now?'

'There's another bike … you can ride, I hope?'

'I haven't for some time, but …'

'There won't be much traffic, I'll go ahead … you just keep me in sight, that's all.'

The two cycles were propped together against the wall, round the side of the house. Ryall's messenger led the way into Brook-side Road, then towards the common. Garth followed, unsteady at first but soon finding it surprisingly easy, after a lapse of ten years. They crossed Wimbledon Common and went on towards Roehampton and Kingston.

Too absorbed in keeping up with his guide to look about him, Garth had not noticed a workman who had cycled out of Brook-side Road a few seconds before him, and whom they had passed. The 'workman' was still in sight when they reached Robin Hood's Gate—an entrance to Richmond Park. Nearby stood a Lanchester coupé, sleek and brightly polished: Ryall's 'taxi'.

The guide climbed from his cycle and waited for Garth. 'Leave the bikes here,' he said. 'They'll be looked after.'

He scanned the road down which they had come; the workman, passing them, received a long scrutiny. He looked an oldish man and his dungarees were torn and dirty. They passed him a little further along the road still pedalling steadily.

But when the car was out of sight, the workman pedalled more furiously, only stopping when he reached a telephone kiosk. From it, he called Craigie, and identified himself as an agent called Graham. Craigie took his message, told him to get to Chertsey as quickly as he could, replaced the receiver, and turned to Loftus.

'Phone the Kingston police, Bill, to get that car watched.'

'Same registration number?' asked Loftus, dialling.

'Yes. Heading for Chertsey, I fancy. But we'd better make sure.'

By the time Garth and his companion had reached Chertsey, a small police car had passed them at speed: shortly afterwards, its driver reported the address of the house where the wanted car had turned in.

On the bank of the Thames, not far from the small house, two young men sat in a small tent which had been there the night before and so had occasioned no surprise in Ryall or Russi. Russi had, in fact, made discreet inquiries and satisfied himself that the two men were junior R.A.F. officers, enjoying an unorthodox leave.

In fact, they were Department Z men.

Craigie, Loftus and Hammond, although satisfied that everything possible was being done—and done well—remained uneasy. The climax was still to come: in spite of Garth's apparent safety, they would not be surprised to learn that he had been killed.

They had constant reports on the various personalities who might be involved but not once did they hear the name of The Beacon. Nor did they learn that important members of the British Missions in the various Anglo-American problems had received what they believed to be highly confidential messages from the Foreign Secretary, inviting them to a conference to be held in great secrecy. Knowing what had been attempted against their American counterparts, each one of the delegates accepted the instructions regarding absolute secrecy without question. ᐧ

Not a word was said; not a question raised....

Olivia Livesey was at odds with the world—her own particular little world, especially.

Her father's reaction to her visit with Kent to David Garth had angered her; she had never felt the bitter animosity towards him that she did now. Nor had it helped improve her mood when Hammond had called at the Queen's Gate house and reported Garth's escape to her father, Catesby, Washington, George Kent—who had come to discuss the M.O.P. questions—and Olivia herself.

Hammond had explained how Garth, being taken from the police station to Scotland Yard at dawn, had surprised his escort and managed to get away. Hammond's brevity and matter-of-factness had made it seem the easiest and most likely of things.

Livesey had raged at the carelessness of the police and Hammond's Department, having little effect on Hammond but making Olivia wince, inwardly. The news of the escape seemed to all the others proof positive that Garth was guilty, and Hammond did nothing to make them think differently.

Olivia had tried to convince herself that she was being prejudiced and unjust. Dick *had* been right to report seeing Garth—if it was indeed Garth—in the flat. The new development *did make* it seem that Garth was guilty.

But she could not—and did not want to—believe it.

When Hammond had gone, her father and the others had at once plunged into details of their arrangements. Livesey wanted much more of the reports published than Kent, as the M.O.P. representative, thought wise. Olivia made notes until her fingers ached. Finally, Livesey lost his temper with Kent—who left the house in high dudgeon—and telephoned for a more senior member of the Ministry to be sent over. Then the argument started again and Olivia, realising that her father and Catesby appeared to have found a working agreement, at long last, wondered how much of the discussion was even necessary.

The food was ready and more would be stored before the word 'go' sent hundreds of laden ships to the starved continents. That was all that mattered, as far as Olivia could see.

While the others were still discussing it hotly—Livesey pressing for more disclosures; the Englishman against it—the telephone had rung. Olivia answered it, to hear an American voice drawl:

'Mr. Livesey there?'

'Who is that?' she asked.

'The Embassy. Mr. Kelly wants to talk with him.'

Livesey broke off in the middle of a heated argument and took the receiver as Olivia said: 'It's the Ambassador.'

'Fire away, Kelly!' he growled, and showed no sign of interest, at first. But almost immediately his hand tightened about the instrument and his eyes sparked angrily. His lips were compressed and veins stood out on his forehead and neck. The others stared at him, knowing that something serious had happened.

Then abruptly, he let fly.

'What in hell's name is the use of working my guts out if *that* kind of thing gets by?' he bellowed. 'They're as bad back home as they are in this goddam country! ... What's that? ... No, by God, I won't be discreet! It's time we forgot being so pussy-footing discreet! ... Oh, of course ... sure ... Yeah ... I'll keep it pretty close. That all? ... 'Bye!'

He banged the receiver down and glared at them all. Olivia's resentment and depression were gone; she was as intent as Washington, Catesby, and the Englishman.

Softly, Livesey said:

'Yes ... it was the Ambassador, in case you're interested! The report Kent lost reached someone it shouldn't have done.'

Catesby stared at him.

'What report?'

'The report Garth stole, you fool!' roared Livesey, pushing his chair back and beginning to pace the office. 'The one that gave details of where the food is stored in the States. And now ... *half of it has been destroyed by fire!*'

There was a shocked, incredulous silence.

Olivia's mouth was dry, Catesby's eyes nearly popped out of his head. The Englishman swallowed hard and Livesey brought a clenched fist crashing on the top of his desk.

'*That's* what your precious Garth has done! Sold the details ... sold us out! My oath, if I could get my hands on him for just one minute ...! And you ...!' He turned on Olivia: 'You wanted to warn him ... give him a chance of getting away!'

The Englishman said:

'Surely the stores can be replaced, Mr. Livesey? It isn't so great a quantity as all that.'

'Replaced!' roared Livesey, 'It's destroyed, understood? It's all gone up in smoke. It was food ... F-O-O-D! It needs growing. It needs *buying*. Someone's going to make a heck of a profit out of it and it could be a helluva long while before it can be replaced. And it'll be needed a damn' sight sooner than that—this war's going to crack open almost anytime now—and you babble about replacing it!' He glared at the affronted Englishman, then turned to Olivia, who was moving towards the door. 'Livvy! Where are you going?'

'Out,' said Olivia.

She drew a deep breath when she reached the passage. Her father was right about the food, she knew. Was he right, too, about Garth? Was Garth responsible for what had happened? The very possibility sickened her. She went to her room, closed the door and crossed to the window, staring blindly out.

She did not hear Washington come in, was unaware of his presence until his soft voice startled her.

'Is it as bad as that, Olivia?'

She swung round, startled.

'Ben! I ... I didn't hear you.'

'I don't like to feel that you and your father are quarrelling,' he said, gently. 'Tell me, does this man Garth mean so much to you?'

'I ... I don't know.' She shrugged defeatedly. 'I'm all mixed up.'

'So are we all,' Washington smiled. 'I did not see a great deal of Garth, but I like him. I find it difficult to believe he is the villain he appears. But don't let it come between you and your father, Olivia.'

'I... I'll get over it, I guess!'

'Of course. You are feeling the strain, I know—but believe me, your father is labouring under an even greater one. You see, Olivia, he is afraid that there is a leakage of information *here*. He has told me. Other papers have been stolen—less important ones, but which could do harm in the wrong hands. He hardly knows whom to trust.'

'Are you *sure*?' Olivia protested, amazed.

'I am quite sure. He does not even trust Hammond and the other men who came the other night. That is why he has been so difficult, lately.'

'But... why didn't he *tell* me?'

'He had no desire to worry you. And, my dear, I am not sure that he is right. The man Kent has had an opportunity for taking the papers. None were lost until he began to call here—and he and Garth are close friends. I wonder if Garth could be suffering for something Kent has done?'

Olivia stared at him without speaking.

'I wish there was a way of making sure,' he told her. 'Perhaps something will transpire. But meantime, I wanted you to know the truth, because the sight of you and Arnold so hostile to each other is disturbing. And you mean so much to him, Olivia—since your mother died....'

'Yes, yes. I know.'

'You remember how sudden her illness was. You know your father was only advised just before he was to board that ill-fated airplane? Her death saved his life and mine—he has not been quite normal since then, Olivia.'

'Why are you reminding me of all this?' she demanded, harshly.

'Because I'm afraid you may not fully appreciate its importance,' he said, gently. 'It affected him deeply. He is more arbitrary, less amenable to ... shall I say, reason? ... than he was. Anything unusual affects him much more than it did; but the underlying reason for it is her death. You understand?'

'Yes,' Olivia's voice was muffled. 'Yes, of course. I'm sorry, Ben ... and thank you.'

'You have no reason at all to reproach yourself!' he said, quickly. 'The fault is his. Both of us know that; and I think he does, too. But to return to the immediate problem—do you think you could face George Kent?'

'About what?' asked Olivia slowly.

'To see if you can find any kind of clue ... any reason for thinking that he, not Garth, is concerned with this.

He might have sent the report of what was stored in the States *before* anything was stolen. The theft might have been arranged because Garth was seen at the flat—and an opportunity thus presented for finding a scapegoat. It is no more than a possibility, but whoever *sent* that message must have had access to private wires from here to the States.'

Olivia looked startled.

'Why?'

'Because it is not two days since the report was stolen, and that would not be time to get the information across, except on privileged lines,' Washington told her, gravely. 'Whereas if Kent knew anything about it and sent word across as soon as he saw the report—over a week ago, now—all that has happened would be more easily understood. Will you see Kent?'

Chapter 22

The Strange Behaviour of George Kent

Olivia was not sure whether Kent was still suffering from the shock of Anne Duval's murder or whether there was something else on his mind.

She wanted to believe the latter: that Washington's suspicions had some foundation. She did not believe there was much she could do. Indeed, when she called at Kent's flat, she wondered whether she would be welcome. But he received her in friendly fashion, expressing the hope that his differences with her father would be settled quickly.

I'm sure they will,' she told him.

'I'm so glad.' Kent gave a quick smile. 'It is worrying, Miss Livesey ... most worrying. You will convey my best wishes to him, won't you?'

'Of course,' Olivia smiled back, reassuringly.

'Thank you so much. I ... oh, excuse me!' he added, as the telephone rang. He lifted the receiver—and a moment later, said in a sharp incredulous tone:

David! What on ...!'

Then apparently realising what he had said, he glanced over his shoulder. Olivia was staring at him, wide-eyed.

'I can't listen to ...' Kent began hastily.

But he did listen, and after a while protested in more urgent tones:

'No, no! I can't do it. I tell you I can't! David, I'd no idea that *you* …'

Olivia stared, wishing desperately that she could hear what Garth was saying. The effect on Kent was remarkable: his forehead was beaded with sweat and his voice unsteady. Before he replaced the receiver, he said in a low-pitched voice:

'Oh, all right, all right!' Then rang off.

He did not immediately turn to Olivia. When he did, his eyes looked as if he were suffering from a mental torment too great to be endured. She knew that whatever Garth had said had shocked him deeply. He seemed to be breaking up in front of her eyes.

'You must go, please!' he said thickly. 'Please …!'

'What did Mr. Garth want!' she demanded.

'I … I can't tell you. Miss Livesey, please go. I have most important work to do and … and …'

'*What did he want?*'

'He wants … help. He …' Kent licked his lips: 'He wants money.…'

'Are you going to give it to him?' she asked tensely.

'I … I don't know. He says he can prove his innocence if … if only he can get money.'

'Do you believe him?'

Kent drew a deep breath.

'It … it's hard to say. I've known him a long time, but… surely he understands *I* can do nothing! If I were seen with him, *I* should be suspect! I'd like to give him a chance … but I can't see how I can do more than I already have.…'

'Where is he?' Olivia asked, with an effort.

'At… at the house of a friend … in Chertsey.'

'How much money does he want?'

'Five hundred pounds. He ... Miss Livesey, there is nothing *you* can do! You *must* not become further embroiled in this unhappy business.'

'What is the address?' she demanded, evenly.

'I will not give it to you! I will not do anything which could encourage you to meet Garth—and perhaps lay yourself open to grave suspicion. I should never forgive myself if...'

'You'll give me that address,' she told him. 'Or I shall tell the police that you know where he is. One or the other! I won't let him hide away, with no one to help him and without the money he wants. Better the police get him again!' Her voice was flat: 'Do you want the police to know that you've heard from him?'

'I ... I can't *betray* him!' gasped Kent.

'Give me the address,' she insisted.

He argued pointlessly for some time, but eventually submitted: she had known that he would. She found herself actively disliking George Kent. Behind that facade of pompous propriety, there was something sly and furtive. He would go to any lengths to justify himself in his own eyes: he cared only for himself.

When she reached the street, she did not know quite what to do.

Was there any sense at all in seeing Garth?

She could send him the money by post; even by special messenger. But she *wanted* to see him. And although she argued with herself, she knew that she would go.

The banks were closed, but there was plenty of money at Queen's Gate and she had a safe-key. She could take what she wanted and replace it next morning; probably no one would even know she had taken it. But at all events, her

I.O.U. was quite sufficient. She could face up to any consequences as to the reason afterwards. She considered the wisdom of consulting Washington, but decided against it: it would be moral blackmail to take advantage of his loyalty.

Both her father and Washington were out, when she reached Number 27. So was Catesby. She scribbled her I.O.U. and took the money from the safe, wrapped the wad of notes in brown paper and put it in her bag. Then went out, found a taxi, learned from the driver that the London terminus she needed was Waterloo, and had him take her there.

She reached Chertsey station about five o'clock. One dilapidated taxi and another—gleaming limousine-type—were waiting. The driver of the latter approached her:

'Taxi, ma'am.'

'Yes, please. Do you know ...' she glanced at her note of the address: 'The Haven, Riverside Drive.'

'I know Riverside Drive, ma'am. We'll soon find the house.'

He held the door open, and she climbed in. Leaning back on the cushions, she felt an increasing tension. And, fifteen minutes afterwards, when the taxi pulled into the narrow driveway of a small house near the river, her heart was beating so fast that it threatened to suffocate her.

Then she saw George Kent.

She was getting out of the taxi when she caught a glimpse of him at a window. For a long moment, she just stood there, staring, trying to imagine why he had forestalled her. Then suddenly instinctively aware of being in far deeper waters than she had suspected before, she wanted desperately to get away. She turned to the driver.

'I've decided to ...' she began, and he gripped her arm tightly and forced her forward.

He acted so swiftly that she was in the porch before she knew what was happening. The door opened and as a neatly-dressed maid stood aside, he thrust Olivia forward into the hall. Before she had recovered her balance, the door was closed behind her—and three men appeared from a doorway on her left.

One was Garth; another, Kent. The third, who pushed through them to the front, was a vast, shaggy-looking man whose teeth showed very white against his dark beard.

'My *dear* Miss Livesey,' he said softly. 'How nice it is to see you!'

She stared at him, mesmerised. She wanted to look at Garth, but she could not take her eyes from this giant of a man in front of her. His smile was a menacing, evil thing: he was like a great bear, frighteningly powerful and fully aware of it.

He gripped Olivia's arm and drew her into the room. Garth stood aside, his face set. Kent looked frightened, but now she was more than ever aware of his cunning, and repelled by it.

'When Kent told me he had given you the address, I felt I had to be here to greet you myself,' Ryall went on. 'You are anxious to help Garth, I understand? Most touching! Garth happily, has no sentimental regard for you—he agreed with me that it was much wiser that you should come here than be allowed to remain at large.'

She looked at Garth, something like horror in her eyes; but she could read nothing in his face.

'What ... what *is* all this about?' she demanded, forcing herself to keep her voice steady.

'Your impetuosity has led you astray, I fear,' said Ryall. 'Just as Garth was led astray by being too sensitive about his own skin—and Kent, because he needed money. Both of them have been good enough to give me some help: I hope you will do the same. Because my *dear* Miss Livesey, I think you can be very useful to me. Very useful indeed!'

'I'll have nothing to do with …'

'I think you will, my dear. All I want is for you to make contact with your father's friend, Washington. I know he will come hurrying down here the moment he knows where you are. He is very fond of you, is he not?'

Olivia moistened her lips nervously.

'Don't be frightened, my dear. You will be quite well cared for provided you attempt nothing foolish and do what I …'

'Ryall!' Kent exclaimed: 'If you do anything to harm her.…'

Ryall swung round on him, a man transformed. Olivia went cold as she saw the glare in his eyes, heard the viciousness in his voice.

'Hold your tongue! There will be no sudden flood of remorse from *you*! You brought her here … knew I wanted to get Washington here and saw how it could be done through her. That is all I want from you!'

Kent backed away like a whipped cur.

Garth remained silent, but looked out of the window. Ryall, suave again, turned to her and pointed to a telephone.

'Call your dear friend "Ben"!'

'What do you want with him?' she demanded, harshly.

'That hardly concerns you, my dear,' he purred, menacing again. 'Call him! Give him that address'—he touched a slip of paper by the telephone—'and tell him it is most important that you see him quickly. Is that quite clear?'

Olivia's chin lifted.

'I won't do it!'

'Now, Miss Livesey,' he purred again, 'I do not wish to make it unpleasant for you. But believe me, I shall not shrink from doing so! There are ways and means of persuading you, none of which is likely to fail. Be sensible, please!'

'I won't do it,' she repeated, doggedly.

She stared into his eyes. Her heart was pounding with fear and she felt weak at the knees. She did not know what methods he would use, but she had no doubt that he would, indeed, find a way of making her talk. She was vaguely aware that she was in a state of emotional shock.

Her mind refused even to contemplate David Garth's involvement and all that it connotated. And her loathing for Kent had been replaced by a kind of numbness that admitted only fear.

Then Garth spoke for the first time.

'I'll phone Washington,' he offered. 'He'll come if I tell him what the trouble is.'

Ryall turned on him and barked:

'You will do nothing of the kind! He will come for his precious Olivia without hesitation. If *you* call him, he will probably arrange some trap ... might even go to the police! If you wish to help, convince *her.* You know what will happen to her if she refuses!'

Garth looked at her.

The numbness remained, but rising through it came a sickening wave of loathing and shame combined. This was the man in whom she had believed—whom she had been ready to help at whatever cost to herself. How would she be able to trust her own judgement ever again?

She was revolted, too, by the cold-blooded deliberation with which Kent had inveigled her here. He had used Garth's alleged need of help as the bait—deliberately, calculatedly, leading her into a trap: leading her here, as the bait to trap Ben Washington.

But why *Ben?* What could Ben do for Ryall.

'You'll be well-advised to telephone Washington,' Garth told her, quietly. 'Otherwise ...' He glanced at Ryall: 'It will not be pleasant, Miss Livesey. I know Washington would far prefer that you did call him.'

'I won't...' she began again; pale-faced now, and very, very frightened.

'Miss Livesey,' Garth began again. 'You ...'

'Enough!' cried Ryall. He strode forward and slapped her hard across the face, sending her reeling against Garth and almost deafening her. His second blow, across the other cheek sent her crashing into Kent.

Both men stood still, doing nothing to help her. As she staggered, trying to keep on her feet, he struck her brutally again. And this time, she fell so heavily against Garth that he lost his own balance.

They fell together, Olivia on top.

'Get up!' Ryall snarled. 'Get up, my *dear* Miss Livesey! I am trying to make you see sense without too much inconvenience. But I can very quickly call on others who will show much less finesse, I assure you!'

She was conscious of the threatening tone of the words, but hardly knew what he said: another voice was whispering in her ear. Garth, one arm about her as he pushed her from him, apparently slipped and fell again so that her hair fell about his face. He spoke softly and urgently.

'Phone him! Trust me ... phone him!'

'Get ... *up!'* Ryall snapped. And bending, gripped her arm and jerked her to her feet. She stared dazedly at him, hardly seeing his face and hearing nothing of what he said.

Garth's voice was in her ears: seemed to be speaking, still. She certainly would not have given in so easily but for that whispered exhortation. She hardly knew whether she even believed she could trust him. But she was miserably conscious that she would not be able to withstand Ryall's pressure for long.

She would make the call, sooner or later. And she wanted, so much, to trust Garth: wanted, too, to show him that she did. *Dear God*, she was thinking, *don't let me be wrong!*

'... Or do you want further persuasion?' Ryall's voice reached her again as she saw Garth get slowly to his feet. And listlessly, she moved towards the telephone.

'Excellent!' Ryall purred. 'You had better have a drink of water, my dear ... and give yourself time to recover. It would not do for you to sound unhappy, would it?'

She was glad of the water; and when she spoke to Washington a few minutes later, her voice sounded normal enough. She gave him the address on the paper—also in Chertsey—and finished on an urgent note:

'I must go! But Ben ... you *will* come?'

'Where are you?' Washington asked evenly.

'I'm ... in a phone booth. Ben, it's terribly important ... you *must* come!'

'I'll be there as fast as I can arrange it,' he assured her. 'Be careful, Olivia! Don't do anything hasty!'

He rang off at once and Olivia replaced her own receiver slowly. She could not look at Garth. She looked dully towards Ryall and dropped into a chair and buried her face in her hands.

She was half-carried, half-dragged out of that room to one on the next floor. Its one small window was barred on the inside. But even if she had had anything with which to lever a bar free, there was one man 'working' in the garden immediately below and she heard Ryall instructing another to keep watch at her door.

Then Ryall went away and she was left to her thoughts and her fears and the uncertain assurance of Garth's voice:

'Phone him! Trust me ... phone him!'

Ryall did not go downstairs immediately.

Instead, he went to a room not far from Olivia's and entered it—surprising even Russi by the silence of his approach. The plump-faced American jumped up from his armchair.

'Has it worked?' he demanded, tensely, and Ryall's bearded face parted in a beaming smile of self-gratification.

'Washington will be there in about an hour,' he announced, his eyes gleaming. 'You will make the arrangements to bring him here, my friend ... and after that, we shall have *nothing* to worry about!'

Russi said: 'You're sure he *is* Brown?'

'Of course I'm sure!' Ryall growled. 'I will admit I realised it with something of a shock. But there is now no doubt, my friend. You see how excellently it has all worked out. Washington will come here ... and we shall deal with him *as* Washington. Not as Brown! Then we shall take over the whole thing, ourselves. There is no way our plans *can* fail!'

'And you can make a deal with the others?'

'I have told you that I can make all the money that you or I are ever likely to need!' snapped Ryall. 'Nor is it an income that will suddenly stop. And tomorrow night at The Beacon, my friend, we shall be putting the finishing touches.'

'Sure, that's all fixed.'

'Then surely you can see how easily the deal, as you put it, can be made?' Ryall shrugged. 'It matters little which representatives are unable to continue their work. Had you been successful with the Americans, of course, it would have saved us the necessity of continuing....'

'Listen, Ryall ... don't give me that! I'm not dumb. You're working this racket two ways, I know.'

Ryall said, deceptively gentle:

'Indeed, Russi! And just what do you mean by that?'

'I mean that I know you're working for Berlin,' Russi retorted. 'Hell, what do I care? I've got no country ... all I want is a rakeoff. But don't take me for a fool, Ryall. You're killing the bunch at The Beacon because Berlin wants it done ... it'd make no difference to the other racket, if they lived. The maid and the chauffeur ... they're Nazis, too.'

Ryall stared at him, unblinking.

The silence in the room was tense and Russi's round eyes were watchful. Ryall smoothed his beard thoughtfully for a moment or two, then smiled: a slow, mirthless smile.

'How clever you are, my friend! And since you would not make the statement unless you were certain of your facts, I shall admit it. How did you find out, may I ask?'

'I did some hard thinking,' Russi smiled, thinly. 'I told myself that it wasn't as simple as it looked. I knew Brown was aiming at destroying food to push up prices ... wanted agreements held up till the prices reached the level to suit him, and he knew where the stuff was stored, in the States. But I know you've got other interests in the States, Ryall.'

'I control a large Corporation in America, yes,' Ryall agreed, softly. 'It is one of the biggest growing and distributing combines in the world, and it has other members who, like myself, are of German blood. So we could help our own people by damaging the Allied war effort—and take our due rewards, at the same time.'

The massive shoulders lifted in a contemptuous shrug.

'We allowed Brown to make the preliminary arrangements—the fool! He is so obsessed with preserving this melodramatic masquerade that he has not even dreamed that we, too, have been play-acting! Using him, until we were ready to take over! We did not know for whom he was working, but now that we know our 'Brown' is Washington, we can be sure it is the Livesey Corporation. You see, my friend ... it is all very simple!'

Russi grinned: 'That's the word, I guess. Simple!'

'Exactly ... as with your own arrangements. You have your men, you train them well, no? *Some,* of course, are my own German friends.' Ryall laughed, softly. 'You did not know that, did you?'

'I don't give a damn,' said Russi. 'I knew some of the guys were German ... so what? All I'm interested in, Ryall, is getting my cut.'

'You need have no fear, my friend! Your men are primed for the attack at The Beacon?'

'They've got their orders, sure.'

'Just what are they?'

'Like we arranged,' Russi shrugged. 'All those people who've had the letters, they get together at The Beacon ... in the Assembly room, like it says in the invitation. Then ... up it goes.'

'Just *what* goes up?' Ryall asked.

'Aw, hell ... what does it matter. I've got guys with machine-guns at all the corners ... up in the gallery. They just squeeze the triggers, and that's it! Then when they've all stopped squealing, they set the place on fire. Don't worry ... my men know just what to do.'

'You have no further instructions for them at all.'

'I tell you, it's all done. They don't need wet-nursing on a job!'

Ryall beamed upon him.

'Admirable! I knew you were a first-class workman, Russi—and I shall always be grateful for your help. But now …!' He beamed again … 'Really, my friend, I do not think I need you any more.'

'Say, what the hell…?'

Russi's hand darted to his shoulder-holster, but before he could draw out his gun, Ryall shot him, from his pocket, through the chest and stomach. Russi staggered; his lips opened but he uttered only a gasping, choking sound. Ryall fired again: Russi crumpled up and then sprawled forward on the floor.

Ryall looked down at him dispassionately.

'We might have worked together for a long time had you not known all the truth, my friend,' he murmured. 'But perhaps it is as well. Now, I have only to deal with Mr. Washington-Brown. The *clever* Mr. Washington-Brown!'

Then he went calmly to instruct the 'chauffeur' to collect 'Washington-Brown' from the nearby rendezvous. And that done, he hummed a little to himself, as if he were thoroughly happy.

CHAPTER 23
NEARING THE END

R yall, Garth knew, was upstairs: either in his own room or talking to Russi in his. Somewhere on the same floor, he also knew, was Olivia. Kent had gone up with Ryall—and a more frightened man Garth had never seen.

When he took the time to think of George Kent, he was filled with an anger and loathing which threatened to destroy all his self-control. It had been obvious, after he had been ordered by Ryall to summon him to the house by the river, that Kent was implicated.

Since then, what he had heard from both of them had made it clear that Kent had been working with Ryall for some time.

The theft of the papers had been a trick to make police and the Department look elsewhere—a simple trick which might easily have worked. Also it had been a means of putting him, Garth, further in their clutches. Had he himself made any admission to the police it would have cleared Kent of suspicion, since he would hardly be likely to arrange for an accomplice to steal papers to which he already had access.

Garth, who had heard of the destruction of the warehouses in the States, wondered what madness had allowed Hammond to let the papers be stolen. He could see no rhyme or reason to that particular tactic; and already appalled by the destruction of current stocks, he could hardly bear to think of the long-term effects, if these cold-blooded devils were allowed to go on.

One thing was certain, he thought bleakly: it was nearing the end.

Ryall had admitted by implication that he knew Washington to be the man 'Brown'. And Ryall, he gathered, was planning a *coup* which would leave him in complete possession.

There was something else afoot, too: some other project on the very brink of success. Garth sensed it unmistakably, while gleaning no least idea of what it was about.

He considered the situation as dispassionately as he could.

Hammond would probably think he had done a worthwhile enough job, simply to have learned the true identity of 'Brown'. But Russi and Ryall had been cock-a-hoop even before they had successfully lured Washington into the trap.

When Ryall and Washington—alias—Brown were together, he told himself, he might well have a chance to look through the house … perhaps get a word with Olivia.

That was the most difficult part of all: to make himself accept the logically obvious truth that the personal safety of Olivia was as unimportant as his own. Of vital importance, was the need to discover what other devilry they were planning—and do his utmost to prevent its taking place. And as time wore on, the necessity obsessed him.

If he had only been able to sneak away, he could telephone the number Hammond had given him. But the place was too closely watched by Ryall's men.

He wondered anxiously whether Washington-Brown would fall so easily for the trick. He certainly hoped so: he had urged Olivia to make the call in the belief that one of Hammond's men would follow the little American, if he came. But in Washington-Brown's place, he knew, he himself certainly would not be likely to fall for it.

A car drew up outside: Ryall's 'taxi'.

The house by the river, like The Elms, was surrounded by tall trees and thick shrubberies. It was impossible to see anything save patches of roof, from the road.

Garth watched, grim-faced, from the window as the chauffeur opened the door, leaned inside, and lifted a figure he knew must be Washington's out of the back seat. The little American was unconscious; his head lolled back against the driver's shoulder, his hooked nose was pointing towards the sky, his mouth hung open.

The front door was opened by that soft-speaking, neat-looking, remarkably self-possessed but punctiliously-correct 'maid'.

Garth stepped forward to the door of the room and opened it a fraction as Washington was carried upstairs. As Ryall's voice boomed out and a door closed, he almost ground his teeth in frustration. Ryall's arrogant self-satisfaction made him feel he would rather make a dash for it—take the risk of being shot at—than stay there, helpless, while that great brute got away with God knew what new crime. Hammond *had* to be warned!

Restlessly, he swung back into the room.

A car passed along the road. It slowed down, then went off. Sudden hope, just as suddenly dashed, he stared bleakly out of the window. It was hopeless: he would never reach a telephone alive. He could see stealthy movements in the shubbery: Ryall's gunmen were everywhere.

Then he suddenly stiffened. A very small man with a puckish face—dressed in black and wearing black gloves—darted from the shrubbery to the door. Garth heard a key quietly inserted in the lock; then complete silence for several seconds, before the door of his room opened....

Standing in front of him, the black cloth mask already over his face, was 'Brown'!

And Washington was upstairs!

Garth recovered his composure quickly enough, conscious of the steady gaze from those strange eyes: he must not be found wanting, now. He took a step forward as the little man closed the door behind him, letting his amazement show.

'Surprised, Garth?' said the man, drily. 'I did tell you I would communicate with you again.'

Garth exclaimed:

'I thought ... I thought you were *Washington*! They were boasting about trapping you! I tried to get out, to warn you ... it wasn't possible.' He gulped: 'I was going to telephone *him*! He ... *he's* upstairs, now!'

'I know perfectly well that he is upstairs! Why else do you think I timed my arrival for this critical moment. Ryall imagines that he has me there, in his power! Poor, *poor* Ryall ... he is such a fool. Many Germans are.'

'*Germans?*' Garth had no need to affect shocked incredulity.

'Oh, yes! Ryall is a German. He is working for Berlin. I am not, Garth: I draw the line at treason. I am prepared to prevent absurd agreements being reached on food and commodity prices, but that is all. I used Ryall, not knowing what he was, but I have learned now. We have to act quickly, my friend.'

'I'm ready,' Garth said grimly, and meant it.

'Of course you are! And I shall be very soon. We shall have to be careful, however. My taxi will have been seen by one or more of their guards, and that will have been reported at once. So they will know that someone is here ... but they will not know who! Is Olivia Livesey also here?'

'What *don't* you know?' demanded Garth, unsteadily.

'Very little.' The black lips actually parted in a smile: 'I was told that she telephoned Washington.'

'But who....'

'I have a very good friend at Queen's Gate,' said 'Brown', gently. 'So I am usually advised of what is happening. But I am concerned by something which has nothing to do with Ryall or the Liveseys. I am concerned with Department Z. You remember the man Hammond, who interrogated you?'

'The plainclothes man.' Garth nodded.

'He is no policeman,' 'Brown' told him. 'He is a Secret Service agent—and a very able one. I have had to work behind the cover of Ryall and Russi to ensure that Hammond and his colleagues did not find me. I have more respect for them than for any other body of men in the world! But it will soon be over—they will have Ryall and Russi and their whole organisation and they will be satisfied there is no one else. They will, of course, be convinced that Washington, who will be dead, was the mysterious "Mr. Brown"!'

He laughed: a ghostly, almost inaudible sound. 'I talked with Russi a very little while ago. His arrangements for their joint great venture are all made. His apprehension will make no difference to the final success of what I am planning. Don't you find that reassuring?'

'I find the prospect of their apprehension reassuring!' Garth said bleakly. 'I'm sorry ... what *are* you planning? What's going on?'

'You will find out,' murmured 'Brown'. 'I wish ...'

He broke off abruptly as a high-pitched scream came from somewhere outside.

The window was open only an inch or two at the top, but the cry sounded clearly. It was a woman's voice and Garth's thoughts sprang to Olivia. He darted to the window, but before he opened it 'Brown' said sharply:

'Do nothing impetuous, Garth!'

'But someone …!'

'Your loyalty is to *me*!' snapped 'Brown'. 'Haven't I made that clear enough? The sound came from outside—so if you are thinking of Olivia Livesey …'

'Never mind who I'm thinking of!' Garth rasped.

He pushed up the window and climbed through. He could not be sure whether 'Brown' would not shoot him. But he had to take what would probably be his only possible chance. As he stood in the garden, he saw what had happened.

Three people were in the river.

A small boat, upturned, was floating downstream and he saw two men swimming strongly towards a third person—a girl. Her long hair floated on the water for a moment—as fair as Olivia's was dark—then darkened as it submerged, waterlogged. The two men reached the girl and pushed her towards the near bank. He was half-way down the garden when they climbed ashore, all three gasping and the girl beginning to wail accusingly at the two men.

They were in uniform—Army subalterns—he noticed with relief: at least there was no chance of their being a couple of Ryall's thugs off-duty.

He reached them, and took the opportunity for a covert glance at the house.

'Brown' was not at the window, but he had no doubt that he was under observation. Still, unless they were prepared to shoot all four, neither Ryall nor 'Brown' could very well afford to shoot him, there.

'Listen, chum!' he said urgently, as he neared the first man. 'This is terribly important! Can you get a telephone message to ...'

He was about to quote the number which was burned in his mind, and to give his name, when the man turned to the girl, ignoring him. As he stared—astonished for a moment and then indignant—the man turned back, scowling belligerently. But his voice in no way matched the scowl as he murmured:

'You're Garth? I'm from Hammond. Anything up?'

Garth gasped and then pulled himself together.

'Get him here!' he said, urgently. 'Tell him "Brown" is here ... he's the man Hammond wants. It's hellish important ... so is speed!'

'Right!' said the other, promptly. 'We've men nearby. Lend a hand with the girl, will you?'

The upsetting of the boat, the girl's cry ... Garth suddenly realised, had been part of a deliberate ruse to let Hammond's men into the grounds to make contact with him. The relief of it swept over him as one of the men plunged into the river to retrieve the upturned boat.

The girl was sobbing hysterically, now, and the second man was bending over her, reasoning with her. Then with a show of sudden impatience, he slapped her cheek sharply. Her loud sobs changed abruptly to a whimper—just as the chauffeur and maid appeared in the garden.

'We'll have to get her into the house!' said the man with her, sharply. 'She'll catch her death of cold in those things ... can your maid lend her something?'

The chauffeur cut in, quickly: 'I'm sorry, sir, but...'

Then Ryall came blundering from the house. The driver and the maid drew aside as he took charge of the situation, declaring himself most distressed by the accident.

It was very inconvenient, he confessed, since he was due at an important conference, but a room and a change of clothes must be put at the lady's disposal. He quelled his driver's unspoken protest with a glare, and was most gracious and helpful.

He left the driver and the young officer to carry the hapless girl into the house and went ahead with the maid on one side and Garth on the other.

'We must get her out of here as quickly as possible,' he muttered, urgently. 'A damnable thing! But we could not have turned her away ... it would have attracted attention, which we *must* avoid! Ethel, go to Miss Livesey and make her undress, quickly ... then give this girl her clothes. Garth....'

They had reached the small passage at the side of the house. The far end was in shadow—but it was just possible to discern something—someone—even blacker than the background. Ryall froze in his tracks and the maid exclaimed, incredulous:

'Brown!'

'A slight miscalculation on your part, Ryall,' murmured 'Brown' mockingly. 'And a most unfortunate little interruption. Hush! Don't talk now, And don't be foolish enough to try to shoot me—the young couple coming in will want to know why!'

Ryall leaned against the wall: even then he looked as if he was staying upright only with a tremendous effort. The maid's face was deathly pale and she was trembling—the first time Garth had seen her discomposed.

'Hurry!' exhorted 'Brown'. 'They will be here in a moment! When we have disposed of them, I am sure your ingenuity will not be found wanting. We can talk, my friend ... about Washington, and other of your peculiar delusions.' He moved towards the stairs.

'Disposed of them,' thought Garth. And aloud, he warned quietly: 'There's another fellow … he went after the boat. He's taking it back to the hirer's … he's expecting them to meet him …'

Ryall, breathing heavily, straightened up with an obvious effort. The young officer who was helping to carry the girl reached the door and called out to ask was it all right to come in? Then did so, and deposited the girl on a hall seat as Ryall muttered:

'Get… those … clothes! Do nothing else, Ethel … understand? Do nothing else, yet!'

They were still standing in the hall, like actors in a dramatic tableau. The influence of 'Brown' was about them all: uncanny, and uncannily effective. Even Garth was so affected by his remarkable knowledge of events that he felt it was only too possible the man would have seen through the mishap on the river.

Then the sitting-room door was suddenly flung open and a man burst into the hall—the 'gardener' from beneath Olivia's window. His face was strained and he saw only Ryall as he gasped out:

'Several men … four or five … coming fast!' He was clearly almost frantic: 'Excellency! You …'

The gutturals in his voice betrayed his nationality. Yet his words came so unexpectedly that for a moment, Ryall only stood and gaped at him. The 'taxi-driver' started for the stairs and the 'maid' shrank back against Ryall. And the next moment Garth was as startled as the others as the laconic voice of the young 'subaltern' drawled:

'How very interesting … a luvverly bunch of little Nazis!'

They turned with one accord—to see the automatic in his hand, the smile on his lips. On the floor beside him was the gun's water-proof holster. The girl who had screamed so realistically was sitting up and smiling widely. And before anyone could move, the hall was suddenly filled with men. Footsteps sounded, windows crashed in, as more approached from all directions.

Garth recognised the Errols and Hammond; the rest were strangers. Two of them held automatics at the ready; others started to put theirs back in their pockets. There was a languid air about them all; Garth had an absurd impression that on the whole they were disappointed at achieving entry without a fight.

Then he though of Olivia.

He whirled towards the stairs as footsteps thundered in the passage above. A man started to scream; the cry was cut short. A thud followed—and the men who were putting their guns away thought better of it. Hammond and the pseudo-subaltern kept Ryall and his party covered, while Garth started up the stairs with the rest in his wake. With three or four yards' start he was the first to see 'Brown' at the stairhead ... with something in his hand.

'Look out!' he roared, over his shoulder. *'Look out!'*

The missile was small and round: a Mills bomb, or the like. 'Brown' tossed it over Garth's head towards the hall, then turned to run. Garth followed; afraid for the rescuers below, afraid for Olivia. George Kent lay stretched out in the passage, a knife sticking up from his throat, his sightless eyes wide open.

'Brown' disappeared into one of the rooms.

As Garth sprinted after him, the explosion came. The floor shook, pictures crashed, smoke and dust and flying debris filled the air. He heard cries and curses and the sound of falling bodies, but dared not pause or look back. But as he pounded into the room after 'Brown', a second door on the far side snapped shut and he heard a key turn in the lock.

Then he heard a voice calling ... Olivia's voice.

'David!' she cried. 'David Garth! *David!*'

He found the room, easily enough. She was hammering on the door, which was locked. But the key was there. Gasping and choking, he turned it, fairly sure she would be unhurt in there: fearing what had happened in the hall.

CHAPTER 24
THE BEACON

Olivia was not hurt.

She did not exclaim when she saw him.

She just stood there, quite still, her fists clenched as if to strike the door again. Her beautiful, violet-blue eyes bright with tears of relief as she whispered:

'You ... all right! Oh, you're *all right!*'

'Yes.' Garth nodded, reaching her: holding her, hardly knowing what he was saying. 'Olivia, I ... look! Wait here ... *please*. Don't move out of this room!'

He held her only a moment longer, then pulled himself free and ran out. Back in the room where 'Brown' had disappeared, he tried the far door again. Then turned as he heard steps behind him ... the Errols: apparently unhurt, but with faces blackened and clothes torn and dishevelled.

'All right,' murmured Mike, and Garth stood aside as he levelled an automatic and fired three times at the lock.

The door sagged open.

The Errols reached the room beyond ahead of Garth, who saw Mark step over a little man stretched out on the floor.

It was Washington. His hands and feet were tied together, but he was conscious, and he jerked his head sharply to indicate a small staircase which led from another door.

Garth followed the Errols, but to no purpose. There was no sign of 'Brown': no indication of what way of escape he had taken.

They hurried back to the hall below, Mike leading the way down the stairs. The last few treads were damaged, so he leapt them. Beyond him, as he followed suit, Garth saw a scene of unparalleled horror.

The centre of the hall had disappeared.

Three men were lying against the wall, unconscious and badly injured. The girl from the river was bending over one of them. There was blood on the walls, the ceiling and what was left of the floor—blood and worse. Garth surveyed the scene with a sudden nausea.

How many had been killed he wondered? Hammond had been right there ... *Hammond....*

No! Hammond was there! Standing by the front door, obviously unhurt.

Later, Garth was to learn that it was his own shouted warning which had saved Hammond from injury or worse: he had flung himself backwards, jerking one of the Department men with him through the sitting-room doorway.

There had not been time to pull Ryall or his party out of the way.

'We can't get across there,' Mike Errol pointed out, stopping short at the great, jagged hole in the floor. The ceiling was completely down and part of each wall sagged inwards. 'See you at the door, Bruce!' he called.

Hammond raised a hand in acknowledgement.

Garth went with Mike Errol to meet him. The front door itself was badly marked, and debris was strewn about the front garden. Hammond's face was set, but he forced a smile as he recognised Garth.

'Hallo!' he said warmly. 'Glad you've got through. Nice work!'

'It wasn't Washington,' Garth said, wryly.

'We know that now. We've been learning quite a lot. Washington is a Federal Bureau man ... Livesey's personal bodyguard, as well. He told us he'd been called to Chertsey ... that's why we had so many men on hand. And this place was watched of course.' This time, his smile came more easily. 'Solving your difficulties?'

Garth swallowed.

'Some of them.' He could think only of the man in black: '"Brown" ...'

'He's got away,' said Hammond. 'He did it nicely. There was a power-boat in that mooring-shed at the end of the next garden ... no one thought of it. So he got clear. The river police have been alerted, of course, but he won't fall for anything easy. Ah, well, at least Ryall and company are out of the game. And Russi, dead upstairs ... did you know?'

Garth grimaced.

'No ... I saw they'd killed Kent. "Brown" did that. I suppose.' His head was aching abominably and his eyes seemed filled with tiny, painful specks of sand. 'Is it ... is it all you wanted? Apart from Brown?'

'It is not,' said Hammond, decisively. 'He's killed them to stop them from talking. There's something else brewing and we haven't any idea what. How's Olivia?' The smile brightened his face again, fleetingly.

'She's all right,' Garth frowned ... 'Listen, Hammond: "Brown" talked freely. He told me he had a contact at Number 27. If it wasn't Washington ...'

'Livesey or Catesby or one of the staff,' Hammond shrugged. 'We'll find out, in time.'

'They might know what "Brown" knows!'

'Yes, of course. Don't worry, Garth … we'll do everything we can. We certainly won't miss the obvious! I've telephoned London and things are in motion. There isn't much else we can do except start tidying up,' Hammond said as he surveyed the ghastly chaos.

Then he and the Errols began their task.

The delegates were on their way to The Beacon, that large house on the outskirts of Staines.

They went separately, of course; although it was not surprising that a number of them were on the same trains from Waterloo and that once they reached Staines there was a rush for the single taxi. By the time the big Assembly Room at The Beacon was half-full, word had reached Craigie and Loftus at Whitehall that men whom the Department was watching were gathering there. Hammond was back with the Errols at Chertsey—following the first 'tidying-up', he had gone for a session with his chiefs and returned early that morning.

He received the news about half-past four, and did not, of course, know that the meeting was timed for five o'clock. He did know that something important was afoot—and instinct told him it was bad: dangerous. He was obsessed by a sense of urgency—as if he had been awakened by the shrilling of warning alarm-bells.

Yet he had not the faintest idea what was likely to happen. Nothing had been revealed at the Chertsey house. He had found no papers, no clue at all to the 'grand finale' he knew intuitively was certainly planned. He had not the remotest clue as to 'Brown's' identity, and no sure knowledge of the spy at Number 27.

Olivia Livesey had been reunited with her father. Catesby remained at Number 27. Washington could offer no help.

At Hammond's request, Garth had 'cleared the air'—and preserved Washington's F.B.I. cover—by telling Olivia that he had believed him *to* be 'Brown' and had persuaded her to send for him so that he would be 'exposed' to her for what he was.

All of them knew they were being closely watched—except Garth, who was in Craigie's office, going through a great stack of photographs.

He was seeking one of 'Brown', whose puckish face he had glimpsed at Chertsey as he darted from the shrubbery into the house.

The tension in Craigie's office was an almost tangible thing: it affected them all.

Photographs—photographs—photographs. It seemed incredible that there were so many small men who could conceivably be implicated. British—American—the Axis and neutral countries alike—men of all nationalities.

To Garth, after an hour of staring at them, every face seemed the same.

Then he turned one up—and his reaction was so spontaneous that Craigie half-rose from his chair and Loftus crossed swiftly to his side.

'Got him?' he asked sharply.

'Yes ...' Garth's voice was strained: 'Yes, this is the chap.' He stared at the photograph of the small, faintly-smiling man. He looked something of a dandy and there was a carnation in his button-hole. 'Yes!' he shouted, suddenly realising how enormously important the discovery was: *'This is the man!'*

Craigie said, in a curiously soft voice:

'Well, well, well ... Sir Herbert Grey!'

The silence lasted only a few seconds, but it seemed an age. Then Loftus broke it:

'*Aunt Mabel's* husband!' he drawled, and his eyes were hard but bright. 'So he's not dead!' He reached for the telephone: '*Now*, we're moving!'

It was a quarter to five.

The Assembly Room at The Beacon was filled with well-dressed and somewhat impatient men and the buzz of conversation was beginning to rise a note or two. It was apparent to them all that something of outstanding importance was to be discussed at this conference and they were eager for the arrival of the Foreign Secretary and his entourage— and, rumour had it, the American Ambassador too.

There was some surprise at the fact that there were no Americans yet in the room.

Outside, several of Craigie's men who had followed their charges to The Beacon gathered in little groups among the shrubs and trees, Hammond was with them, considering the wisdom of trying to get some of his men into the building.

From the moment that 'Brown' had thrown his bomb, Hammond had been filled with a sense of foreboding which deepened with every passing second. He did not think that this meeting was a genuine one. And the more he thought of that bomb, the more vividly he realised the havoc a larger one would wreak in this house.

High up *in* the gallery surrounding the room, the machine-gunners were hidden behind plush-covered chairs. They had been there, waiting, for some time—still acting on Russi's instructions: with no slightest inkling or suspicion that he was dead. At a given signal, they would rise and begin their dreadful work.

That would be at five o'clock—and it was fifteen minutes to five.

It had taken half-an-hour to make 'Aunt Mabel' talk.

At first she had denied all knowledge of her husband's activities and insisted that he was dead. Loftus and Craigie had not been kind to her. Garth had heard and watched them, realising how necessary it was, yet hating the pressure they exerted.

Then, without warning, she cracked. She flared into a towering rage which suddenly turned to uncontrollable tears as she admitted the truth. He was alive, but she had seen him very rarely and had no idea what he was doing.

He had told her that it was vitally important she keep his 'resurrection' an absolute secret—that he was involved in Secret Service work for the Government. She had begun to disbelieve it only in the past few days, in which she had had to face the fact that the chief of Department Z actually believed him dead....

She did not know where he was living, but believed he might be at The Beacon. The place was his—he had inherited it shortly before going to America.

'We would know if he were living at the house!' Loftus rasped. 'He's not!'

'He ... he might be at the cottage!' she gasped. 'We stayed there, once, when we went to The Beacon for a few days ... to save opening the big house. But he wouldn't do anything wrong!' The racking sobs had started up again: 'I *know* he wouldn't do anything wrong. ...!'

That had been at ten minutes past four.

Forty minutes later, a powerful car roared through the outskirts of Staines towards The Beacon. Hammond, near the gates, heard the sound and glanced along the road. He recognised the dark green monster as Loftus's Bentley—and knew at once that Loftus had *news!*

He sprang into the roadway as the car slowed down to turn into the drive. Craigie was sitting next to Loftus and Garth was in the back: Hammond scrambled over the side to join him as Loftus put his foot down again and the big car raced towards the house.

It did not pull up at the doors, but swung left along a secondary drive. Some distance away, half-hidden by trees, was the 'cottage': Aunt Mabel had described its situation exactly. Two or three Department Z agents, recognising the car and guessing at important new developments, sprinted to the scene as the Bentley screeched to a halt.

It was only seven minutes short of five o'clock.

Hammond asked: 'What is it?' as Loftus climbed awkwardly from the car, impeded by his artificial leg.

'Herbert Grey's alive,' said Loftus, shortly. 'He might be here.'

'*Might!*' Hammond beckoned to the men who had come running and as they converged on the cottage, more came from the grounds and joined in the assault. As windows crashed in and men jumped through, revolver and Tommy-gun fire began to add to the din.

Gordon Craigie directed a sortie against the big house by another group of agents, among them, Wally Davidson. Davidson—as always, in a crisis, belying his lethargic appearance—shinned up a cedar tree by the south wall and climbed along a branch to a window. Other Department men were approaching the ground-floor windows as Davidson made a flying leap, balanced on the window-sill, then jumped down into a wide hall where two doors stood ajar.

From somewhere below, startled voices were exclaiming. And along the passage, a man came running: a little man, his face covered in a black mask....

'*Start now!*' he was shouting. '*Start now! Start now!*'

Davidson shot him. The man's impetus carried him forward a step or two more, then he stopped short and dropped in his tracks. As Davidson leapt for the nearer of the open doors, he saw a man with his back towards him, at a machine-gun. Davidson fired again, and the man fell.

But a split-second later, from the other three corners of the high gallery, a hail of fire streamed towards him. As he ducked out of sight, bullets pitted the floor about him, the walls, the gallery.

In the Assembly Hall below, there was a sudden stampede for the doors and what threatened to be a disastrous crush.

A few well-judged bursts of machine-gun fire then would have put a finishing touch to all that Ryall had planned. But Davidson, now down on one knee and sheltered by a massive chair, brought down a second machine-gunner—and brought more withering fire on himself, in the process.

Then Craigie came in through another door, with several of his men. Three bursts from automatic pistols were enough. The stampede below grew more frantic, but the Department men who had broken in on the ground-floor began to restore some kind of order. Craigie, himself, tight-lipped and anxious ran along the gallery towards Wally Davidson, whose head he could just see.

Davidson was still kneeling, when he reached him. His eyes were open, and there was a curiously twisted smile on his lips. The chairs and carpet about him, like the wall behind him, were pitted with bullet-holes. Only his face had escaped: Craigie saw at a glance the wounds in his chest and stomach.

'Stopped 'em,' he croaked. 'Stopped 'em, Gordon. Nice … work!'

And as he fell forward at Craigie's feet, the living voices of the men below became a valediction for Wally Davidson.

David Garth, knowing nothing of what was happening at the big house, rushed the cottage with Loftus and Hammond and the others. The resistance broke quite soon, with little damage on either side. Russi's men went scuttling away like rats into the grounds—where they could only fall into the arms of police or other Z agents.

Watching some of them flee, Garth caught a glimpse of one that he recognised.

'Catesby!' he shouted, pointing him out. 'Catesby!'

Hammond, by his side, grunted and fired at the running figure. He missed once, but his second bullet brought the American down and they raced towards him. They reached him as he put his hand to his mouth.

Then Garth felt Hammond grab his shoulder and drag him away. He was still gasping for breath as Hammond, standing back and looking at Catesby's writhing body, said as if to himself:

'We miss too much … a lot too much!'

'What's that?' asked Mike Errol, coming up to them.

'Catesby's killed himself … as he killed the gunman who tried to get Garth. Remember? We thought the fellow had swallowed the poison himself, but Catesby, I fancy, managed to drop it into his mouth.'

Errol stared: 'My oath, yes! He *did* slap the fellow across the face. I … oh, well! Is Garth all right?'

'He will be. What about…?'

'It's all over, I gather. And not a minute too soon!' Mike looked grim and dishevelled, but there was a bright light in his eyes.

A similar gleam was in the eyes of Loftus, Craigie, Hammond and Garth, when, a few hours later, they were seated together in Craigie's office. Graham Hershall who had insisted that they resume their seats, was leaning against Craigie's desk, a cheroot jutting from his lips.

The Prime Minister had said little: Craigie had done most of the talking.

'We've a lot to learn yet, sir,' he was saying, now. 'But we have the bones of the story. Sir Herbert Grey went over as our representative on Lease-Lend—but also representing certain British interests. He saw a chance of sabotaging much of the scheme. It would slow down supplies but it would put money in the pockets of himself and his principals. He did not board that aircraft which crashed, but someone who could be mistaken for him *was* on board. And as no one doubted it was Grey, neither the man's presence aboard nor the crash itself can be considered accidental.'

'H'mph,' said Hershall, moving the cheroot to the other side of his mouth.

'Thus, having arranged the crash of the airliner, Grey delayed Lease-Lend agreements and gave himself and his principals time to arrange to provide supplies from foreign and British companies abroad in which they had controlling interests. Ryall, who worked for Grey in this country, was also a representative of Berlin. He discovered what Grey was doing and arranged for pro-German interests in America to do the same—delay production of foodstuffs and other non-military commodities till they could cash in on it. Some American isolationists and certain obstructionist politicians, with commercial interests over here, helped them—unwittingly or wittingly. Ryall himself was out to slow down our war effort, as well as making fat profits for his pro-German faction in the

States. Who, of course,' Craigie added, drily, 'were carefully disguised as excessively patriotic "good Americans", fighting to preserve their great country's heritage of private enterprise and industrious commerce.'

'H'mph!' Hershall growled again. 'Go on!'

'Well, for the rest ... I think we shall find that Grey proposed to appear again when it was all over—and when his interests had made their profit. I don't know how. But what he said to Garth suggests that he expected to be in favour with the Government. Kent, by the way, was badly in need of money. He first sold information from the M.O.P. to Ryall—then got further into the mess and didn't have the guts to get out. Garth was told to take the papers from Kent's flat to incriminate himself—and steer suspicion away from Kent.'

Craigie glanced at Garth.

'Catesby, working for Brown, didn't know about that.'

He turned back to the P.M.

'You, sir, and the President, knew that plans for immediate post-war food and basic-commodity distribution had to be finalised urgently. You arranged these conferences, to that end—and with so many British and American key men together, Ryall saw his chance to do lasting harm to the Allies. Grey saw what he was doing and encouraged it. Clearly he had only one aim: to ensure that *his* Empire and foreign companies—the controlling interests were still "his", held in his wife's name—would finally be the only ones in any real position to supply the wanted goods.'

Craigie's hooded grey eyes were bleak.

'At a guess, the man was no longer wholly sane. No Englishman who could condone, let alone assist at such a thing, could be. The murder of so many really key men—leading world specialists, many of them, in their own fields—didn't trouble him one iota. And the fact that his plan could mean death by starvation of millions of other human beings didn't even affect him.'

He grimaced:

'From what he said to Garth, he seemed to feel that he was proving his patriotism by ensuring that his Nazi associate did not live to profit by post-war Anglo-American shortages, and world want.'

Hershall nodded, his pugnacious face creased in a scowl.

'It could hardly have been a darker crime—except in the event of its success. I don't need to tell you how I feel, Craigie,' he added gruffly. 'Well, I must be off, I've a meeting across the road.'

He nodded to Craigie and his two chief lieutenants, then suddenly strode across to Garth and held out his hand: 'Well done, Garth!' he said. 'It won't be long, now, before you'll be able to say exactly what you like, on any platform!'

He was chuckling as he went out, and Garth was smiling. But it was a preoccupied smile, which faded as he turned to Craigie.

'*Why* was Kent's copy of the report allowed to get to Ryall? Since I heard of the destruction of that food ...!'

Loftus chuckled.

'No destruction, Garth. The report you "stole" was a fake, anyhow. Livesey was told the stuff had been destroyed, to get the story circulating at Number 27. We hoped it would help us learn who was the man we wanted there ... who of course was Catesby. Anyway, thanks to Aunt Mabel, we got moving in time to get him along with all the rest. He worked for the American interests controlled by Grey. We used Lady Grey *because* of her present control of those American ... and other ... interests, all of which could obviously one day matter very much indeed. We had no idea at all, of her husband's continuing existence!' he added drily.

'She didn't know much more than *that*, herself,' Craigie said quietly. 'I well believe she thought he was on "hush-hush" work—he told *her* that British Intelligence had supplied a "double" for him, so they could use Grey on some very secret work and after the crash had allegedly given him permission to tell her he was alive only on condition he could guarantee she would not divulge the fact.'

Garth was shaking his head in amazement at the ramifications of the whole business ... and at the extent of the Department's awareness and control of events.

'We don't often miss the obvious,' said Hammond, with a crooked smile. 'Although things didn't go just as we expected with you, Garth. We didn't think they'd move so fast. You looked a safe man to plant inside Ryall's organisation ... and I don't think Ryall himself knew just how quickly they would move. He made contact with you at first because Kent was reaching the end of his sphere of usefulness and he wanted someone else who could get the information for him. There's just one thing ...'

Hammond hesitated and Garth asked: 'What is it?'

'Miss Duval discovered what Kent was doing,' Hammond told him, quietly. 'That was why she was killed. Her murder was used to intimidate you, Garth ... but you were not the cause of it, Some sort of satisfaction, I hope, in knowing that?'

Garth said slowly: 'M'mm ... Or shall we say, some sort of consolation.'

He left Craigie's office, not long afterwards, but he did not go to his flat. He went to Queen's Gate, where Olivia was waiting for him.

DARK PERIL

JOHN CREASEY

CHAPTER 1
THE MEN WHO COULD NOT SEE

The round-shouldered man sitting at the large, littered desk, drew in his breath and pushed his chair back. The electric lamp, immediately above his head, reflected from his bald pate and cast the shadows of his bushy eyebrows on a sheet of paper covered with figures. Except for his heavy breathing, the large, book-lined room was very quiet, but now and again a howl of wind outside disturbed the silence.

The man closed his eyes. He sat like that for fully five minutes, then opened them and leaned forward, looking down at the paper. The rows of figures remained clear for only a few seconds; they gradually merged into one another, and he could not read them. He stood up abruptly, with his hands clenched.

"I can't go on like this!" he muttered, "it's fantastic. I can't even *see!*"

He took off his glasses and rubbed his watery eyes. They were painful and red-rimmed. He went out of the room and walked along the dimly-lighted passage, but before he reached the landing he blundered into the wall, and stopped short.

"It *can't* be as bad as that!" he said aloud.

He replaced his glasses, and peered ahead of him. At first, the richly-carved balustrade along the landing showed clearly, but gradually the dark line thickened and moved until it merged with the oak panelling of the wall behind. He stood quite still, with his lips parted and one hand stretched out, as if to fend off some evil thing.

A door opened downstairs.

He heard voices, and the light laughter of a girl, yet they hardly registered on his mind. He did not move as the voices drew nearer and footsteps sounded on the stairs. A deep voice alternated with the girl's.

"I'm not a bit sure that I ought to worry him now."

"Oh, Daddy won't mind," said Julia Hartley, confidently. "Don't be put off by his forbidding manner, Mike, and don't be offended if he suddenly looks away from you and starts scribbling: I don't think he really cares tuppence about anything but his work."

"A pillar of reconstruction," said the man called Mike.

"Daddy!" gasped the girl.

Sir Basil Hartley had not understood the conversation, and had not realised that they had reached the landing. He had not moved from the moment the wooden balustrade had become part of the background. At the girl's exclamation, he started and looked towards the sound, and he could vaguely discern the shapes of his daughter and her companion.

"Daddy, what on earth—"

"It's–it's nothing, my dear, nothing," muttered Hartley. "I have a severe headache, and I must go and rest." He turned abruptly–and walked straight into the wall. He reeled back and put his hand to his forehead, his whole body trembling. "I–I have been overworking," he went on. "My eyes have given out, but a night's sleep will put them right. Lead–lead me to my room, Julia, will you, please."

The girl went forward and took his arm, then shot a glance at her companion, a tall, good-looking man, who was dressed in a well-cut suit of light grey. His hair, a little untidy, was inclined to curl.

"I'll see you in a few minutes," she said.

"All right," said Mike Errol, quietly, "but you ought to send for a doctor. Your father mustn't take risks with his eyesight." He was looking oddly at Hartley, frowning and paying little attention to Julia. She was as tall as her father, and her dark, wavy hair showed up against Hartley's baldness. "Can I telephone for you?"

"Do you really think it's necessary?" asked Julia, dubiously.

"No, there is no need to send for Lewis," said Hartley, sharply; "it is just that I have been overdoing it. Perhaps–perhaps if you will make a solution of boracic acid powder and tepid water, Julia. I will bathe my eyes. "

"Yes, of course," said Julia. "Oh, Mike, would you mind going into the bathroom, and—"

She had started to speak while looking at her father, but now she turned her head, and saw Mike Errol walking down the stairs. She opened her mouth to call him back, but changed her mind. She led her father to his bedroom, which was next to his study, and, when he was sitting back in an easy chair, she went to the bathroom and opened the first-aid box and the medicine cabinet. She took out what she wanted, and hurried downstairs. There was no sign of Mike Errol, and she went to the kitchen to put on a kettle.

"I hope he *isn't* telephoning for Lewis," she said, uneasily.

Mike Errol was at the telephone; he had just replaced the receiver, after putting in a call to a Whitehall number. He stood with one hand in his pocket and a cigarette jutting from his lips, frowning towards the door.

Lyddon House, on the outskirts of Woking, was large enough to need a staff of three or four. Only one old servant, the housekeeper, remained, and she was out for the evening. Julia Hartley had prepared dinner, taken a tray up to her father, and had enjoyed having her meal with Mike Errol, a comparatively new acquaintance who both appealed to and puzzled her. It had been an unconventional evening and Mike had sprung another surprise when he had said that he would very much like to ask her father one or two questions. He had been vague, but he had a way with him, and she had assured him that her father would not object.

There was a brief delay on the Whitehall call. As Julia walked along the hall, with the small glass of boracic acid solution in her hand, the telephone bell rang. She heard Mike answer it, and went straight to the drawing-room, which was long, narrow, and furnished in neo-Jacobean style.

"You aren't telephoning the doctor, are you?"

"Oh, no," said Mike, with an engaging smile. "Orders are orders! I forgot a call I should have made earlier, and I didn't think I need worry to ask you just now. Do you mind?"

"No, of course not."

"Can I help?"

"No, I shall be all right," she said, and hurried out.

Mike Errol's smile faded as he spoke into the mouth-piece again, and he did a curious thing. He spelt his surname, backwards, very quickly. Gordon Craigie, the man at the other end, did not seem to find this peculiar, for he said:

"Yes, go on, Mike."

"It's happened again," said Mike Errol, in a voice which was barely audible two yards away from him. "I didn't have a chance to see Hartley before it was too late. My fault, I'm afraid, I didn't expect anything to happen so quickly. The

symptoms are the same, as far as I can tell. I met him a few
minutes ago. He was as blind as a bat, and looked as if he
had just discovered it. What's my best move?"

"Have you sent for a doctor?"

"Hartley rejected the idea at once. He doesn't want to
admit that it's anything serious. I don't know either him or
Julia Hartley well enough to show the iron hand, unless you
think it's worth causing offence."

"Stay there and do whatever you think best until
Faversham arrives," said Craigie. "I'll get him to come over
at once. You'll have to handle the situation as best you can,
Mike—sorry."

"No need to be sorry," said Mike Errol. "Right-ho, old
chap. I'll get well dug in. Shall I say I've sent for Faversham?"

"There's no reason why you shouldn't."

"May Hartley know that it's not the first time such a
thing has happened?"

"It won't surprise me if he knows about the other cases,"
said Gordon Craigie. "I give you a free hand, Mike. I must
go, a bell's ringing."

Craigie rang off and Mike Errol replaced his receiver, then
shrugged his wide shoulders and stubbed out his cigarette.
Julia Hartley was an unpredictable young woman who might
resent any high-handed action on his part; his best plan would
be to tell her a little of what he knew, and thus justify himself.
Even after that she might accuse him of trying to worm his
way into her confidence on a false pretext, and might not be
appeased. He was thoughtful as he went into the hall, in time
to hear her calling from the head of the stairs.

"Mike!"

"Can I help?" He hurried up, taking the stairs two at a
time.

"Yes–would you mind helping him into bed? He really can't manage, and he doesn't want me to help him. I–I hate asking you."

Mike smiled and squeezed her arm before hurrying along to Hartley's room. The old man was sitting in his shirt-sleeves and struggling to unfasten his shoe-laces. A surgical eye glass and a piece of cotton-wool were on a bed-side table.

"Let me give you a hand," said Mike, cheerfully.

"There is no need—" Hartley began, but his protest faded.

Five minutes later he was in bed, with his eyes closed. Mike put out the main light, but left on a subdued bedside tablelamp, and went out. He closed the door softly. Julia was not in sight, and he stepped across to the bathroom, and looked through the medical cabinet swiftly. He took out a small, blue bottle bearing the label: "*Eye Lotion–For Tired Eyes.*" For a moment he hesitated, then he slipped the bottle into his pocket, and went out.

Julia was coming up the stairs, carrying a tray with a glass of milk; steam was rising from it. Mike said: "That's a good thought," and opened the door for her, but he did not go into the bedroom again. Instead, he waited near the open door of the study until she came out with the empty glass. Her fine grey eyes were narrowed, and her full lips set.

"I'm beginning to think we *ought* to send for Dr. Lewis," she said. "Daddy seems absolutely exhausted. I told him a hundred times that unless he rested much more than he did, he would crack up."

"If he'd rested for a month it wouldn't have helped him," Mike said.

"It wouldn't have—" she broke off, frowning. "What do you mean? What are you making a mystery about?"

She was a striking-looking woman when she was frowning, and a creature of contrasts, for in her light moods she was almost kittenish. There were people who said that her father had thoroughly spoiled her, and that he had been wrong not to allow a relative to bring her up, after her mother had died when she was four–twenty years before. Instead, Hartley had employed a woman who was partly a foster-mother and partly governess, and had kept the reins of control himself. She had a wide face, a fine complexion, and a short nose, which was quite straight. None of her features was particularly good, but the general effect was pleasing.

Some said that she was headstrong; Mike, who had known her for a little less than a week, agreed. She was also generous to a fault, often impulsively so, and he did not think it wrong that she held some strong opinions.

"Will you please explain?" she demanded.

Mike grinned.

"Not while you're fixing me with the evil eye!"

In spite of herself, she smiled.

"Mike, what *are* you driving at?"

"Well, it's like this," he said, lightly. "I am not soldier, sailor nor airman, as you perceive, but I have a job to do, and in my humble way I do it as best I can. Often it sends me to strange places, and often it gives me work which is distasteful. I didn't *like* pretending that I was only attracted by the glow in your eyes when we met at Chubby Foster's, but I had to pretend that was so. Actually I wanted to meet you because you are who you are–daughter of Sir Basil Hartley. My mission was purely protective. It's failed, horribly. You see, three other men, working along similar lines to him, have been suddenly afflicted by blindness."

She took the shock well. Her hands clenched and her head lifted a little, thrusting her square chin forward.

"I see," she said slowly. "So you expected this to happen?"

"I didn't so much expect it as feel afraid that it might," said Mike. "I was detailed to try to find out whether there was any suggestion of eye trouble with your father. How long has he used that eye lotion?"

"For years. I–what do you mean?"

"In at least two cases the trouble was caused by an irritant put into an eye-lotion which was in daily use," said Mike, "and the same thing might have happened again. Julia, don't ask me dozens of questions, because I don't know the answers. I'm only doing my little bit in the work of finding out what is behind it. I think you'll have to take it for granted that the trouble with your father's eyes is not the result of overstrain, but has been deliberately contrived."

"Are you suggesting that someone has tampered with the lotion?" demanded Julia.

"It's possible. I've the bottle here, and I'll have it examined," said Mike, taking the bottle out of his pocket to show her, and then putting it back. "It's not easy to advise this course or that, and I know you must be feeling pretty worked up. Actually, I've gone further than I should have done in saying so much. You'll keep it to yourself, won't you?"

"I see no reason why I should," she said, coldly. "I don't even know that you are telling the truth. You may pretend to be working under orders for some Government department–that is what you're implying, I suppose?–but actually you may be doing nothing of the kind."

"I can't complain about that reasoning," admitted Mike. "Let's put it this way: will you keep quiet until I've had the chance of proving that I'm on the square–say, until tomorrow mid-day? That isn't asking too much, is it?"

"I suppose not," she conceded, "but I can't admit that you were justified in tricking me. Nothing you say will alter the fact that I resent it very much. You should have come to me and told me what you suspected, and I would have done everything I could to help."

Mike grinned.

"You would probably have told me that I was talking nonsense, and shown me the door! You would certainly have told your father and worried him when worry might not have been necessary. The main point is that I acted under orders." He stood up, and rested a hand lightly on her arm. "Julia, I've come to know you fairly well. I know now that you're quite trustworthy, but I didn't a week ago, and I might not be able to convince everyone concerned. They're a cynical, hard-bitten crowd, who take a lot of convincing. Yes," he added, squeezing her arm gently, in spite of her growing anger, "they *will* think it possible that you doped the eye lotion! Until, of course, we've convinced them to the contrary."

"I have never heard anything so ridiculous!" stormed Julia, wrenching her arm away.

She broke off abruptly, for downstairs there was a bump, followed by a muttered imprecation, then silence as Mike stepped swiftly to the door.

Want another perfect mystery?

Get your next classic crime story for free...

Sign up to our Crime Classics newsletter where you can discover new Golden Age crime, receive exclusive content and never-before published short stories, all for FREE.

From the beloved greats of the Golden Age to the forgotten gems, best-kept-secrets, and brand new discoveries, we're devoted to classic crime.

If you sign up today, you'll get:

1. A free novel from our Classic Crime collection.
2. Exclusive insights into classic novels and their authors and the chance to get copies in advance of publication, and
3. The chance to win exclusive prizes in regular competitions.

Interested? It takes less than a minute to sign up. You can get your novel and your first newsletter by signing up on our website www.crimeclassics.co.uk.

CPSIA information can be obtained
at www.ICGtesting.com
Printed in the USA
LVOW12s2204041217
558590LV00005B/1320/P